NIGHT HUNTERS

Also by Oliver Bottini in English translation

Zen and the Art of Murder (2018)
A Summer of Murder (2018)
The Dance of Death (2019)

OLIVER BOTTINI

NIGHT HUNTERS

A Black Forest Investigation: IV

Translated from the German by
Jamie Bulloch

MACLEHOSE PRESS
QUERCUS · LONDON

First published as *Jäger in der Nacht*
by S. Fischer Verlag GmbH, Frankfurt am Main, in 2014
and in a new edition by DuMont Buchverlag in 2015

First published in Great Britain in 2021 by MacLehose Press
This paperback edition published in 2022 by

MacLehose Press
An imprint of Quercus Publishing Ltd
Carmelite House
50 Victoria Embankment
London EC4Y 0DZ

An Hachette UK company

ISBN (MMP) 978 1 52940 917 8
ISBN (Ebook) 978 1 52940 918 5

This book is a work of fiction. Names, characters, organisations, places and events are
either the product of the author's imagination or are used fictitiously. Any resemblance to
actual persons, living or dead, events or particular places is entirely coincidental.

10 9 8 7 6 5 4 3 2 1

Designed and typeset in Minion by Libanus Press, Marlborough
Printed and bound in Great Britain by Clays Ltd, Elcograf S.p.A.

There are fewer uglier traits in human nature than this tendency . . . to grow cruel, merely because they possessed the power of inflicting harm.

Nathaniel Hawthorne, *The Custom House, and Main Street*

Prologue

One glimpse of the dark, silent water of the Rhine and everything was momentarily forgotten. The hatred, the pain, the fear.

Eddie dropped his bike onto the grass, wandered down to the river and sat. What would he do without the Rhine? For a few minutes it made everything go away, leaving only his thoughts.

His thoughts and the beating of his heart.

Killing his father.

Eddie lit a cigarette, stretched out his legs and dangled his feet in the water. As his Nikes got soaked a coolness crept up his legs.

Whenever he felt overwhelmed by the hatred and the thoughts inside his head he would go for a night-time swim. Into the water in Germany and out in France. First the Old Rhine, then the island, and finally the Grand Canal of Alsace. The canal was dangerous. One hundred and fifty metres of darkness and cold, straight across the waterways between barges, fishing boats and pleasure cruisers, all the time battling a strong current. Sometimes an angry voice might bark at him from one of the vessels, but mostly nobody ever saw him. Then he would swim back, freed of the hatred and his thoughts.

In winter, when the water was too cold, he ran.

As he filled his lungs with smoke, Eddie allowed his gaze to wander. The forest in the sunshine opposite, the moorings downstream on the German side, then a slight bend to the left up to Breisach. Upstream a splash of white on the riverbank – Dennis, who was always the colour of mozzarella even though he spent every spare minute of the day sunbathing. Who always looked like a wobbly jellyfish even though he ate next to nothing.

A flabby white arm was raised aloft. Eddie waved back. When he heard a man's voice he held his breath. A woman laughed. The noise of bicycle tyres on the path above. Then it went quiet again.

He flicked away his cigarette, sank back down into the grass and imagined what life would be like without his father.

"Eddie?"

He opened his eyes and sat up. His heart was pounding and he could feel how tense his muscles were.

But it was just Dennis, a yellow bag in one hand, the other holding his bicycle. He carefully laid the bike onto the grass and came down the two metres of bank to Eddie. "I've got beer. Want one?"

Eddie nodded, Dennis took a bottle of Ganter from his bag and opened it.

The bottle was cool and wet. Even Dennis's voice was white and fat, Eddie thought as he sipped the beer.

Letting out a burp, Dennis sat beside him. He burped and farted every few minutes – because he was so white and fat, it seemed to Eddie. Dennis must think that if you can't help being ugly, you might as well go the whole hog.

Eddie didn't care. He swam in the Rhine at night; Dennis burped and farted. You had to do something.

Dennis farted. "You're bleeding."

Eddie touched the wound on his left cheek. He'd scratched it open in his sleep and now it was hurting again. He held out his blood-smeared hand and they both looked at it for a while.

"Cool," Dennis said. "Mine's much lighter."

"White?"

They grinned. Eddie leaned forwards and dipped his hand in the water. The Rhine washed the blood away.

He turned his head and their eyes met.

Although they didn't discuss it, Dennis seemed to have guessed how the wound had appeared. Which was why Eddie never wore shorts or short-sleeved T-shirts, not even in summer.

It struck Eddie that he liked Dennis without having any inkling why. Perhaps because he didn't ask questions. Or because he burped and farted all the time. Or because they were almost like brothers. His father was fucking Dennis's mother.

She never went into the sun, ate like a horse and was just as white and fat as Dennis. Nobody knew what Dennis's father looked like. Not even his mother, Dennis said. I was made from behind, he said, as if that explained everything. The white skin, the fat, the poor grades at school, and why life was so shitty.

Eddie turned away and washed the blood from his cheek.

"You can watch the match at mine tonight if you like," Dennis said.

The second semi-final. Mexico against Argentina in Dolby Digital on a plasma screen that took up half the sitting-room wall. Lots of men fucked Dennis's mother and some left her money.

"O.K."

Eddie stared at his distorted reflection in the water and his heart started racing again. The first semi-final was yesterday. Germany had played well, but the Brazilians had won. When the final whistle went his father had leaped up and struck him.

"Mama's making goulash."

"O.K."

Eddie sat back down, took a sip of Ganter and for a moment he felt almost happy. Watching football, drinking beer, smoking and eating goulash from huge soup bowls. Later he would come home, wait for it to get dark and then swim across the river to the French side.

They sat there for a while in silence, watching solo canoeists on the water. Eddie's moment of happiness had passed. His wound was sore and the hatred had returned. Adriano's goal. His father's rage, the apathy in his mother's eyes.

This morning began with the usual poking, shoving and threats. Then his father started laughing: What's that on his face, did he fall out of bed? Come on Eddie, his mother said, you've got to laugh, it's funny. Then his father said, Look at him pouting, and didn't stop laughing. Eddie went to the door, turned and said: I'm going to kill you one day. His father wasn't laughing anymore.

"I'm off, then," Dennis said.

Eddie nodded.

"Do you want to come to the village with me?"

"I'm going to stay here for a bit."

"I'll leave you a beer if you like."

"O.K. Got any fags?"

Dennis opened another Ganter. "I'm out," he said. There was a curious expression on his face and Eddie wondered what he was thinking.

"You can come to my place if you like."

Eddie shook his head.

"Alright, then. See you later."

"O.K."

He heard Dennis get on his bike on the path above. A fart, a burp, a screech, then the noises faded away. Now he realised what Dennis had been thinking and he hated him for it. Dennis felt pity for him – you only felt pity for the weak.

It looked as if his father had been waiting for him. He was sitting on a chair in their narrow front garden, a bottle of beer within reach, his cowboy hat pulled down over his face. Eddie couldn't enter the house without brushing past him.

Then Eddie heard snoring and thought his luck was in.

He followed the fence around the house until he found the fist-sized, almost round stone that he'd put here months ago. He wiped away the mud and rubbed it clean on his trousers so it wouldn't slip from his hand. Holding the stone in his right hand he went back to the garden gate. The stone felt cool and calming, as cool and calming as the water of the Rhine. The stone was made for him, just like the Rhine, he thought.

At the garden gate he stopped and looked at his father. He was wearing shorts and a vest, allowing a view of his muscular arms and legs. Eddie gripped the stone tightly. The key thing was to hit him as hard as possible with the first strike; even if his father tried to defend himself he wouldn't have a chance.

A movement in one of the upstairs windows made him glance up. Although the white curtain was drawn he could see the shadow of his mother behind it. She stood there motionless, her face turned in his direction. Then she raised a hand and grabbed the curtain, before standing motionless again.

Eddie took a few steps towards his father. His heart was thumping and the hatred was throbbing inside his skull. He stopped again and looked up at his mother. Her hand clutching the curtain had twisted the material.

In his sleep his father grunted softly and deeply, like a pig, and Eddie turned back to him. His father was going to die in a very apt way, he thought: grunting like a pig.

He advanced. Again he heard a grunt, but realised that his father had woken up and was grunting now because he'd seen the stone. At that moment he raised his head slightly and Eddie could see his eyes beneath the brim of the hat. They stared at him expectantly and full of scorn. Come on, they were saying. Just you try it.

Eddie froze. All of a sudden he knew that, like him, his father had been waiting for the right moment.

And now it had come. Finally, the eyes said, and it dawned on Eddie that he'd lost and his father had won. Everything was decided; there was nothing he could do to affect the outcome. As ever, his father was too strong and he was too weak.

His father smiled, looking very pleased with himself.

Eddie lifted the stone, drew back his arm and hurled it at his father. But the stone missed by a metre. When it crashed against the wall of the house his father jumped up. Eddie turned and fled.

*

His father didn't follow. For several minutes Eddie stood at the other end of the village in the shadow of a tree. His heart was racing, the hatred was back, accompanied by even more fear. But his father didn't come. Why would he bother? Eddie thought. All his father had to do was wait and see if he dared come home.

For a moment he pondered what to do. He had no money or clothes. To run away he would have to go back home first. But how could he go back home?

Banishing these thoughts, he followed the road to the centre of the village to retrieve his bike, which he'd left by the dovecote. The Rhine would have some answers.

As he was taking off the lock his mobile played the opening bars of 50 Cent's "Candy Shop".

Dennis.

"I've got something to show you," he said, and now his voice sounded mysterious rather than white and fat.

Eddie didn't respond. The hatred and fear of his father sat in his throat like a fist, preventing him from speaking.

"Come to the old barn."

Eddie shook his head to get rid of the fist. "I'm going swimming."

"You can do that later."

He thought of the pity in Dennis's face. An hour ago he'd hated him for that, but now Dennis was the only person he had left.

"I've found something."

"What?"

"Come," Dennis said again, "but make sure nobody sees you."

Eddie put the phone in his trouser pocket. As he cycled through town he thought of the old barn. There had been good days in his life and many of these had involved the barn. Getting drunk, fights with boys his own age from Hausen and Oberrimsingen, fumbling with girls, watching porn films on a mini T.V. until the batteries gave up the ghost. For a few weeks they'd abducted dogs and cats and battered them to death in the old barn. It was here too that they'd shared out the money they'd stolen from the offertory boxes and collection bags in church.

And then all those quiet nights after he'd been beaten by his father.

The old barn stood two hundred metres to the west of the village, in the middle of an uncultivated field. Crows flew up from the knee-high, parched grass as Eddie cycled down the narrow path across the field, accompanied by their shadows and greedy cawing.

He laid his bike beside Dennis's and entered the barn. Sunlight broke through the endless cracks and gaps in the wooden walls. Dust danced in the shafts of light.

Dennis was sitting cross-legged, leaning against a wall. Eddie sat next to him. "Well?"

Dennis pointed his chin at the wall facing them. Only now did Eddie realise they weren't alone. On the floor lay a woman. Her face was pointing upwards and she wasn't moving. She looked as if she was dead.

"Who's that?"

"No idea."

"Is she dead?"

"No."

Eddie went over. The woman was wrapped in a red blanket and her eyes were closed, but now he could hear her breathing. The blanket had slipped; he saw a bare shoulder and bare legs. Bruises and scabs were visible on the tops of the legs. There was blood on her face too, one eye was swollen, and the nose looked crooked. Her lips were split and from the copious amount of blood Eddie reckoned her teeth must have been knocked out. The face was so disfigured that he couldn't have said whether the woman was pretty or not. Only that she was in her early twenties at most and slim.

"Pretty cool to be honest," Dennis said.

Eddie said nothing. He wondered why Dennis had called him

rather than an ambulance or the police. Why he'd sat against the wall and done nothing.

"Check out the left leg," Dennis said.

Eddie bent forwards. From the knee down the leg was bruised on one side. The woman was barefoot and her feet were covered in mud and dirt.

Now she moved her head slightly and her eyes opened, one fully, the other halfway. They stared at him in sheer terror. He got the impression she was trying to move, but without any success. As if all she could move were her head and eyes.

He couldn't help thinking of the dogs and cats that had lain tied up on the floor in the barn. They'd looked similar to this woman: helpless and utterly terrified.

He kneeled beside her. The blanket wasn't fully covering her tummy and he could see a narrow strip of skin. He lifted the edge of the blanket. She had bruises and scabs on her stomach too.

When he pulled back the blanket he thought he heard the woman whimper briefly, but he wasn't certain. He stared at her left breast, which was now uncovered and was red with bruises. He pushed the blanket away from her other breast, then from her waist. The woman made a strange sound, but that was all. He could make out blood between her legs, which were slightly apart. Holding his breath, Eddie laid his hand on her right thigh. Beneath his palm he felt a shudder run through the woman's body. Again, that was all.

It struck him that he could do what he wanted and nothing would happen to him.

He inched his hand up her body. Because of the bruising and scratches he only faintly touched her skin, even though he'd have liked to have a better feel of it. He knew how painful wounds like that were and he didn't want to hurt her.

It was only when his hand reached her breast that he gave in to his urges and cupped it. Another shudder shot through the woman's body and her shoulders spasmed, but not her arms. When Eddie took a closer look he saw that there was bruising on her arms too. Again he heard the peculiar, soft sound from her mouth, and when it stopped so did her movements. From the corner of his eye he saw that the woman had turned her head away and closed her eyelids. Once more he thought he could do what he wanted and nothing would happen to him.

With his hand still on her breast he wondered how he could touch the woman all over without hurting her, because he really didn't want to cause her any pain. Seconds passed without him finding a solution. At some point he stopped thinking because all other sensations were blanked out apart from the sight of his hand on her breast, the feel of that breast, and the idea that he could do more without anything happening to him.

"Eddie." Dennis's white, fat voice brought everything else back.

He turned around. Dennis eyed him with one of those inscrutable Dennis looks, and it crossed Eddie's mind that he'd love to bash that look from that face.

"We've got to go now. Dinner will be ready soon."

"You go ahead."

"Eddie . . ."

They looked at each other in silence.

"You go ahead," he said again.

Dennis awkwardly got to his feet, supporting himself on both hands, and knocked dust and bits of hay from his shorts. Eddie fancied he could see him trembling, but he might have been mistaken. Perhaps it was just the fat wobbling. Then Dennis looked at him again and his expression was no longer inscrutable, but uncertain and perhaps a little shocked. "Come on now."

Eddie didn't respond.

"Someone's going to be looking for her, and if they find us here . . ."

"You go ahead."

Dennis shook his head and Eddie realised that he wasn't going to leave him alone with the woman. That he knew what was going through Eddie's mind and that he'd been thinking the same thing at first too, but not anymore.

Eddie took his hand from the woman's breast, stood up and left the barn.

Dennis followed him. No sooner was he outside than he burped and farted prodigiously, as if he'd been keeping it all in inside the barn. "To be honest, I think we should call someone."

"I'm not asking you."

"A doctor, I mean. Or the police."

"Later," Eddie said, thinking that Dennis might become a problem and he didn't yet know how to deal with that.

Near to the barn he found a plank which must have come from one of the walls or the roof. He slotted it behind the handles of the double barn doors so that they couldn't be opened from the inside unless you threw your entire weight against them. He didn't think the woman was in a state to be able to do this.

"Because of the animals," he said.

"Uh-huh," Dennis said quietly. Then they got on their bikes and rode back across the field to the village. Once again the crows flew into the air, cawing angrily, their shadows swishing beside them across the grass.

During dinner the only thing on Eddie's mind was the woman and the thoughts that had entered his head in the barn: he could do what he liked and nothing would happen to him. Whenever his gaze met Dennis's he knew that his friend was thinking about the woman too.

Dennis's mother didn't notice any of this. She barely said a word. Pale, fat and sweaty, she sat between them, focused on the giant portion of goulash she'd heaped into her bowl. After dinner she went to her room. Eddie heard her talking on the phone for a while, then crying, and then she seemed to have fallen asleep.

The football match began at six o'clock and even during the game all Eddie could think about was the woman in the barn. On a couple of occasions he was about to get up and go, but changed his mind.

At half time Dennis turned down the volume and said, "I wonder what's happened to her?"

Eddie shrugged. He was thinking how he might be able to stay in the barn for a few days. At some point during the night he would slip back home to fetch food and clothes, then he would stay in the barn with the woman for a few days.

"To be honest . . ." Dennis didn't finish his sentence, and instead said, "Hopefully she won't snuff it."

"She won't."

"But we ought to call—"

"Tomorrow," Eddie interrupted him.

"O.K." Dennis went into the kitchen and came back with some beer and his mother's cigarettes. They drank and smoked in silence. The second half had begun and Dennis turned the volume back up. Eddie felt himself being carried away by the beer, the huge T.V. screen and the stadium noise coming from five speakers. Despite this the woman was still in his head, lying naked in the dim light of the barn.

Dennis burped and said something.

"What?"

"I wonder if anyone's looking for her."

"Who?"

"The guy who did it."

They looked at each other. There it was again, the pity in Dennis's face.

"We'll look after her," Eddie said.

The game went on for ever. There was extra time and penalties, then Argentina scraped victory.

Eddie stood up. "Let's go."

"I'm not sure," Dennis said, not moving. As he sat there pale and flabby, Eddie knew that he really had become a problem. "I'm not sure," he said again. Then he switched off the television and was about to get up.

"If you don't want to come," Eddie said, "I'll go on my own."

Surprised, Dennis sank back into his chair, as if dragged down by his own weight. "I'm not sure," he said a third time. "To be honest, we shouldn't."

"Shouldn't what? You're not doing anything."

"But we ought to call someone."

"Yes," Eddie said. "And then they'll ask why we waited so long."

Dennis looked at the black screen as if to say, "Because of the football."

He let out a loud, long fart – a fart of despair, Eddie thought. "I'll tell you who she is. One of those French gyppo slappers."

"Do you think?"

"She made trouble and the other gyppos beat her up."

"But she doesn't look like a gypsy."

"Of course she does. Didn't you see her eyes? Gyppo eyes."

Dennis didn't reply.

"Right then, are you coming or not?" Eddie waited another moment. He knew Dennis was thinking about the woman. About the opportunity suddenly on offer, which no girl would ever freely give to him, the fat, ugly fifteen-year-old.

But then Dennis shook his head.

"You're not going to call anyone, do you hear me?" Eddie warned him.

Dennis turned to him. "What about you?"

"Later. In the morning."

"Alright."

Eddie went to the door. "Come later if you want."

Dennis nodded. For a moment there was a glimmer in his eye and now Eddie knew that there wouldn't be any problems later. That Dennis would come and take advantage of the opportunity.

*

Outside it was getting dark. Eddie found himself keeping an eye out for his father as he cycled through the quiet streets of the village. But there was no sign of him.

When he got to the field he stopped. It was hard to make out the barn against the dark woods behind. For a moment he thought he could see a light moving where the barn stood. But he was mistaken. There was no light.

He cycled along the path. The wind whistled through the tall grass and in the distance he heard a car engine. The crows seemed to have gone; either that or they were hiding silently in the shelter of darkness.

Clouds gathered and suddenly it was dark.

It was only when Eddie got off his bike that he realised one of the double doors to the barn was open. He gave his bike a shove and it fell to the ground. On his way to the barn he felt the plank underfoot. Bending down, he saw it was intact. The door must have been opened from the outside.

He spent a while just staring at the entrance. It was even darker inside than outside. Eddie couldn't hear any noises. He thought of the light he fancied he'd seen from a distance. But there was no light.

Finally he went in. Although he was enveloped by darkness, he'd been here so often that he could have found his way around blindfolded.

He walked over to the wall opposite. The woman had gone. The stench of urine filled his nostrils and he thought she must have pissed herself. He slowly made his way along the rear wall, then one side, the front, the other side, before finally zig-zagging his way across the barn a couple of times. After a few minutes he was convinced that the woman was no longer there. He wondered whether to look for her outside. But if someone had come and taken the woman he wouldn't find her.

Eddie turned to the entrance and froze in shock. A human figure stood out against the bluish shimmer of the night. Blood rushed to his ears and he was covered in goosepimples. But he remained calm.

Too tall to be the woman, he thought. Too slim to be Dennis.

A man, at any rate.

His father?

Without making a sound, he kneeled. He wasn't scared and this pleased him. The barn was his domain. And he knew the man couldn't see him.

But he must have noticed the bicycle.

"Come out," said a deep and friendly voice he didn't recognise. Then the man vanished from sight.

Eddie didn't move a muscle. This was the strangest day of his life, he thought. A day on which so much had happened, but in some respects also nothing at all.

He crept to the door and peered outside. The man was standing beside his bike. Wearing jeans and a leather jacket, he looked large and old. "Come here," he said, beckoning him over with his hand. A curt gesture, and yet one with a certain familiarity. Even his voice sounded trustworthy. The voice of a tired, gentle, old man.

"Come on then," the man said, and Eddie stepped out of the barn. He saw the man nodding. "What's your name?"

Eddie just raised his eyebrows.

The man wiped his eyes. In his jeans and leather jacket he almost looked like a copper. "You know . . .?"

"What?"

The man pointed at the barn.

"Oh, right," Eddie said. "Yes, very well."

The man didn't understand at first. Then he smiled, but said nothing. They looked at each other in silence.

"What's *your* name, then," Eddie asked.

"Willie Reimer."

Willie, Eddie thought, then giggled. Willie and Eddie. "Are you a copper?"

The man smiled again. "Kripo." He held up something that in the darkness looked like an I.D.

Eddie grinned. Willie – if that was his real name – must think he was really stupid. "What are you doing here?"

Willie pointed at the barn again. Eddie nodded and said, "Are you going to buy it?"

Once again Willie didn't understand straightaway. Then he said, "I saw the blood."

"That's from the cats and dogs."

Instead of responding to this, Willie just stood there very still, waiting.

"The kids from the village kill them in there."

"Yes," Willie said.

Eddie wondered if Willie had been responsible for the state the woman was in. The way he stood there – weary, gentle, friendly – it seemed most unlikely.

"The barn's empty now. Was that your work?"

"The cats and dogs?"

"You know who we're talking about, young man," another male voice said behind him.

Eddie spun around but couldn't see anybody. The second man must be in the barn.

"Another copper?"

"Yes," the invisible voice said, but it didn't sound convincing.

Eddie wasn't going to hang around to see what the two men would do. Head down, he began to run towards the woods, because Willie stood between him and the village. To begin with he heard footsteps and panting behind him, but the sounds soon fell back. It wasn't until he got to the woods that it struck him the men might have pistols. But they hadn't fired a shot so it didn't matter.

He leaped into the undergrowth and kept running without looking back. He wasn't going to stop until he reached the Rhine, and even then he wouldn't stop; he would jump into the river and swim to the island. They definitely wouldn't follow him there.

Arms aloft, he ran through the woods. Twigs and branches lashed his forearms, shoulders and head, but he didn't care. He'd been through worse.

Soon he could see lights ahead of him – the lamps along the riverside path. He laughed to himself. The Rhine was waiting for him.

He'd almost reached the edge of the woods when a body rammed into him from the right. He went crashing into a tree and there was a crack as something in his arm broke. He fell with a cry. Pain was shooting through his left elbow, but he got back to his feet. All that mattered was to get to the Rhine. The Rhine would save him as it had so often before.

Two hands dug into his T-shirt and hurled him to the ground. Now he knew that he'd lost.

He lay on his tummy. At first he thought that his father had attacked him. But it wasn't his father and it wasn't Willie either. It must be the man from the barn.

"Out with it," the man whispered.

Eddie gasped for air. "Go fuck yourself."

When the man kicked him in the side with the toe of his shoe Eddie realised that he would have to talk if he didn't want to end up like the woman.

He said that he'd seen the woman in the barn that afternoon and that by the evening she'd gone. He didn't know her and they hadn't talked because she was too badly injured to speak.

Eddie didn't say anything else.

As he spoke he wondered who the woman could be. Whether anybody else had found her. He wished they had. In some funny way, he thought, they belonged together, the woman and he, and he didn't want anyone else to have her.

He was still lying on his tummy, the man beside him.

"Did you tell anyone else about her?"

"No."

"Why not?"

Eddie said nothing.

The man gave him another kick. "Did you lock her in, eh? What, did you think you could fuck her later?"

Eddie didn't answer.

The man laughed. "Why didn't you just there and then?"

"Dinner was ready. And then the footy was on the box."

"So you were going to come back after and fuck her?"

"Yes."

The man laughed again. "Were you alone with her?"

In his mind Eddie saw Dennis's fat, white face and for some reason he found this image comforting. He thought that maybe he liked him because he was a kind of brother or because Dennis never stopped burping and farting. Whatever the case, he liked him and the truth was that Dennis was the only person he had left after today.

"Yes."

Bending over him, the man pulled up his head and slapped him again and again. Now Eddie was certain he had lost, but so long as he didn't betray Dennis then he'd won a minor victory too.

So he didn't.

At some point Eddie must have lost consciousness. He came to because there was something cool on his head.

Water.

He tried to breathe, but took water into his lungs instead of air.

Water from the Rhine, he thought, and there was something comforting about this too.

Then came desperation and he began to defend himself against the hands that were holding him underwater with the strength of iron.

But it was too late.

I

Eddie and Nadine

1

A narrow strip of light in the darkness, barely twenty metres away on the other side of the road. In the middle of the light, the outline of a man, blurred in the pouring rain, but not a soul about apart from him. No dogwalkers, no drunks, not even any homeless people strayed here.

A virtually empty car park, a brightly lit security guard's cabin. A sad place, Louise Bonì thought, in happy Freiburg.

In the twenty minutes she'd been watching him, the uniformed security guard had hardly moved. No-one had come, no-one had left.

Night shift in St Georgen.

Fifteen minutes ago, when he picked up his mobile phone and dialled a number, she wondered who he was calling. A short conversation – four or five minutes – then he put the phone down.

When she switched on the ignition the L.E.D. display on the radio came to life. All those buttons and dials for a bit of music. All those tiny symbols. Too small for the eyes of a forty-four-year-old.

She pressed this and turned that. When nothing happened she switched off the ignition. A new car after so many years – the change-over couldn't be completely smooth. A factory-new Peugeot that stank of plastic, paid for by an unpleasant, autocratic Bavarian, for whom it was worth the fifteen thousand euros to finally get her out of her apartment in Gartenstrasse so it could be renovated.

Her gaze fell on the glowing numbers of the digital clock. A quarter to twelve, fifteen minutes left. She felt a strange tingling run up and down her arms and legs. The molecules were on the move again.

Louise leaned back. Much was new in that summer of 2005: the

27

car, the apartment, a zest for life. A man she could definitely try to make a go of it with.

In that order, she owed it to herself.

Actually, she thought, life was pretty good. Apart from all the new things, it was a bespoke summer: hot days, followed by cooling storms at night. No danger of a relapse. No serious crimes: a case of arson in Littenweiler; a burgled villa, everything removed; and a missing student who, so it seemed, was just taking some time out. Nothing that would be likely to open up the abysses inside her again.

She took the photograph of the student from the file that lay on the passenger seat. Nadine Rohmueller had an elegant face, pretty in a childish way, and looked more like a schoolgirl than a student. Shoulder-length, chestnut hair, enviably full lips. A touch of the spoiled brat and pride in her eyes. A rich Bonn family: the money flowed without the daughter having to do any more than go to the cashpoint. American Studies, German and Psychology, in her sixth semester, middling grades, she'd had enough now, a friend of hers said, she hadn't been enjoying her course for quite a while.

Louise browsed the documents.

Her parents had rung that morning. They hadn't been able to contact their daughter for three days, they said, and no-one at the university had seen her since Friday. The father was expected tomorrow lunchtime. They would go with him to the apartment, two bedrooms with a kitchenette on Wintererstrasse in Herdern, owned rather than rented, of course, to prevent the daughter from succumbing to the temptation of soaking up real life in a flatshare.

Quite clearly she'd just done a runner.

Louise glanced at the security guard, still immobile, staring into the darkness beyond the window of his cabin. What could he see? Tel Aviv? Priština? Sarajevo?

Years as a detective, then deployment abroad in crisis regions. Now a tin shack in St Georgen, Freiburg ...

And yet it was a job. At some point the shift began and at some point it finished. In-between lay nine hours during which you knew you were needed, even if it was just to guard an empty car park at night.

It was a beginning.

She looked at the documents again. I reckon Florida, the friend had said. Apparently Nadine worshipped Jack Kerouac.

Does he live there? Thomas Ilic had asked.

He's buried there, the friend had said. In Saint Petersburg.

Saint Petersburg in Florida, Ilic had noted.

Louise smiled. This was new too – Illi had been back at work for a few weeks. Still slightly awkward, pale because of his medicines and quiet, but he was back.

American writer, 1922–1969, he'd noted.

Karin, a trainee inspector, checked out the car hire companies, airlines and the railway. Although Nadine had a car, it was important not to rule anything out.

The alarm on her mobile started beeping. Midnight. She put on some lipstick, reached for the umbrella and paper bag and got out.

"Hi," she said.

Ben Liebermann smiled. "Hi."

"Lunch." She passed him the paper bag through the opening in the glass.

He looked inside. One cheese roll, one salami roll, as ever. She shrugged. "You dare complain!"

He laughed, closed the bag and stood up. "Shall we take a little stroll?"

A kiss, then they linked arms. She still found all of this slightly strange, and Ben Liebermann must think so too. Out of practice, both of them. But the molecules were leaping wildly all over the place.

At the edge of the car park they walked a rectangle in the darkness. Around them the rain was hammering down, the puddles sploshed beneath their feet. When they'd gone halfway she said, "You were on the phone."

"Yes."

She waited. This was what she feared most: shadows from the past. Ben had lived in Hamburg, Cologne, Berlin and Freiburg, not to mention Tel Aviv, Priština and Sarajevo. His past must be full of all manner of shadows.

Quite apart from the fact that he'd been married twice. Somewhere were two women who'd spent years with him. Who knew him in a way she might never do. Who'd been with Ben to places she would never go with him.

They hadn't talked about their past histories, but that would come at some point. Then she would also explain why she couldn't trust him yet and why she asked for night-time phone calls. She would tell him about Mick, who'd been married to a gullible chief inspector and had abused her trust dozens of times.

"A friend in the Ministry of the Interior. I want to know why they won't take me."

She nodded.

Ben had applied to regional police headquarters in Freiburg. If possible he wanted to work for Freiburg Kripo, but he was prepared to go anywhere, even to a village outpost in the High Black Forest. Hunting poachers instead of Bosnian war criminals.

No vacancies, police H.Q. replied weeks later.

In truth they knew the real reason why. Ben Liebermann had left the police service in May 2004, and they didn't want anyone back who'd left of their own accord.

They returned to the cabin in silence, then did another round of the car park.

Still, no shadows from a past life. Just the darkness of the night.

At half past midnight she was back home and opened the window wide. The new car smelled of plastic, the new flat of paint.

And the new man?

She got into the shower. Of Zino Davidoff, cigarettes, worry and possibly of pain from some period in his life.

But also of possibilities.

She washed her hair. This was a peculiar urge too. After all these years she wanted to be beautiful and feminine again. Wanted to dress elegantly, buy nice things. Wanted to feel beautiful and feminine.

Danger alert. She resolved to watch out.

Under the jet of water she thought once more of Nadine Rohmueller. The friend's statement suggested that she'd absconded abroad for a few weeks or months of adventure. Rich, bored daughter, sick and tired of studying and the carefree life.

But perhaps Louise just wanted to see it this way. It fitted the picture. Young, rich, beautiful, bored, vacuous. The world was her oyster. Why not make a pilgrimage to Jack Kerouac's grave in Saint Petersburg, Florida, rather than only ever going to St Tropez?

Nadine hadn't withdrawn any money from her various accounts since Saturday afternoon. The last transaction: 16.34, Deutsche Bank A.T.M., 262 Kaiser-Joseph-Strasse, three hundred euros. No activity on her accounts from the past few months that pointed to a trip.

That could mean a lot or nothing.

Credit card? Thomas Ilic had noted. Tomorrow a financial investigator with the relevant contacts would make some telephone calls.

As she stood in front of the mirror, Ben Liebermann edged his way back into her thoughts. She saw him sitting in his guard cabin, staring into the darkness, eating rolls, cheese and salami like every night. His hair was now short, an unofficial condition of employment – well, *that* will have to go.

If you're forced to get your hair cut at the age of forty-three . . .

You've got to start somewhere, Ben, she'd said.

Yes, Ben replied.

She wondered how long he would play along. She'd given him two months; it had already been four.

Which was good and bad at the same time.

The start had become day-to-day life.

*

At one o'clock she sat on her new balcony, looking out over Annaplatz. A one-bedroom apartment with a kitchenette. Period block, newly renovated with stripped floorboards, seventy square metres. Big enough for two, but you had to like living together, and neither Ben nor she did. He often came over as a guest, especially at half past five in the morning after his shift when she had to be at H.Q. early. They would have breakfast and then set off together. He had a small apartment in Stühlinger, slightly rundown and devoid of charm, possibly ideal for someone who claimed to feel most comfortable living in cities which had been through war.

The war in Freiburg didn't count. Too long ago. Ben wanted to see war in the façades of buildings and in people's eyes. One of the many puzzles about him which she'd yet to solve. The only one she couldn't take quite so seriously.

Tel Aviv, Priština, Sarajevo, she thought with a shake of the head. For her the little wars were enough, those private wars that individuals conducted against others because for some unfathomable reason they'd decided to surrender to the urge for violence.

Ben arrived at half past five. His face looked pallid in the gloomy light of the stairwell. She knew that Freiburg wasn't good for him.

But he smiled and she got the impression he was happy to see her.

Louise pulled Ben into the apartment and began undressing him. Clothes were sent flying through the darkness and floorboards creaked. The telephone table fell over, the sitting-room door crashed into the wall. Louise laughed. Two desperate individuals full of desire.

Some people said that a relationship shouldn't be based on sex. But after meeting Ben she no longer gave a damn about such reservations, about caution and prudence. Frequent sex was definitely a good start for *this* relationship, into which both of them had plummeted without a safety net. She'd spent December with him in the Croatian town of Osijek and since February he'd been living in Freiburg. They were kindred spirits, both at risk of falling into the abyss. Having found each other they had to make the most of it, naked and entwined. Sex was a good way of banishing the fear of failure. Their bodies could get closer while their souls still had a few obstacles to overcome.

Ben was anything but a hero of women's dreams, but what they did in bed, on the floor, in the bathtub or in the car was thoroughly satisfactory, because somehow everything fitted, because each body seemed to shape itself to fill the hollows of the other, because they just did what they fancied.

"Ow!" Ben said.

"What?"

"You bit me."

"It was just a nibble."

He laughed.

She bit him again.

"Ow!" Ben said, and it struck her that one day, in the very distant future, she might be able to love this strange, lugubrious, gentle, homeless man.

2

At seven a.m., worn out, she trudged through the empty corridors of police H.Q. Alfons Hoffmann was already in his office; apart from that it was quiet. Some of the team were attending seminars in preparation for next year's World Cup or busy with the Confederations Cup in Leipzig or Frankfurt, where the third and fourth place playoff and the final were being played this Wednesday. Language courses, panic training, dealing with violent fans, security strategies – these were the topics of the summer. Squabbles that lasted weeks – who was going to be part of it next year and who wasn't? Grown men running down the corridors, their eyes bursting with excitement like children. Rolf Bermann, head of section 11, suddenly had friends. It was Rolf this, Rolf that, fancy a beer, Rolf? The stakes were high.

"Morning," Hoffmann said as he chewed. In his hand was a chocolate croissant, as every day at the top of the hour.

"Morning."

"Fancy a bite?"

She just nodded.

"Anything new on Nadine?" she mumbled, her mouth full.

"No."

Bonì kept going. She didn't meet anyone else on the way to her new office, which she was sharing with Thomas Ilic. Now she remembered. They were visiting a training camp that morning, followed by a meeting with French and Dutch colleagues.

"I need one more woman," Bermann had said at one of their last meetings.

"Me, me, me!" Peter, Richie, Tommy and all the rest of them cried.

"A *woman*, idiots."

"Why?" Louise said.

"To escort the players' wives."

"Me, me, me!"

"Louise?"

She'd stared at him, picturing Heidi Klum clones whose purpose in life consisted of basking in the shadow of their football star and giving birth to lots of little future football stars. "Are you actually serious?"

Bermann had grinned.

"Kiss my arse, Rolf!"

"Not in a million years."

Bonì entered the office and sat at her desk. Ilic wasn't here yet either. She sank into the chair and yawned into the pleasant silence. Bermann occupied her thoughts once more, Bermann who a few months ago had again shown that deep inside his macho soul sat the grain of a lonely but stable personality. She'd told him about her trip to Slavonia and Bosnia at the beginning of December. About the hunt for Antun Lončar, alias Heinrich Schwarzer, who she'd finally encountered in the Bosnian village of Štrpci, also known as Schutzberg.

Bermann ranted and raved.

Then he stopped ranting and raving, and sat down. They drank coffee in silence.

Eventually Bermann said, "Let's not talk about this again, alright? It never happened."

And so it hadn't happened.

Claus Rohmueller came in the morning rather than at lunchtime. At eight o'clock he was sitting opposite her, beneath the poster with the laughing Asian children in red monks' habits, drinking espresso, his anxious eyes clutching onto her. At his feet lay a collie, clearly old, and the dog was on edge too. It kept lifting its head and looking at the door. "He can sense it," Claus Rohmueller said.

Louise nodded. People and their dogs. Another puzzle she would never solve. She didn't have anything against dogs, though, just so long as they didn't start sniffing around her with their filthy snouts.

The dog whimpered enquiringly.

"Quiet, Cesare."

"Cesare?"

"After Cesare Pavese."

She raised her eyebrows.

"An Italian writer I greatly admire."

"I see."

A family that admired writers.

Claus Rohmueller put a briefcase on his lap and opened it. "PRADA" was emblazoned inside a silver triangle.

The dark-grey suit, dark-blue tie and elegant black shoes were evidently from top designers. Rohmueller himself was a slim, pale, handsome and very rich man with taste. Louise didn't have anything against rich people, just so long as they weren't condescending towards her.

He took a number of documents from the briefcase and placed them on the desk. Photographs of Nadine, lists of names and addresses, school reports, various C.V.s. Twenty-two years reduced to numbers and letters.

His hand trembling, he held up a list. "Friends and acquaintances, so far as we know." Another list: "Fellow students, tutors, professors." The next list: "Men in chronological order."

Louise nodded. No wonder the daughter felt the need to get away. From all that wealth, elegance and fastidiousness.

She took the last list: "Men in chronological order." Names, addresses, dates of birth, photos, time frames. Three entries, all valid for about two years. A good, respectable girl.

Harald/Bonn, Richard/Bonn, Serge/Freiburg.

She wondered how the girl's worship of Jack/U.S.A. fitted in here. *Alcohol, drugs, hitchhiking, Buddhism, jazz, psychological problems, married three times, possibly homosexual,* Ilic had noted.

"So far as we know, she's not with anyone at the moment."

Bonì nodded.

"Talk to me," Rohmueller whispered.

Surprised, she looked up.

"We haven't had a wink of sleep in days. We . . ." He rubbed his brow. "My wife is sick with worry."

"I know. I'm sorry, I'm just . . ." She broke off. "Worn out" wasn't a friendly term to use right at that moment.

"I know, you're doing all you can to—"

"We are. But there's no evidence that points to a crime. Not a single piece. And I hope it stays that way."

"Yes," Rohmueller said.

She knew what he was thinking. Nadine had been abducted. Back home in Bonn the mother was sitting by the telephone, waiting for a ransom call. Because everything in the Rohmuellers' life was linked to money, this must be too.

"I don't believe she's been abducted, Herr Rohmueller. You—"

"Yes," Rohmueller said.

"Demands for ransoms are almost always made very early on. Before the relatives inform the police."

"Yes," Rohmueller said for the third time.

She looked closely at him, then suddenly it dawned on her. For as long as the Rohmuellers kept believing in an abduction they didn't have to contemplate anything worse – murder, or suicide.

Louise poured herself a glass of water and took a large gulp. Wealth clouded people's view – the view of both the wealthy and those who had dealings with them.

All the same, she told him, of course they would have the forensic team inspect Nadine's apartment, and they would also talk to friends, neighbours and fellow students. But they had to keep a slight distance. Nadine was an adult. She was free to do as she pleased. If she wanted to go away, nobody could stop her.

"I don't understand."

"What if she just wanted to go to ground for a few weeks without telling her parents? She—"

"Go to ground?"

"Get away."

Rohmueller nodded. "You don't know her."

"I know other girls."

"Nadine is slightly . . . fearful of life," he said softly. "She lives through books, do you understand? One day she might find the courage to live a little less intensely, but not yet."

"Do you know that, or do you believe you know?"

He waited a moment before saying, "Are you looking for proof of a feeling?"

Louise couldn't help smiling. Not her, no, certainly not.

Shortly afterwards there was a knock at the door. Meirich, a grey-bearded veteran from the Organised Crime squad, popped his head in. "Could I speak with you for a sec?"

She nodded. As she went to the door she tried to recall his first name, but without success.

Behind her Cesare whimpered, as if he didn't want her to go. "Quiet, Cesare," Rohmueller said.

"Hans," Meirich said, offering her his hand.

Louise took it. "Now I remember."

"Hans the office messenger." Meirich smiled cheerfully. "Here," he said, handing her the fax of a missing person report. "A boy from Oberrimsingen."

She read it in silence. Eduard "Eddie" Holzner, resident in Grezhausen, Oberrimsingen, Breisach, born 15/3/1990, last seen Sunday 26 June 2005 around 4 p.m.

Bonì stared at the sheet of paper in her hand. Nadine Rohmueller on Saturday afternoon, Eddie Holzner on Sunday afternoon. *Two* young people fleeing their lives?

"The mother has just been with our colleagues in Breisach."

Louise looked at the mother's name. Gabriele Edwina Holzner. The signature could have been that of a ten-year-old. "It took her three days?"

Meirich shrugged. "Fifteen-year-old wanders off and doesn't come home . . . Happens every day."

"We've got another one. A student from Freiburg." Louise told him about Nadine Rohmueller.

"Could be a coincidence," Meirich said. "You do get the strangest coincidences."

Oh yes, Louise thought. Tell me something I don't know. "Her father's in there. I've got to go back."

Meirich nodded. Without his cheerful smile he looked tense and exhausted. Worn out, she thought.

"Anyway, thanks for this," she said, waving the sheet of paper.

"About Breisach . . . someone ought to go over there."

"This afternoon. What's it got to do with Organised Crime?"

Meirich raised his hand and pointed at the corridor, grinning.

She nodded. There was nobody around from D11.

"We've got a bit of slack right now," he said. "You can borrow me for a few days if you like."

Did they want to? She didn't know. Quite apart from the fact that Hans Meirich was above her in the police hierarchy, he was an old-school copper. One of those she didn't get on easily with.

But who *did* she get on easily with apart from Thomas Ilic and Alfons Hoffmann?

And they could always use someone with Meirich's experience.

And she found him quite likeable, in a way.

"As a team player," Meirich said with an innocent air.

"Fine."

"What can I do?"

She smiled. It might be fun bossing around one of the old-timers from Organised Crime. "Go and see our colleagues in Breisach. Illi and I will talk to the mother."

"Illi?"

"Thomas Ilic."

"The lad who was at Heuweiler when the S.W.A.T. guy was killed? Wasn't he . . ." Meirich left his sentence unfinished.

She nodded. Trauma, sick leave, eighteen months off work. But he was still her favourite colleague.

"He was, but everything's alright again now."

"O.K. If you need more people I could get you another colleague or two."

She just stared at him.

"It's still your case," Meirich said, raising his hands defensively.

"Good."

"I'll go to Breisach with one of my colleagues, then."

She nodded. "I'll have to speak to Rolf first."

"Do you want me to do it?"

"No."

Meirich smiled. "Your case."

"Yes," Louise said.

Claus Rohmueller sensed it, the dog sensed it. Everything was different now.

Swearing him to secrecy, Bonì disclosed what they'd found out. She felt somehow that Rohmueller deserved to know.

"*Another* child?"

"Could be a coincidence. You do get the strangest coincidences."

"For heaven's sake, another child . . ."

"Please calm down, Herr Rohmueller. Who knows what's happened? Maybe there's nothing to link the two of them. Maybe . . ." Louise stopped. She knew she wasn't a convincing liar.

"Yes," Rohmueller said.

"Have you ever heard the name Eduard Holzner? Eddie?"

He shook his head. The name of the village didn't mean anything to him either. Grezhausen, Oberrimsingen. He had no idea where it was.

"I need your help. I need you to be strong," Louise said.

"Yes."

"I need you to keep hoping, do you understand?"

Rohmueller nodded, but she could see that he was battling his tears. Bonì offered him a tissue. He shook his head and took a cloth handkerchief from his bag.

Her gaze fell on the dog. He was staring at her with silent eyes. Yes, the dog sensed it too.

Everything was different now.

Ten minutes later Ilic arrived. He stayed with Claus Rohmueller while Louise went into the next-door office to call Bermann.

Bermann already knew. Anselm Löbinger, head of Division One, had let him know during the flight to Frankfurt. Hans Meirich and another colleague from Organised Crime would be joining their team.

Bermann knew about Eddie Holzner too.

She hung up.

Of course, her case.

said. "I've no idea," Ilic said.

3

"Right," Ilic said, opening the folder with the sheets covered in blue ink, which she so loved. He was sitting in the passenger seat of his car; she was driving. An old tradition, a new reason. He was still on medication and unable to concentrate for long periods.

Early that morning he'd been to Nadine's bank with a financial investigator from section 31. From there his colleague had called Mastercard and American Express; Nadine used both these credit cards. There had been a few transactions in the previous week – shopping, restaurants, nothing out of the ordinary. Eight hundred euros on Saturday lunchtime, handed over to a small, expensive boutique near Münsterplatz.

"But there might be more stuff," Ilic said.

She nodded. They would have to wait another few days, especially if they were working on the assumption that Nadine had gone abroad. Credit card transactions in the U.S. took a while to make their way across the big pond.

But was that still their assumption?

"Yes. No. I don't know," Ilic said.

"No," Bonì said.

He laughed uncertainly. "Is that a hunch?"

She shot him a glance. Ilic was one of the few of her colleagues who took hunches seriously. But this was about probabilities and experience rather than hunches. Eighteen months away from the force, all the medication, loneliness, self-doubt – it must be deeply unsettling. Maybe worst of all were the looks when you came back. Victims of crimes and psychopaths had traumas, police officers didn't.

Police officers helped others, they were strong and psychologically invulnerable.

The same look had been in Hans Meirich's eyes earlier. A mixture of empathy, disgust, contempt and amusement.

"You're right," Ilic said. "We can forget abroad."

There was a pause, then Louise said, "We've lost a whole day."

"You can't look at it like that."

She braked at a traffic light. In front was Claus Rohmueller's black Volvo, taking them to his daughter's apartment. She sensed that he was looking at her in his rear-view mirror. That he could do with an encouraging smile. But she didn't feel like smiling.

"What about Rohmueller? Should we cross him off too?"

She shrugged. In theory fathers belonged to the pool of potential suspects. Like Serge/Freiburg, her most recent ex. "I think so."

"But shouldn't we investigate him? His financial circumstances, that sort of thing? Where does all his money come from? Does he still have any money, in fact?"

"We ought to have started on that yesterday too."

"Louise . . ."

She looked at him, unable to make out the eyes behind his sunglasses. He looked so different from two years ago. A few years older, many years wearier. His face pale and bloated, fatter in the belly and on the hips. A permanent film of sweat covered his brow, even though he generally felt cold if she touched him.

"Why do I keep making these sorts of mistakes, Illi?"

"You're not making mistakes, you're just not all-knowing."

"We've lost a whole day because I didn't take it seriously."

Ilic didn't respond.

"I shouldn't have taken you to the Rappeneck that time."

"Let's not start all that again."

She focused on the road. The Volvo pulled away and she put her foot down. "And as for the Niemanns . . ."

"Is everything your fault now?"

"Am I not concentrating enough? Am I too loose with the rules? With you I should have—"

"Rubbish, Louise."

"Hey, that's *my* word."

Ilic giggled. "It's a nice word. You can really put your soul into it."

"I say it better."

"Go on, then."

"*Rubbish!*"

"Yes, you do say it better."

"It has to come from below, from the chest."

"*Rubbish!*" Ilic said from his chest.

"You got it!"

They both gave a subdued laugh.

"Do you want a few of my pills?" Ilic asked. "They help against depression and a bad conscience."

"Rubbish."

Ilic nodded with a smile.

"Let's do it how we used to, Illi."

"What? You talk and I listen?"

"Yes."

Although she felt slightly better, the questions had taken hold inside her head. All the *if onlys*.

She talked, he listened. "At eight o'clock on Saturday evening she and her friend went out to eat at Café Wiener. At ten they moved on to Oscar's, and at one to Kagan. Everything perfectly normal, nothing unusual to report, Nadine same as ever, the friend says."

"Beatrice."

"Beatrice. Where did you get the name from?"

"Rohmueller."

"Of course. So, 'same as ever' means cheerful, but diffident, a bit uptight, insecure and rather conventional, because she hasn't yet wrestled free from her upbringing, her home, and the expectations of her parents. Men like her, but she's too shy to notice or to play along. She leaves at five on Sunday morning, intending to take a taxi back to her apartment."

"Yes."

"Did she get home or not? Did she leave again? Was anyone in her apartment?"

From the corner of her eye Louise could see Ilic writing. And she knew what: check cab companies. Another thing they hadn't yet done. She shook her head in anger.

"By eleven on Sunday morning she hadn't turned up to Aran, where she was supposed to be having brunch with Beatrice and others."

"Like every Sunday morning."

"It happened in the interim. Between five and eleven on Sunday morning."

"Yes."

"Have we been in touch with the telephone companies?"

Ilic started writing again.

"Dammit," Louise said. "Call Karin and tell her to get onto it right away. The cab firms, the phone calls."

Ilic took out his mobile. "Could you put the heating on, please?"

"But it's summertime, Illi."

Ilic dialled the number.

"Are you really cold?"

"I don't know. Yes, I think so."

She turned the knob. "The blower too?"

"If you don't mind."

Karin the trainee inspector had some information. Nadine Rohmueller's name hadn't turned up in connection with any car rental company or airline, and nor had she booked a train ticket, at least not online.

Not a rich daughter trying to get away.

No trip abroad.

"Suicide?" Ilic said incidentally.

45

"Then it would all be coincidence. Nadine on Saturday, Eddie on Sunday. A bit too much coincidence."

Ilic nodded.

They didn't say anything else until they got to Herdern. The word hung between them like a lead weight. Suicide, but in a different context, and both of them knew it.

She wondered what it was that might have saved Ilic.

Claus Rohmueller stopped in a winding, quiet street below Freiburg forest. When they got out he pointed to a modern, three-storey building with wide balconies and floor-to-ceiling windows.

The dog went ahead.

"Let's see if her car's there first," Louise said.

Rohmueller unlocked the front door. They went into the underground garage via the cellar steps. Rohmueller stopped beside a nearly new black Golf.

"Don't touch," Louise said.

He nodded.

They took the lift to the third floor. Sun flooded through the glass façade of the stairwell and the marble floor was dazzlingly bright. Houseplants stood at regular distances along the glass wall. No noise was coming from the apartments; the entire building was rigid with silence and neatness.

The dog went ahead again, then gave a restrained bark by one of the apartment doors.

Rohmueller took a key wallet from his pocket.

"Wait," Louise said. She took the wallet, got him to show her the right key and unlocked the door. The dog pushed past her, Ilic stayed close behind her, while Rohmueller stayed where he was. She saw the dog trot into the first room that led off from the hallway, then come out, enter the next one, come out again, then disappear once more.

Useful, she thought.

"Where is he?" Rohmueller croaked. In a mirror on the wall opposite she saw that he was standing on the threshold behind her, his hand on the doorframe, his face deathly pale.

They waited. The dog didn't reappear.

Ilic followed the dog, his hand on his holster. "He's here," she heard him say.

Bonì entered the room – the sitting room. The dog was lying beside a sofa, wagging his tail.

Ilic stood at the entrance to the kitchen, shaking his head.

She went back into the hall, checked the bedroom, the bathroom and dining room. Nadine wasn't there.

Rohmueller, who was still standing in the doorway to the apartment, looked at her anxiously. Only now did Louise realise that he'd contemplated the possibility of suicide too.

"She's not here," she said.

Nadine's apartment was pretty much how Louise had imagined it when she met the father: a restrained dream of design, aesthetics and understatement, without any showiness. An elegant leather sofa, Bang & Olufsen hi-fi, designer shelving, everything in tones of brown and matt white, apart from the Apple laptop on the desk that shone brightly. No dust, no items of clothing lying around on the floor, not even a pencil that had been overlooked.

The large kitchen contained a few splashes of colour and stainless steel, jazzy chairs and expensive Rosenthal porcelain. On the wall was a poster of a Jack Kerouac exhibition at New York Public Library from several years back. In the bedroom she took a peek at the large wardrobe – Max Mara, Edcada, Ralph Lauren, handbags by Gucci and Louis Vuitton, Armani jeans, Hermès scarves, everything folded, piled and hung up with the greatest of care.

Fastidiousness was a family trait.

Louise momentarily felt shabby in her never-changing outfit: blouse, jeans, Converse.

Rohmueller was sitting on the sofa, staring into the distance. He seemed to have crumpled on entering the house, out of relief perhaps that the worst hadn't occurred, or maybe it was just exhaustion.

His gaze fell on her hands, and his face filled with anxiety again. Like Ilic, she'd put on a pair of disposable gloves.

"Where's the phone?"

The telephone was on a small antique table. No messages on the answer machine. She took the cordless receiver from the dock. The last ten numbers Nadine had called were saved, along with the name and length of conversation. The previous Friday: "Papa office", "Papa mobile", "Mama mobile", "Home", "Pizza", "Taxi", "Beatrice". On Saturday: "Beatrice", "Inge", "Rudi".

Bonì noted the names, numbers and dates.

"Do you know an Inge and a Rudi?"

"Inge Rovak is on one of my lists. They're studying together. But I don't know Rudi."

Ilic came into the sitting room from the hallway. "Louise?"

He took her to the bathroom and opened the mirror cabinet above the sink. One of the compartments was full of medicines. Luvox, fluoxetine, citalopram, Seroxat, she read.

"Anti-depressants," Ilic said quietly.

They went back to the sitting room.

"Did you find anything?" Rohmueller asked.

Louise shook her head. Her eyes met Ilic's. "Would you describe your daughter to us? What should we know?"

Rohmueller rested his crossed hands on his stomach and rubbed his thumbs together fitfully. Nadine was slim, terribly pretty, intelligent. Shy. An introvert. She did yoga and went jogging every other day. Physically, she was very fit.

Any illnesses?

No.

Drugs?

What are you implying? Absolutely not!

Any medication?

Medication? No. What sort of medication do you mean?

Louise shrugged as if to say: Just asking.

"Are you going back to Bonn today?" Ilic asked.

"No, I'm going to stay here until . . ." Rohmueller paused.

For a moment there was silence in the room.

"Go home, Herr Rohmueller," Louise said. "Look after your wife."

"She's coming here tomorrow."

"In that case you ought to have all your calls forwarded to your mobile. In case someone rings your home in Bonn."

"Of course." He took a notebook from his pocket, jotted something down, then put it away again. "Can I stay here? In Nadine's apartment?"

"Not tonight."

"But I—"

"Our colleagues from Forensics will be coming later. You can move in after they've finished up here."

"Alright, then. I'll wait here for your colleagues and—"

She shook her head. They'd already destroyed enough evidence these past few minutes.

They parted company by the Volvo.

"Call us when you know where you'll be spending the night," Ilic said.

Rohmueller nodded. "So you . . . you're going to Grezhausen now?"

They didn't reply.

"Couldn't I come along?"

"No," Louise said.

"But if—"

"No."

49

Rohmueller turned away, opened the rear passenger door and let the dog into the car.

Louise touched his arm. "If I see you in Grezhausen . . ."

"O.K., I understand."

"I hope you do." She waited, but Rohmueller didn't say anything else. They watched the Volvo drive off.

"We can rule out suicide, then."

"Nobody kills themselves in an apartment like that, Illi."

"No?"

"That's not an apartment for blood, the stench of a corpse, urine stains. If she's killed herself, she did it somewhere else."

"But where? Where would you commit suicide, Louise?"

"You tell me."

Ilic frowned. "In the bath."

They got into the car. Louise was going to probe further, but let it go. Not now, she thought. Let's not get distracted again.

One evening, over a glass of something.

In any case she had to tell him that Ben Liebermann, who he'd studied with, was now living in Freiburg and that the two of them were an item. Six months ago Ilic had tracked Ben down in south-eastern Europe, then sent him a woman who was on an unofficial, sensitive mission. Sometimes she wondered whether he'd had an inkling of what would happen. Whether he'd hoped there would be a spark between her and Ben.

"In the car. She takes sleeping pills and gets into the car."

"The car's in the garage." Ilic cleared his throat.

A patrol car from Freiburg North stopped behind them. Ilic got out and gave a policeman Nadine's key to hand to the Forensics team which would be there sometime that morning.

When he returned to the car Louise said, "Or maybe some particular place. A favourite place that has an association with some writer she adores. Here Schiller wrote his . . . his . . . whatever. Here Nadine passed away."

"That's cynical."

She shrugged and put the car into gear. People who confused fiction with real life gave every reason for cynicism. They worshipped dead authors and couldn't get a grip on their own lives.

4

The sun was shining on Grezhausen, a hamlet in the triangle formed by the Tuniberg, the A5 and the Rhine, originally the possession of the Cistercian Order of Günterstal, who established a number of granges here, Ilic read from his papers. Louise smiled – so much had changed, but some things were just the same. A well-prepared Ilic.

Between a moss-covered stone wall on one side of the road and houses set back on the other they drove slowly into the village.

"Look, there's the chapel," Ilic said, pointing to the left.

She nodded. "And there's Meirich."

Hans Meirich was sitting in the sun beside Sandy, a colleague from Organised Crime, on a bench opposite the chapel. He had called from Breisach. The constable who'd filed the report had noticed that Eddie's mother showed signs of physical abuse and had obviously come against the will or knowledge of her husband. Eddie's father had a widespread reputation as a drinker and a thug. He used to have a job at a petrol station in Oberrimsingen, but was sacked for theft. Alcohol, casual labour, social security. And twenty years ago he'd served time for manslaughter.

Just be a bit careful, the constable had advised Meirich.

Louise had suggested that the four of them should carry out the interrogation together. Meirich agreed.

She parked in the shade in front of the chapel.

"I heard about Heuweiler," Meirich said as he shook Ilic's hand. "It's great to have you back." His eyes weren't visible behind the dark sunglasses, but there was sympathy in his voice.

"Yes," Ilic said, surprised.

"Must have been dreadful," Sandy said, rocking her head so that the blonde plaits danced on her shoulders.

"Yes, yes," Ilic said.

They discussed how they would proceed. Although they were a *single* investigation team, it was the Serious Crime squad's investigation, not Organised Crime's. Which meant Bonì and Ilic would lead the interrogation, while Meirich and Sandy would remain in the background.

"If we forget or miss something, then you step in."

"Wouldn't it be better if us men—"

Louise raised her eyebrows as a warning.

"I mean, with *this* sort of individual."

"He won't be intimidated by a woman," Sandy said.

"If it goes tits up, you can save us," Louise said nicely.

Meirich and Sandy exchanged glances, then nodded.

On the drive to Grezhausen Louise and Ilic had discussed how to proceed. In different circumstances they would have summoned Eddie's mother back to Breisach police station, or sought her out while shopping or met her at the social security office so they could speak to her alone. She was unlikely to tell the truth in the presence of her husband.

But they didn't have much time.

Quite apart from the fact that Louise was especially keen to speak to Eddie's father.

"We can walk there," Meirich said. "It's just down the road."

She didn't want to make a habit of disagreeing with Meirich, but four Kripo officers arriving on foot wasn't going to make much of an impression. Four officers leaping from two cars, on the other hand, would have a much greater impact. "We'll drive." They got into their cars.

"What was that about?" Ilic said.

"What?"

"Heuweiler."

"You're going to have to put up with it for several months. Maybe your entire life."

Ilic didn't respond.

"What do you think of Sandy?" Louise said. "Meirich's busy little bee?"

"My God, the plaits," Ilic said, shaking his head.

"Blonde and plaits."

"Maybe she's moonlighting at I.K.E.A."

"But she's meant to be really good, so I've heard."

"Oh, she's alright," Ilic said.

Louise smiled. Ilic never made good jokes.

Eddie Holzner's family lived in a small detached house beyond the Möhlin, on the road to Hartheim. A red shingle roof with a satellite dish, a small strip of grass around the house, bordered by a wooden fence with sharp stakes. Much of the paint had flaked off the front of the house, the curtains had yellowed in the sun and in the tiny front garden was plastic furniture from a cheap D.I.Y. store. On the garden table were a half-drunk bottle of beer and an ashtray disappearing beneath a mountain of cigarette butts. Stubbed-out cigarettes littered the lawn too. No marble, no floor-to-ceiling windows, no Max Mara or Gucci. If there were a connection between Nadine Rohmueller and Eddie Holzner, it was well hidden.

The door was opened by a short, squat woman in a pink dressing gown, with dyed orange hair. Her eyes flitted from one person to the next, finally alighting on Louise. She didn't need to be told that there were four police officers standing at her door. "For heaven's sake," she whispered. She put a hand over her mouth and bowed her head.

"There's no cause for concern . . ." Louise said to reassure her.

But the woman wasn't thinking about Eddie. "You can't come *here*! Go, now, before he wakes up!" She was about to close the door.

Louise raised a hand and held the door open. "Are you Gabriele Holzner? Eddie's mother?"

"He'll . . ." the woman whispered. "He'll . . ."

They looked at each other. Only now did Louise notice the yellow marks on the left-hand side of the woman's forehead and around her left eye. There was also a slight swelling beneath the eye.

Anger rose inside Louise.

It's a man's world.

She hadn't thought about the phrase for a long time. Many years ago she'd seen it on a rear-window sticker. An abducted girl had lain in the boot. Annetta, folded like a sheet of paper, raped, beaten, strangled.

"Your son is missing, Frau Holzner, and we—"

"But I *can't* let you in."

Louise nodded. She hated situations like this, but she had to find Eddie and Nadine. She couldn't make any allowances, even though she knew what would happen in this house after they'd gone.

"Illi, call the public prosecutor," she said, without taking her eyes off the face of the terrified woman. "We need a search warrant." A mean little trick that usually worked.

"For God's sake . . . But be really quiet, he's sleeping!" Gabriele Holzner whispered as she let them in.

She took them down a dark hallway into the sitting room. About fifteen square metres, Louise thought, loads of plastic and synthetic fibres, the furniture from a D.I.Y. store or off a skip. The windows were closed; the air was thick with stale cigarette smoke and mustiness. Two wasps were circling a half-eaten jam roll on the dining table, while old editions of *BILD* newspaper were heaped beside the tatty sofa. As if in mockery, the sunlight slanting through the little windows made parts of the room appear friendly and cosy.

"Sorry," Frau Holzner mumbled, before hurrying back into the hallway. They heard a door shut.

And they heard her being sick.

"Shit," Louise said. She thought about going to check on her, but she didn't move.

The lavatory flushed.

"It's hard to believe there are people who live like this," Sandy said quietly.

"This is how poor people live," Ilic said.

Meirich nodded. "Give them money and they change." He was looking at Louise. He ran a hand across his grey beard. For a moment she had the impression that he wasn't being serious. That he'd said it because of her.

Frau Holzner came back.

"Everything O.K.?" Louise said.

"Yes, yes." Frau Holzner shot her a hostile glance then looked at the floor. She might be in her late thirties. Her face was grey and limp, her hands looked dried out and neglected, the fingernails chewed.

"You are Eddie's mother, yes?"

"Yes."

"Have you heard anything from him since?"

Frau Holzner shook her head.

"Who might have heard from him? Does Eddie have any friends in the village?"

Gabriele Holzner shrugged. "Don't know." Her eyes wandered and then she blushed, as if only now aware of the state her sitting room was in. "Maybe Dennis."

"Dennis?"

"Ostermann. From school." Frau Holzner sat at the table. She stared at the half-eaten roll, the wasps. "You shouldn't have come here."

Yes, Louise thought. Once again her eyes met Meirich's and she guessed he was thinking the same thing. That he doubted she was competent to head the investigation team.

She had no desire to discuss this.

"We need to speak to your husband," she said.

Frau Holzner looked at the floor, then raised her head and it looked as if she were gazing into the distance through one of the windows.

"Frau Holzner, please get your husband."

Gabriele Holzner looked at her. "Can you take me away?"

"From here? Of course."

"Good." Frau Holzner stood up. "Because he's killed my child and now he's going to kill me."

"What do you think?" Meirich said.

They were standing in the street, in front of the rundown house. Sandy had driven to Breisach police station with Eddie Holzner's mother. Ilic was on the phone to Marianne Andrele, the duty public prosecutor, who apparently had her reservations. Their conversation was dragging out, and she heard Ilic explain the situation several times, repeatedly emphasising the need for protective measures. Surely Eddie and Nadine's lives took priority, he insisted, and maybe . . .

Bonì shrugged. What should she think? She couldn't yet see any connection between Eddie and Nadine, let alone between Eddie's father and Nadine. All they had were two missing young people from different places and strata of society, as well as a statement from a woman who'd evidently been battered by her husband for years.

Two patrol cars appeared on the thoroughfare, the officers from Breisach Louise had asked for. They were driving fast with their lights flashing. Children ran behind the cars and were already on the bridge. A handful of Grezhausen residents stood about twenty metres away, watching what was unfolding outside the Holzners' house.

"No," Ilic said eventually, putting his mobile away. "No search warrant. We need more."

Yes, Louise thought with a sigh.

A body.

*

Eddie Holzner's father opened only after they'd rung six times. He was wearing a black cowboy hat, shorts, a T-shirt in the German national football colours, and he stared at them with his red eyes. In his hand was a lit cigarette. "Coppers," he said disdainfully. "Seven of them, too."

They showed their I.D.s.

Holzner took a drag of his cigarette and waited.

"Could we talk inside?" Louise said. She could smell the alcohol, and sense the aggression.

His eyes strayed lustfully over her. But she'd long stopped feeling intimidated by the looks people gave her. By men.

"No way."

"Herr Holzner, your son has been reported missing, and we—"

"'Herr Holzner.'" Eddie's father laughed. He sized up Ilic and Meirich. "Do I have to speak to her?" he asked Meirich, nodding in Louise's direction.

"Yes, you do."

"Reported by who?"

"An unknown source."

"*Unknown,* my arse. Where's the bitch? Have you taken her away?"

Louise didn't reply.

"Let's talk inside," Meirich said.

Holzner flicked his butt into the grass. "You're not coming into this house. Piss off."

"We're getting a search warrant," Meirich said.

"You know where you can stick your search warrant. Fucking police." Holzner grinned.

Louise heard Ilic clear his throat as a warning. But she knew he wasn't going to butt in. "You've got two options," she said. "Either you talk, or we're going to take you into custody on suspicion of abducting two people."

"I'm not talking to anyone apart from my brief," Holzner said, rubbing his stomach with a grin. Then the penny dropped. "Two?"

"Your son and a female student from Freiburg."

"Am I guilty of everything now, or what? Doesn't it matter that the little shit was going to kill me? He threw a fucking stone at my head, the bastard." Holzner had raised his voice and taken a step forward.

"You stay right where you are."

"Piss off, bitch."

"You'd better watch it, Herr Holzner, or we'll be talking at—"

She didn't get any further. Holzner struck out so quickly that she barely registered the movement. But instinctively she'd recoiled and the fist met with thin air. Ilic pulled her aside as Holzner stumbled forwards. Recovering, he raised his fist again, flailing around wildly. From the corner of her eye she saw Meirich collapse, then the uniformed officers were in front of her, wrestling Holzner to the ground. There were shouts, threats and insults, but she couldn't tell who they came from.

"Shit," Meirich stuttered faintly. He was sitting on the ground holding his mouth. Blood dripped onto his jacket.

Bonì laid a hand on his shoulder. "Are you alright?"

"Shit." Meirich had turned deathly pale and was trembling.

"Show me."

He took a handkerchief from his pocket and pressed it to his mouth. "Just my lip," he said, struggling to his feet.

The handkerchief soon turned red.

"Come on, show me," Louise said.

Meirich lifted the hand with the handkerchief. His lips were split and his grey beard dripped with blood.

"You need to see a doctor."

"Shit."

The constables marched Holzner past them. Meirich took a step backwards as if afraid of being hit again. Holzner began to laugh, loudly and with satisfaction. Meirich lowered his gaze.

It's like that, then, Louise thought.

"You can lead the interrogation," she said, patting his shoulder.

5

"Alone again," Ilic said as the two of them watched the patrol car drive off.

Louise nodded. Her mind was on Ben Liebermann. She wanted to be with him now, to be in bed with him. When he came to Freiburg she realised that there were ways to offset the hatred and aggression she was confronted with every day. And that she really needed this kind of respite.

Ilic sighed. "What a brute—"

"Dennis Ostermann, Illi."

"Yes." He took out his mobile.

She looked at the Holzners' house. While Ilic spoke to Alfons Hoffmann, she recalled what Eddie's mother had said. *Because he's killed my child and now he's going to kill me.*

She rubbed her eyes wearily. Nadine on Saturday afternoon, Eddie on Sunday afternoon.

Nadine and Eddie.

A student from a rich Bonn family, and a secondary school kid from a Grezhausen family on benefits. What if it were a coincidence? What if Eddie and Nadine had never met and there was no connection?

Two missing people, two cases.

She wondered what role the fathers played. Claus Rohmueller, who seemed close to death with worry; Holzner, who beat his wife and maybe his son too.

What if the son were like the father? What if Eddie had met Nadine in Freiburg and abducted or killed her? Nadine, the pretty, rich student?

Ilic was off the phone, and was now leafing through his folder. A computer printout of a map of Grezhausen.

She turned on the ignition.

"Right up there and then right again," Ilic said.

Dennis Ostermann had a cold. With a woollen scarf wrapped around his neck and in dark-blue pyjamas, his greasy hair was dishevelled and sticking up. He'd half opened the door and on a wall behind him Louise could see enormous faces on a television. The volume had been muted.

"Why, what about Eddie?" Dennis asked with a blocked nose.

"Are your parents in?" Ilic said.

"No." Dennis gave a loud cough and closed the door slightly. A snail retreating into its shell.

His face was now in darkness. The cough sounded artificial.

The white door brightly reflected the sunlight. Louise screwed up her eyes. "Could we have a word with you?"

Dennis kept coughing. She could just about see that he was shaking his head. Too ill, can't talk, it no doubt meant.

"Eddie has been missing since Sunday, Dennis."

Dennis coughed and coughed; it sounded as if he wouldn't be able to stop any time soon.

When the door closed another few centimetres the light bouncing off it was even more dazzling.

"Can we speak to your parents on the phone?" Ilic asked.

Dennis shrugged and went on coughing.

Louise took a step forwards and pushed the door open. She felt some resistance initially, but then it opened easily. Only now did she notice how fat Dennis was, and how empty his little eyes looked. A lonely, overweight boy. Only fifteen or sixteen years old but already virtually resigned to life.

The coughing stopped and Dennis stared at them. "I didn't do anything."

"This isn't about you, it's about Eddie."

"Louise," Ilic said softly.

She nodded and stepped back. Don't make any mistakes, Bonì . . . At least the door was no longer reflecting the sunlight. "Dennis, how can we get hold of your father or mother?"

"Why?"

"Because you're still a minor."

Dennis gave them a phone number. Ilic took out his mobile and moved a few metres away. Louise heard him speaking but couldn't make out what he was saying.

She looked at Dennis. "Got a cold?"

He nodded.

"Hopefully you don't have to go to school."

"No."

"Have you been off all week so far?"

"Yes."

"So you don't know if Eddie . . ." She sighed. "You don't have to talk to us, Dennis. You don't have to say anything that would incriminate you."

"What's happened to Eddie?"

"We don't know. He's disappeared."

"He wanted to . . ." Dennis said in a reedy voice. His face had turned red and she could see a touch of panic in those empty eyes.

Ilic came back. "That was his mother. She's fine with it, but she can't come now."

Louise nodded. "*What* did he want to do, Dennis?"

"You don't have to say anything that—" Ilic said.

She interrupted him. "He knows."

Dennis took a step towards them. "I told him we shouldn't, but he really wanted to. And then he took her away."

Louise felt a cold shudder run down her spine. "Took who away, Dennis?"

"The woman."

From his jacket pocket Ilic took the photograph of Nadine. "This woman?"

Dennis stared at it. "I don't know, maybe."

"Hold it and take a good look," Ilic said. Dennis obeyed and spent several seconds inspecting the image, before shrugging.

"Don't you recognise her?" Louise said.

"She was . . . Her face was . . . Someone had beaten her up."

"Beaten her up? Her face?"

He nodded. "Really badly, so badly that it was hard to make out what she looked like. To be honest . . ."

"Yes?"

Dennis said nothing.

"Could it have been the woman in the photo?" Louise asked insistently.

"I dunno. It's the right colour hair." Dennis gave the picture back.

"So, you're saying that someone beat her up, but it wasn't Eddie. But Eddie took her away. Is that right?"

"Yes."

"Just tell us what happened," Louise said firmly.

Dennis started talking.

The barn stood in what looked like an uncultivated field between Grezhausen and the Rhine. They parked the car by the side of the road and followed a well-worn path that bore the marks of shoes, dogs' paws and bicycle tyres. As it had rained several times overnight since Sunday the footprints couldn't belong to Eddie, Dennis or Nadine. All the same they took care to walk closely behind each other to the side of the path where there were no footprints.

When they reached the barn Bermann called back. A posse of uniformed officers from Lahr was on its way, as well as the canine unit from Umkirch and a helicopter from Stuttgart. France had been informed; their French colleagues would be starting a search on the other side of the Rhine Canal.

"That was quick," Louise said.

"Wasn't it?" Bermann said. "It's . . . twelve now. I'll be with you at five."

"You're coming here? What about the final?" She and Ilic exchanged glances.

Bermann didn't respond. In the background she could hear the clatter of cutlery and glasses. Someone called out, "Rolf!" – it sounded like Anselm Löbinger. Recently Bermann had seemed to draw a shorter straw than Löbinger in every respect. Löbinger had been promoted to division head rather than Bermann. Löbinger was watching the final in Frankfurt; Bermann had to go back to Freiburg.

And it wasn't hard to guess the mood he would be in.

"What are we going to tell the press and the parents? How certain are we that she's alive?" Bermann grunted.

"All we know is that she was still alive on Sunday afternoon."

"It's *Wednesday* today."

"You might well be right."

Silence.

"Graeve is going to come by around two."

She nodded. Reinhard Graeve, the new Kripo boss appointed six months ago, successor to Almenbroich and Bob, another one who made life tough for the alpha males and machos around Bermann.

"Anything else?" Bermann said.

"Not for the time being."

"How's Illi bearing up?"

"What a stupid question."

"You're a pain in the arse," Bermann grunted and cut her off.

Classic Rolf Bermann.

Bonì put her mobile away and walked a few steps to the barn, careful to avoid damaging any potential evidence. Forensics were on their way too.

She stopped by the door.

"Stupid question?" Ilic had followed her.

"He wanted to know if it was raining here too."

"Oh."

They looked inside the barn, which was shrouded in silence. An atmosphere of peace, secrets and gradual decay. Only the dark stains by the opposite wall didn't fit the picture. That was where the woman had lain.

Nadine?

Ilic guessed her thoughts. "Is it her?"

"We have to assume so."

Samples of the blood in the barn and D.N.A. material from Nadine's apartment would be sent to the forensic laboratory, then they would know for sure.

"What does 'looked at and touched' mean?" Ilic said.

The same question had been going through her head since Dennis told them that Eddie had looked at the woman and touched her. Had he raped her? Three days had passed, a long time for a boy like Eddie, who'd grown up amidst violence, poverty and alcohol, to not call an ambulance or the police when he stood beside an abused, defenceless, naked woman. "I don't know."

"What do you reckon on Dennis?"

"I think he'd love to be like Eddie, but doesn't dare to."

"You mean he'd have liked to 'touch' her too, but didn't?"

Louise nodded.

Dennis had found "the woman" in the barn on Sunday afternoon on the way back from the Rhine. She'd been lying on the floor, wrapped in a blanket, bleeding and covered in bruises. Her nose was broken, Dennis said, and maybe that wasn't all.

She wasn't able to talk or move.

Louise had no desire to imagine what had happened to her. What had been done to her between Sunday morning and Sunday afternoon. From a carefree life straight into the depths of hell.

No, that probably wasn't right. Maybe Nadine had long been living in a different sort of hell. A psychological hell made only bearable by anti-depressants.

Dennis had called Eddie, who turned up soon afterwards and "looked at" and "touched" the woman. Then the two of them cycled to Dennis's for supper and to watch a football match.

A phrase barged its way into her head. *Fucking, Football and Food – those are their basic needs.* One of her mother's sayings about men. She'd forgotten one of the basic needs: violence. But then again her mother wasn't a police officer; she didn't know the statistics.

At around 9 p.m. on Sunday evening Eddie cycled back to the barn. What happened then was a mystery. Did Nadine's ordeal continue?

Dennis turned up an hour later. The doors to the barn were open and Eddie had gone, as had the woman. Or at least that's what Dennis assumed, even though Eddie's bicycle was lying on the ground by the barn. Nobody responded when he called out and Dennis didn't dare take a look inside the barn. It was dark, and when he got off his bike he thought he'd heard a man's hushed voice and a rustling like footsteps in dry grass. He couldn't be certain, but it was enough to stop him from going in.

The following morning he'd gone back to the barn. Eddie's bike was no longer there and the barn was empty. Eddie hadn't answered his mobile since Sunday evening, so he'd probably gone away, Dennis said.

Where, Dennis? Where could he be?

To be honest . . . Sometimes he swam across to France, maybe he went to France with her. Paris and that.

Louise shook her head. Paris and that. The worlds that some people dreamed up.

The man's voice preoccupied her.

Yes, maybe Eddie's father's voice, Dennis had said. That's if he really had heard a voice.

They sat in the grass a few metres from the barn, a veil of silence over them: the waiting had begun. Louise gave a restrained yawn, Ilic looked at his fingers. He didn't appear relaxed. His first major case after eighteen months' sick leave. After Heuweiler.

Her gaze roamed the barn, the field and the strip of woodland, beyond which lay the Old Rhine. Where were Eddie and Nadine? Surely they couldn't be far.

A student from Freiburg, a boy from Grezhausen, both missing since the weekend. Here, in this barn, they had met.

Did Eddie take Nadine away? Did Nadine run away?

Paris and that.

Bonì was seized by anger. How easy it was to put a positive spin on the world. To put a positive spin on what you'd done or hadn't done. Even though he was a minor, Dennis would have to answer for his failure to render assistance. What ultimately happened to him was largely dependent on when, or whether, they found Nadine.

On what Eddie had done to her.

But maybe the story was quite different, she thought. If Dennis had actually heard a man's voice, this case was no longer just about Eddie and Nadine.

A call came from Karin, the trainee inspector. Ilic nodded, muttered a few "O.K."s and then said, "Thanks."

"Let me guess. No taxi to Wintererstrasse?"

"No."

"Do we have a list of destinations?"

"Yes."

"Illi . . ."

Ilic smiled. "Sorry. Right . . . " He paused.

"Are you flagging?"

"No."

"Because I have to squeeze every word out of you. If you're flagging, Illi, then . . ."

Ilic had turned away and was rubbing his temples.

"I'm sorry." She put a hand on his shoulder, which felt cold and tense.

"My concentration goes around lunchtime." He gave a faint smile.

"I can imagine."

"But I'm feeling better. I'm well again."

She nodded. He'd said the same thing two years ago when they stood in the rain on the Rappeneck. She'd believed him – a mistake she wasn't going to let herself make a second time.

"It's a long list," Ilic said.

"I thought as much."

The Kagan Club was on the top floor of the Solar Tower by the station. Even though there would barely be any trains or buses arriving and leaving at five o'clock on a Sunday morning, they had to assume that there would be travellers on the list of trips too, not just clubbers.

This was going to be a hard slog.

The staff at Wiener, Oscar's, Kagan. The taxi drivers, their passengers. Serge, the ex-boyfriend. She was going to ask Ilic to see to that one, but now the doubts had surfaced. What could she trust him to do and what not?

"I'm *well*, Louise." His voice sounded slightly grim. Once again he seemed to have guessed her thoughts.

She realised she was about to make another mistake. "Can you look after the list of trips?"

Ilic nodded, but she sensed that he was annoyed.

"And someone's got to talk to the people at Wiener, Oscar's and Kagan."

"Yes."

"We should get Karin or someone from Organised Crime to help you."

Ilic got up and held out his hand. She gave him the car keys.

"But you've got to promise me something."

"I promise."

68

"I want to hear it, Illi."

Ilic sighed. "O.K. What?"

"If you're not right, you're going to tell me."

"I'm feeling fine, Louise."

"If you don't, you say so. Promise?"

"Yes, yes, promise." He sat back down beside her. "I can't go on anymore, Louise. I feel shitty. My life's imploding. It's a disaster."

She said nothing.

Ilic got up, gave a dogged smile and left.

No, he really couldn't make good jokes.

6

An hour later the waiting was over. The technicians in their Tyvek suits were combing the barn, centimetre by centimetre. Uniformed officers from Lahr and Breisach, with help from Freiburg South station, were walking in a long chain across the field towards the woods. The helicopter flew above the Rhine and the woods and fields that bordered the river on the German side. The *brigade de gendarmerie* from Colmar was combing the river bank on the French side. Louise surveyed the scene in awe. Nobody had spelled it out yet, but the background seemed to be clear. Rohmueller had made a few telephone calls, triggering a flurry of activity at management level.

If only it were always so simple, she thought.

Patrol cars and police vans were parked by the side of the road, as well as broadcasting vans from the television networks. Behind a barrier a handful of reporters waited for the police spokeswoman. Louise had just briefed her and now she was striding energetically along the path towards the road, her azure blouse shining against the brownish-green of the field.

Meirich was back with stitches, plasters and a pale face. He was standing on his own, saying nothing; talking was obviously painful. What had happened outside the Holzners' house seemed to have made a lasting impression on him. The old hand knocked to the ground by an oik in front of a group of officers.

She'd asked him whether it wouldn't make sense to go on sick leave. The look he gave her was as ill-tempered as that on Ilic's face an hour earlier. He shook his head and produced some incomprehensible sounds without moving his lips.

Louise had shrugged. She was beginning to get tired of this. Every man a hero – they wouldn't settle for any less.

At around half past one she got a call from Hugo Chervel, who was in charge on the other side of the Rhine.

Chervel was a hero, too.

"*Alors?*" he said.

"*Rien.*"

They'd worked together in the past, most recently in the winter of 2002–03 when the German and French police had busted a child-trafficking ring operating from a Zen Buddhist monastery in Alsace.

"I've had a call from Paris," Chervel said in French.

"I see."

The flurry of activity at management level was continuing every which way. Rohmueller had tossed a pebble into the water and the ripples were now lapping as far away as Paris.

"If it helps," Chervel said.

"Let's hope it does."

They ended the call.

Louise liked Chervel even though he was an alpha male like Bermann. But unlike Bermann, he didn't get carried away, restricting himself to subtle teasing whenever comparisons were made between the French and the Germans. And he countered the endless French bureaucracy with common sense and purposefulness. Like Bermann, Chervel was a relic from an era when men thought that the smell of aftershave, cigarettes and sweat was sexy, and that they were the bee's knees, especially when it came to female desire. But she found it amusing to watch him navigate this extinct world with elegance and humour.

He and Bermann belonged to the same species: pureblood chauvinists – Chervel because he worshipped women, Bermann because deep down he was afraid of them. She couldn't imagine Chervel ever being violent towards a woman. With Bermann she wasn't so sure. It was pure chance that Bermann had ended up on the side of the good guys. If nothing else, his profession had socialised aspects of his personality and this set him apart from men like Holzner. But it wasn't much more than that.

Louise dismissed these thoughts. The case was starting to infect her, get inside her like a virus stealing its way into every cell of her body. Her defence mechanisms weren't working, they hadn't been in a long time. She'd lost the ability to distance herself.

Eddie, Nadine, Holzner, police H.Q., they were one aspect of her life.

Her apartment, the new car, the new man, they were another.

But the distinction between the two no longer existed; the boundaries had disappeared a while ago. The thought of what Holzner and Eddie might have done gave rise to the question of whether Chervel or Bermann might be capable of doing something similar, just because they were men.

She'd hoped that with Ben in her life something would change. Surely the other aspect did exist again, in all its clarity and intensity. But evidently nothing had changed, and this scared her.

Time for a break, she thought, before it's too late.

She scowled. Again? Wasn't she taking a break every year? A few weeks in rehab here, a few months in a monastery there, a visit to hospital when she'd been shot, sick leave for the whole of last November because she couldn't cope with what Antun Lončar, alias Heinrich Schwarzer, had done, holiday with Ben Liebermann in Osijek for the whole of last December ...

She glimpsed a movement and looked up. Meirich was on his way over to her, his eyebrows raised. She shook her head. No news from the French.

"You look terrible," she said.

Now Meirich's eyebrows sank threateningly.

"Go home, Hans."

The battered mouth opened slightly and Meirich mumbled

something unintelligible. He really did look in a pitiful state. Holzner's punch had damaged more than just the lips. Meirich's eyes lay in dark hollows and his look was one of despair, as if all his pride and self-esteem had crumbled the moment he'd been hit. As if that punch had thrown his entire existence into question.

"It can happen to anyone, Hans," she said, squeezing his arm.

He nodded. His eyes were now cold and alert.

"Don't lay a finger on him, alright?"

His eyebrows rose again.

"Holzner. You're not going to lay a finger on him."

Meirich waved his hand magnanimously. Not me, no way.

Exactly: heroes.

Lubowitz, one of the technicians from section 42, stepped out of the barn and motioned for her to come over. He was holding up a bag. As she made her way towards him she tried to work out what was in it.

A cigarette butt, barely more than the filter.

"Pretty fresh," he said. "Marlboro, I'd say. Number seven."

She peered into the barn. Around two dozen evidence markers were stuck into the ground. Number seven was close to the entrance. Louise looked up at Lubowitz, who must be 1.90 metres at least, a scruffy, occasionally cantankerous beanpole. She didn't know anything else about him. Tall, scruffy, grumpy, resourceful – that was it. They saw each other almost daily, but she didn't even know his first name. Nobody, she thought, knew his first name. Lubowitz was Lubowitz.

"What do you mean by pretty fresh?"

"It's been there for a day at most. Take a closer look."

She took the bag, turned it this way and that. It was a cigarette butt, like any other. "Well?"

"Who's Sherlock Holmes here?"

"Tell me."

"It wasn't stubbed out, Bonì, it burned all the way down."

"Have you found any burn marks?"

"None at all."

"Someone was lucky."

"It must have been one of the bad guys then. The good guys never have any luck."

"What about the blanket?"

"Fibres. Red, 100% synthetic. Really cheap, the sort of thing you find in any department store."

She nodded. "The blanket is important."

"Could have been the girl's."

"The girl's?"

Lubowitz rolled his eyes. "Don't wind me up, Bonì."

She said nothing.

"The woman's."

"Either the blanket belongs to the culprit, or she found it here."

Lubowitz nodded thoughtfully.

"What do you think, could it—"

"I don't think, Bonì. I just look."

"Could it have happened here?"

"Do you mean, could she have been beaten and raped here? There are no signs of that. No evidence of a struggle. Someone did lie on the ground over there, but there's not much else to go on."

"O.K. Anything else?"

He sighed. "I give you an inch and you want the whole mile."

"Well?"

"Blood, hair, skin, urine, footprints. A rotten banana skin. Dead mice. Mice skeletons. Rock-hard chewing gum. Almost rock-hard chewing gum. Rusty nails. Cat shit, dog shit, rat shit, rabbit shit, fox shit—"

She raised her hand to stop him.

"No, Bonì, you're going to listen to this," Lubowitz said, looking happy for the first time ever.

*

Half an hour later Reinhard Graeve arrived. For six months he'd managed to discreetly ease into the role of Kripo head, and yet exuded authority at every moment. "We're going to set up a task force," he said. "You'll get everything you need. People, equipment, time."

"That was quick," Louise said.

"Well," Graeve said.

They were on their own in the field, watching their uniformed colleagues head into the woods. Lubowitz had left with his technicians, the helicopter had flown down the Rhine and Meirich had gone back to H.Q. Silence had abruptly returned and, with it, a strangely unreal atmosphere. It felt as if something were lurking here, as if they were being observed. As if the barn, the field and the woods were watching their secrets being pried from them one by one.

"Let me guess. You had some calls."

Graeve smiled. "From Bonn, Berlin and Stuttgart."

"Rohmueller pulling strings."

"Don't judge him. If you were in his situation you'd use all the means at your disposal too."

"Luckily I don't have any children."

Graeve raised an eyebrow and at once looked very paternal. He had a lot of Bob's efficiency and a touch of Almenbroich's humanity. Maybe this was another boss one could go to at six in the morning with personal problems.

She smiled faintly. An option for the future.

Chervel rang. *Rien.*

Ilic rang. Nothing.

He was at the station with a few colleagues, showing people pictures of Nadine. Other officers were visiting taxi drivers at home or on cab ranks, who'd been on duty on Sunday morning. One remembered having driven Nadine in the past, but not a few days ago. Meirich's people were questioning Inge Rovak and Rudi, whose names and numbers were stored on Nadine's home telephone.

Bermann called. I'll be there in an hour. Have you got anything?

Nothing.

When her telephone rang again she saw movement at the edge of the woods. A policeman came running into the field, waving his hand.

"Frau Bonì," Graeve said tensely.

"I see it." She held the mobile to her ear as they went to meet the policeman.

"Bonì?"

"Yes."

An investigator from the Organised Crime squad, whose name vaguely rang a bell: Andi Bruckner. She also recognised the voice, loud and aggressive. Bruckner was in a taxi at the Schwabentor cab rank. The driver had recognised Nadine.

From the edge of the woods she heard shouting. The policeman had stopped. She couldn't make out what he was trying to say.

"What?" Graeve yelled.

They quickened their pace.

"Around five on Sunday morning he took her from Kagan to Martinstor," Bruckner said. "A guy said hello to her. Early twenties, shoulder-length hair, good-looking. Surfer type. She remembered a photo on one of Rohmueller's lists. Serge, the ex-boyfriend, looked like a surfer.

"And he's absolutely sure it was Nadine?"

"Absolutely. You don't forget a sweet thing like that in a hurry, he says."

"Call Thomas Ilic," Louise said and ended the conversation.

Now they'd got to the policeman, a young sergeant who had his hands on his thighs and was panting. He merely pointed behind him.

"Say something, for Christ's sake," Graeve said.

They had found Eddie Holzner's body.

7

Eddie Holzner lay beneath branches, twigs and leaves in the undergrowth near the Old Rhine. Nikes, long tracksuit bottoms, long-sleeved T-shirt, eyes wide open, caked blood by his right ear. Left arm broken, one bone at right angles.

Ants, worms, flies. Putrefaction had set in.

Eddie had been beaten up and strangled. The coroner would have to establish the ultimate cause of death.

Louise stared at the body. Whatever Eddie had intended to do to Nadine, or indeed had done, nobody ought to die like this.

Nadine horrifically abused, Eddie brutally murdered. A criminal without any restraint.

Because he's killed my child . . .

Holzner?

Graeve, who was kneeling beside the body, stood up and looked at her. She nodded and turned to the uniformed officer. "Keep searching. Keep going until you've found Nadine."

Chervel had arrived by boat, Bermann by helicopter. They stood with her and Graeve by the riverbank, watching Lubowitz and a technician search the area where the body had been found. The first evidence markers shone amidst the foliage in the light of the low-lying sun. Lubowitz cursed. They crawled on their knees through the undergrowth.

After a while Lubowitz came over to them. "It didn't happen here," he said to Graeve. With his hand he indicated a line from the woods to the river. "He was dragged here from the riverbank."

"*Merde*," Chervel said. His gaze swept Bermann before alighting on Louise. As ever, his eyes were red, the pupils small and tired. She liked the colour of his eyes: Husky blue. Despite the heat he was wearing a grey suit and black shirt.

She nodded faintly.

If the murderer had killed Eddie by the riverbank, the French were definitely out of this. If he had a boat, they were still in. The boat could have come from the French side via Breisach and returned that way.

Assuming it wasn't Holzner.

"Who's going to talk to Rohmueller?" she said.

"I'll do that, if you like," Graeve said.

"Might be better."

Graeve nodded.

"I'll do Holzner," Bermann said.

"Do you want to be there too?" Graeve asked Louise.

"Of course."

Bermann grinned.

"No objections, Herr Bermann?"

"None. Seven p.m. Don't be late."

A boat from Breisach river police arrived, bringing the coroner. Lubowitz went to meet him.

"Do you think it was Holzner?" Chervel asked Louise in French.

"Speak German," Bermann said.

There was silence for a moment, then Louise said in German, "I'm not sure." Holzner had a violent temper. He exploded and then struck out with his fists. But would he kill his own son like this? Torture a young woman? That required callousness, coldness, a perverse form of intelligence. Holzner wasn't intelligent.

"And a pleasure in torturing people," Bermann said.

"Yes."

"We'll see after the interrogation," Graeve said. "Is everything understood?"

"*Oui*," Chervel said.

"Do you want to be there?" Louise said.

"*Naturellement.*"

"Speak German," Bermann said.

"Any objections, Herr Bermann?"

Bermann sighed theatrically. "No. Make sure you're at H.Q. just before seven. Wait in the double door system, Chervel."

"Being there without being there," Chervel said, smiling again.

Louise nodded. They had experience of this. In winter 2003 she and Bermann had been at a police operation led by Chervel in Alsace – without being there. Official authorisation from both sides took too long.

They liked each other without liking each other.

Classic French and Germans.

Bermann and Graeve got onto the Breisach boat, Chervel onto the French one and Louise walked back through the woods to Grezhausen. One kilometre along narrow, overgrown paths, through small, sunny clearings. As the noises made by the search teams and boats receded, the sounds of the woodland became more distinct. It always seemed to involve forests and woods, she thought. Bodies dumped, hideouts dug, weapons stashed – time and again she found herself walking amongst trees. She knew a woman who wandered through the forest for hours at night, projecting imaginary figures into the darkness. Ghosts, spirits, a robot, and she saw landscapes, cities, memories. Only the murders had been real.

She crossed a footpath and stood there for a moment. How far could you get in three days in Nadine's condition? A few kilometres?

Quite apart from the fact that she had nothing but a blanket. No clothes, no money, no food.

But was she even still alive?

How and where had Eddie's killer come across her? In Freiburg? Did he take her to the barn? If so, he must have a car. And where was she now? Did she escape, was she hiding somewhere? Had he killed her and concealed her body in a different place from Eddie's? How had he got there?

She kept going.

He must have a car. Holzner didn't.

Louise gave a start when her mobile rang.

They'd found a bicycle near the bank of the Old Rhine. Eddie's bike, his mother had confirmed on the telephone.

So preoccupied was Bonì by the thought of a car that she soon forgot the bike. He must have a car. A car that may not have been seen in Grezhausen before.

Now another thought barged its way into her mind. If Nadine had escaped, was Eddie's killer searching for her too?

8

The field and the barn were deserted, reporters loitered by the roadside and further away stood some villagers, including Dennis. She beckoned him over.

"Eddie's dead," he said.

"Yes."

"Who . . ."

She shrugged.

"I heard they took his dad in."

"Not because of that. He hit a police officer."

"What about the woman?"

"We haven't found her."

Dennis coughed, took a tissue from his pocket and blew his nose. Bonì could see tears running down his cheeks. She wanted to comfort him, touch him, but all of a sudden the anger had returned. Dennis could have prevented much of this if he'd just done the right thing. If he'd rung the police from the barn rather than Eddie. Nadine would now be in hospital and Eddie still alive, perhaps.

Paris and that, she thought, and her anger grew.

But now this was about something else.

"Eddie was with the woman in the barn and he's dead. You were there too, Dennis."

"What?" Dennis said in a high-pitched voice. She could see he'd understood.

"I don't mean to frighten you. But I'd like you to go away somewhere with your parents for a few days."

He nodded.

"Are they at home now?"

"My mum."

"Come on, then."

She took him to a patrol car and asked one of the police officers waiting there to drive them.

In the car Dennis said, "But you've got his dad, haven't you?"

"We don't know if it was him."

Dennis nodded again. His small, empty eyes clung to her, as if she were all he had left.

Louise turned away.

"To be honest," Dennis said softly, "I think he could have done that to Eddie."

"Who?"

"His dad. But the thing with the woman . . . I don't know."

She looked at Dennis, waiting for him to go on.

"What I'm saying is, he wouldn't have to do that to get a woman, do you know what I mean?"

"No. Be straight with me, Dennis."

"He's *got* women. Other women."

"Other women?"

"He has sex with."

"Here in Grezhausen?"

Dennis didn't reply.

"Where, Dennis? In Freiburg?"

"Only once in Freiburg, back in the eighties when he was in the nick. Later he never went beyond Breisach, Eddie says."

"In Grezhausen, you mean?"

"In Breisach and over in Oberrimsingen."

"Eddie says?"

Dennis had turned away and was staring out of the window. "We followed him sometimes."

She understood. "And watched?"

"Sometimes. If they did it in the woman's car or in the woods."

82

"Or if you could climb up onto a balcony or if the apartment was on the ground floor?"

"Yes."

What a world, she thought, what a life. Watching your own father cheat on your mother. And Dennis? Had he got anything else from life apart from what had come via Eddie?

She laid a hand on his shoulder. "I'm sorry that Eddie's dead."

"Yeah," Dennis said.

She waited in the car. Dennis went up to the door and opened it with his key. Then he turned around and looked at her. Louise felt sympathy for the boy again. His life without Eddie must be even worse, even if she couldn't imagine either as particularly satisfactory.

In the hallway a short woman appeared. She was as fat as Dennis and started talking insistently to him.

Dennis raised his hand and gave Louise a fleeting wave before closing the door.

She began with the gawkers at the edge of the field. An unfamiliar car that had driven through Grezhausen at some point over the weekend, or maybe on Monday, and might have stood here, beside the field, or maybe somewhere else.

No, nobody had seen a car like that.

She handed out business cards, perhaps someone might ring if they weren't keen on admitting in front of the others that they took an interest in what happened in the street.

Louise then continued with the inhabitants of the houses alongside the Möhlin, at the end of the village. Some were outside with the others, some weren't.

She struck lucky with an elderly lady. Yes, a big blue car with a spare tyre on the back. It passed by a few times around Sunday lunchtime. Then on Sunday evening she'd seen it at the side of the road as she made her way to church. A big blue car with a spare tyre on the back.

"A jeep?"

"Yes, that's right, a jeep."

"Do you know what a jeep is?"

"Yes, of course, a jeep."

"What about the driver?"

The lady hadn't seen him, or maybe she had, how could you tell with all the walkers and day-trippers about? Just the jeep, she had seen that, with a spare tyre on the back.

She called Ilic. Did they actually know who the field and barn belonged to?

They did.

She heard him rustling his documents. Loud club music was thumping away in the background; he was still at Kagan, interviewing the employees. Nothing new, he said, as he continued to leaf through the file. Nadine had left at five on Sunday morning, one of the last as ever, but there wasn't much more to find out here. "Got it!" he suddenly said.

The field and barn belonged to Maria and Josepha Ettinger, sisters from Grezhausen. Born 1925 and 1928 respectively. Ilic's contact at Breisach police station said that the Ettinger sisters were "odd", if not "off their rockers". They were rich – property in Munich – and donated money to the Cistercians, so they could live as they pleased and do as they pleased. They kept themselves to themselves, so people didn't bother them. They didn't want to lease out the field, so it became overgrown. They wanted the barn to fall to ruin, so it fell to ruin.

"They sound nice," Louise said.

"Relatives of yours?"

They laughed.

In the 1940s the entire Ettinger family had spent two years in a concentration camp. They weren't collaborators, but had refused to carry out the Nazis' orders.

"Are they Jewish?"

No, not Jewish. Catholic.

Ilic gave Louise the name of a street in Grezhausen and described how to get there. She remembered: the street they'd driven down that morning with the wall on the left-hand side.

"What's happening your end?"

She told him about her conversation with Dennis, Holzner's other women and the blue car with the spare wheel on the tailgate.

"What I've been wondering all this time . . ." Ilic said.

Where did you go when you'd been through what Nadine had been through?

Home, Louise thought.

"Home, wouldn't you think?" Ilic said.

"But with those injuries?"

"Home means family. All she's got to do is call. So why doesn't she? Because she's no longer alive? Because she's in hiding somewhere and is frightened of leaving her hiding place as we're not the only ones looking for her?"

"I've been thinking along similar lines."

"Yes," Ilic said. "It stands to reason."

"Have you been drinking? This is turning into a lecture."

"Well . . . just one beer."

"That's O.K., Illi."

"I mean, I've got time now. I'm doing Kagan, Meirich's people are doing the rest. This Bruckner guy has a voice like a foghorn and speaks so quickly that I can barely understand a word. He's everywhere."

"If it helps."

Ilic sighed. "It does."

Louise heard the clatter of crockery and a woman say, "Enjoy your meal." Ilic cleared his throat in embarrassment.

Bonì smiled. "Don't forget to pay."

"I don't know," Ilic said, with a hint of bitterness in his voice. "Sometimes I think I've paid already."

*

The moss-covered, head-high wall that surrounded the Ettingers' property seemed to date from a time when Cistercians still lived in the village. The barbed wire that was affixed to the top of it, however, was clearly from the recent past. Chestnuts and maples towered above the wall, casting long shadows onto the asphalt. Signs warned of vicious dogs. The emblem of Günterstal Monastery was forged onto the rusty railings of the gate, and on a weathered wooden sign Louise could just make out "Ettinger". Hidden in the shade beneath the trees was a small, unwelcoming house, beside it a red estate car. Whereas the entire village was now in turmoil, here it was peaceful.

She rang the bell.

A dog barked, two more joined in and the peace was shattered. She heard the rattling of chains, but the barking didn't appear to be getting any closer. A high-pitched voice shouted a strict command and the dogs fell silent.

Footsteps crunched on gravel and from the shadows outside the house a figure emerged. A small elderly woman approached her.

"We don't wish to be disturbed," she said coldly, staying a few metres away from the gate. Her voice sounded cultivated, and she was elegantly dressed all in ivory, brooch, earrings, ruby-red bracelet.

"Who does?" Louise said, holding out her I.D. "Louise Bonì, Freiburg Kripo."

The woman said nothing. Her long, white hair was plaited and she looked emaciated, her cheekbones very prominent.

"Have you heard what happened?"

"Of course."

"It doesn't seem to bother you."

The woman shrugged. "People die." Her face remained expressionless, her lips barely moving as she spoke.

"Yes," Louise said. "But in this instance we're talking about a fifteen-year-old boy who didn't just die, he was murdered."

"A boy who killed cats and dogs, who stole, who beat up other children. I knew Eddie Holzner."

The walls that this woman had put up around herself wouldn't be so simple to overcome, Louise thought, not with five metres and an iron gate between them. She laid a hand on one of the sides of the gate and gently pushed. Nothing moved.

"What about the girl?" Louise asked.

Another shrug. "The world is rotten."

"Not the world, just some people in it."

The woman smiled coldly.

One of the dogs barked again, and again came the high-pitched command. The barking stopped.

"Your sister?"

"Yes."

"Are you Josepha or Maria?"

"Josepha."

Louise nodded. A feeling of helplessness washed over her. Helplessness and anger.

Locked out.

Stay calm, she thought.

She looked up. The railings ended in spikes and barbed wire ran along the top of the wall.

"You'd do yourself an injury," Josepha Ettinger said.

Louise gave a grim smile. "When were you last there? At the barn?"

"Yesterday."

"Did you go at the weekend?"

"Yes."

"When exactly? It's important."

"For you, not for me."

"Saturday or Sunday, Frau Ettinger?"

Josepha appeared to mull this over. "Saturday."

"Are you sure?"

"We were coming back from the Rhine and then did some shopping in the village. So it must've been Saturday." For the first time a hint of Alsatian-German dialect crept into Josepha's crisp high German.

"You and your sister."

"Yes."

Louise realised that both her hands were now on the railings. How ridiculous she must look from where Josepha Ettinger was standing. She took her hands off the gate. "Did you notice anything? A car or a person you'd never seen before?"

"All I noticed was that this world gets less like my world with every day."

"Is that the reason for the barbed wire? Is that why you're letting everything fall to ruin?"

Bonì had the impression that Josepha was about to reply, but she didn't.

Louise sighed. "What about your sister?"

"She'd tell you the same as me. We didn't see anything. What happens outside these walls has not been of any interest to us for a long time."

"A dead boy, an abused girl."

Josepha said nothing.

"Next time you leave these walls, take the dogs with you. We haven't apprehended the culprit yet."

"And if you did get him, there would still be the others." Josepha stared at her. "You don't even know where to look, do you? *Who* to look for."

Louise took a step back. "Maybe you're right. But there's one thing I do know – neither Eddie Holzner nor the girl can do anything about what happened to them."

She slid a folded business card between the gates above the lock and turned away. At least she'd had the last word; that tempered the anger and the feeling of humiliation.

Locked out.

But maybe even that wasn't the worst. Josepha Ettinger had left her alone with the dead and the criminals of the world outside of their walls.

Once back in the car she turned to look at the gates. A flash of white on the railings; the card was still there.

9

The sky had become overcast and rainclouds now hung over the city. Seven p.m., the time when the weather changed on these summer days. Bonì was standing with Bermann, Hugo Chervel and Andreas "Andi" Bruckner in Bermann's office, waiting for Holzner to be brought with his lawyer to the first interrogation. Nobody spoke, everyone was tired, dwelling on their thoughts. Seven p.m.: a cheap alarm clock from Sarajevo was ringing on a plywood bedside table in a bare apartment in Stühlinger. She saw Ben sitting on his bed, staring up at the gathering dusk. If she asked him he would tell her stories from his past, which usually began: back in Tel Aviv, back in Sarajevo. He was someone who, for whatever reason, couldn't escape his past. Usually he talked only about trivial matters, impressions and people that had remained in his memory. An ice-cream seller in the pouring rain, a horse-drawn cart carrying gypsies in commuter traffic. She got the feeling that he liked to talk, that he was delighted someone was listening at last.

She turned to Bruckner. "Where's Meirich?"

"At the doctor's. He'll be here later." From the corner of her eye she saw Chervel twitch. Aggressive voice, aggressive look, jutting chin, neck muscles tensed. Not a cry-baby, Andi Bruckner, more a fighting dog, she thought. A small, furtive, moustachioed fighting dog. A touch of deviousness.

But he was quick and he picked up traces.

"*Les Allemands*," Chervel whispered to her with a smile.

"I got that," Bermann said.

*

Soon afterwards they heard the sound of footsteps in the corridor. The door opened and in walked some Kripo officers with Holzner and his lawyer.

"Four coppers and a brief," Holzner groused. "And now I won't be able to watch the games. What a *shit* evening."

The lawyer grinned and shook all their hands. Richard C. Müller, a well-tanned, supercilious individual in his mid-forties. Ill-fitting cream suit, yellow trainers, whitened teeth and gelled hair. "I love it when my clients have a sense of humour," he said.

Chervel shook his head in scorn.

"I saw that," Bermann said.

"So did I," Müller said with a grin.

Bermann pointed to two chairs.

Holzner was wearing jeans and a light-blue T-shirt. He had shaved. Someone must have gone to Grenzhausen and brought him a few things. "When am I going to get out?" he said, slumping onto the chair.

"Don't say anything." Müller grinned.

Bermann frowned. "You won't."

"Oh, oh, oh, let's be careful about this," Müller said.

"When I lay my hands on that little bastard!" Holzner roared.

"Don't say a word."

Silence filled the room. Louise fixed her eyes on Bermann, trying to understand. Bermann didn't look at her.

She gazed at the window: grey evening light and a pale moon. In some café not too far from here Ben was having his breakfast, bolstering himself for better times. Finally, she thought, finally she had a private life that was worthy of the name, and yet she still had to spend her evenings fighting running battles with men like Holzner and Richard C. Müller. With men like Bermann, who deceived, manipulated and kept secrets, even though he was one of the good guys.

Turning to Holzner, Bermann said what had to be said prior to the first interrogation, according to paragraph 136 of the Code of Criminal Procedure: threatening and assaulting a police officer, verbal abuse, he could comment on the accusations levelled against him, but was not obliged to . . .

Bermann didn't mention suspicion of murder. Officially, Holzner wasn't accused of this.

"My client was provoked," Müller said indignantly.

"You bet I was," Holzner shouted, his face red with anger.

"Rolf," Louise said.

Bermann shot her a menacing look.

"Are you going to do it or am I?"

"Do what?" Müller asked.

"Seven fucking coppers outside my house!" Holzner said.

Bermann rubbed his brow with the tips of his fingers.

Then he told Holzner that they'd found Eddie.

It was now dark outside and a drizzle had set in. Nobody had said a word for several minutes. In the windowpanes Louise could see their outlines, all completely still: Holzner, Müller, Bruckner. Bermann was leaning back, anger working its way into his expression. Occasionally he gave her a glance that spoke volumes.

The telephone rang; Bermann didn't pick up.

"How?"

"We don't know yet," Louise said.

"When?"

"Sunday evening, probably."

Holzner nodded. His legs had started to shake and he placed his hands on his thighs. "So that's why the little bastard didn't come home."

"I do hope you don't suspect my client," Müller said.

Nobody said anything.

Holzner looked at Bermann. "Hey, what's happening in the game?"

Bermann snorted. "Two–one at half time."

"Two–one!" Holzner nodded again. His legs were trembling, his arms were trembling, his face was glistening with sweat. "Who's scored for us?"

"Podolski and Schweinsteiger."

"Wahey, the fuckers!"

Then he fell silent and just sat there, shaking and sweating. Dennis had said he thought he could have done that to Eddie. But not to the woman.

"If you're going to accuse my client of—"

Holzner leaped to his feet. "Can you get me a telly to watch?"

Andy Bruckner stepped in the man's way, his fists balled, Müller got up and Chervel whispered, "*Merde!*"

But Holzner just stood there, his eyes on the wall opposite, and yelled, "I want a telly!"

Müller touched his arm. He'd turned pale. "Everything's going to be O.K."

"I don't believe this," Bermann muttered.

"It can't be that fucking difficult!" Holzner shouted.

"No," Louise said. "It isn't."

Holzner had stopped shaking and bellowing. Now he sat silently in the large cell where he would spend the night, and waited. Louise waited with him on the other side of the bars.

Gregori, the porter, was on the hunt for a television.

Of course it was difficult. "A T.V. for a suspect? We're not a bloody charity!" Bruckner had cursed.

The interrogation was postponed until the following morning, when Holzner would appear in front of the magistrate who would decide whether he should be kept in custody. Müller had left, so had Chervel. Bermann was preparing for the task force meeting, Bruckner was contacting Meirich, and Ilic, who hadn't got back in touch, might still be drinking beer at Kagan and getting annoyed that others were working more quickly.

And Ben . . . She checked the time: just after half past seven. Ben was probably having an espresso, wondering what he was doing as a security guard in peaceful Breisgau. Was that any life at all? Had he

93

ever imagined that this was what he'd be doing once he'd turned forty?

"Time?" Holzner asked.

She told him.

"For fuck's sake." Holzner slapped the tiled wall and the noise echoed around the cell. He stared at his hand. Louise saw it turn red.

"Fucking coppers," Holzner said to his hand.

Then, at the end of the corridor leading to the cells, the double door system opened and Gregori came in panting, carrying a portable television.

At ten to eight the television, placed on the floor outside the cell, was finally working. "Extra time!" Holzner said, propping his elbows on his knees. "Four–three! Holy shit!" He laughed out loud. "The little bastard was right. We're going to win, he said, because the fucking Mexicans are short arses. Look at those fucking Mexican dwarves, he said . . . I mean, can you *believe* it!"

Gregori glanced at Louise, who shrugged. "We're not a hotel," he murmured.

"Just this once. Thanks."

She called Bermann to say she was going to be late.

"What's the score?"

"Four–three."

"How's Holzner?"

"Quite calm."

She asked about Ilic. Yes, he was back now. "By the way," Bermann said. Eddie Holzner had water in his lungs: he'd drowned. Been drowned.

Louise looked at Holzner who was quietly watching the game.

"Tell him," Bermann ordered harshly. "Go on, I want to hear it."

She didn't say anything.

"That'll put an end to the peace, Louise. So?"

She cut him off, turned to the two constables who'd brought Holzner in and were standing with the guard, and said she'd stay a little longer.

Louise went up to the bars and looked down at the television. There was a pause in the game; the players were sitting or lying on the edge of the pitch. Close-ups showed wounds receiving medical attention and leg muscles being massaged. Someone was handing around water bottles. Jürgen Klinsmann was giving one player instructions with energetic hand gestures.

Holzner's gaze was fixed on the screen, as if that's where his fate would be decided, rather than in the task force room on the fourth floor.

The match resumed.

Soon afterwards Germany had won, but Holzner didn't appear to register this fact. He was trembling again, sweat was running down his face, and the chest and sides of his light-blue T-shirt were soaked through. She wondered what battles he was fighting with himself.

He hadn't uttered another word.

She called Bermann and said she'd stay longer. Bermann had a fit and threatened to come and get her himself.

He didn't come. Nobody did.

When the other match began – the final – Bonì sent the two constables away and sat on the chair outside the cell. Almost 9 p.m., Ben would be on his way to St Georgen. In her mind she saw the guard cabin in the darkness, the deserted streets. She was looking forward to midnight and their stroll around the car park. Cheese and salami, Ben, you dare complain . . .

Brazil scored, then again. Holzner didn't react.

At 9.15 Ilic called. The meeting was over. Bruckner and Sandy were going to see Serge, Nadine's ex-boyfriend. Holzner would spend the night in the cell and suspected murder might be added to the charge sheet in the morning. A brilliant actor, Bruckner had said – who else would it have been? A pure sociopath who just lost it.

Sandy had asked Eddie's mother about the alibi. Apparently Holzner had been at home for the whole of Sunday and only popped out briefly on Monday morning. But why should anyone believe the mother?

"Tell Bruckner," Ilic said.

She asked what Bermann's thoughts were. He wasn't sure, Ilic replied. But because Berlin and Stuttgart were applying pressure he wanted to wait a bit longer. Better to have the wrong man in custody · than nobody at all. That was the end of the meeting.

They finished their conversation.

Four–nil, Holzner said nothing. The stench of sweat hung in the air.

Four–one.

Then the game was over. Gregori retrieved the television set; Holzner followed him with his eyes.

Brilliant actor, Louise thought. She'd really had it with men like Bruckner and Bermann. Men like Richard C. Müller and Holzner. And if the children were already like that . . .

She moved to the locked cell door. "I'm very sorry, Herr Holzner."

Holzner was staring at the spot where the television had been. "Look at those fucking Mexican dwarves," he said.

10

To St Georgen in the rain, waiting in the rain. Two rolls on the passenger seat, the aggravation with the tiny symbols beneath the L.E.D.s. The end of a working day.

As Louise watched Ben in his brightly lit guard cabin, she went back over her conversation with Josepha Ettinger. Something had become snagged in her subconscious. Something that had been hinted at, but not stated.

What had she overlooked?

She couldn't put her finger on it.

Ben drank from a bottle, opened a newspaper and leafed through it. It felt strange to be missing someone after only a few hours.

Louise closed her eyes. The wall with the barbed wire, the double iron gates with the crest. A red estate car.

The car? But they were looking for a blue jeep.

The dogs had barked, but they hadn't raced to the gate. The sister's voice. Josepha, who'd stayed five metres away.

No sympathy for Eddie, for Nadine. Only indifference and a touch of mockery when she'd briefly considered clambering over the gate.

But Josepha had answered her questions. *We were coming back from the Rhine and then did some shopping in the village. So it must've been Saturday.*

At the end of the conversation came bitterness, a brief moment of anger. *And if you did get him, there would still be the others. You don't even know where to look, do you?* Who *to look for.*

A kidnapper, rapist, murderer, Josepha. Does that mean nothing? Nothing at all?

An old woman without sympathy. But she gave money to the Cistercians.

The Ettingers had been in a concentration camp, Ilic said. They weren't collaborators, but had refused to carry out the Nazis' orders. Had Josepha lost all sense of sympathy in the concentration camp?

For a moment she toyed with the idea of ringing Ilic. There must be more about the sisters in his documents. But she dropped the idea. It was almost midnight, and if anyone needed peace and quiet it was Ilic.

But she couldn't get Josepha Ettinger's last words out of her head. *And if you did get him, there would still be the others.*

Which others? From the past?

Or from now?

As soon as she was with Ben she stopped thinking about her conversation with Josepha.

The lines around his eyes had expanded. It occurred to Louise that she'd never seen a man with so much joy in his expression.

Ben was hungry.

Louise let him eat. She said nothing, just watched, which was interesting enough. There was little chewing and he swallowed so quickly that the taste receptors on his tongue couldn't have registered all the good things racing past them. But he ate with abandon and seemed happy enough.

He drank only water – she'd made this a clear condition. If you want to smooch, Ben, then no alcohol for four hours beforehand. Beer's not alcohol, he'd protested, raising his eyebrows in feigned horror. Your call, she'd retorted, and so far he'd always made the right call.

When the last crumb had been devoured she said, "You don't have to do this job, Ben."

He stood up and took off his coat. "I've got to do something."

"But not this sort of thing."

98

"It's not so bad. It gives me a lot of time to think."

"Maybe thinking's not such a good thing."

He laughed softly. "Maybe."

They embarked on their first lap of the car park, which was emptier than the previous day. A single car stood in the darkness. Louise thought she'd seen it here yesterday too.

Nobody had come, nobody had driven off. Nobody he could talk to. How could anyone put up with that?

"I prefer it when I've got no time to think," she said.

"Because the shadows appear?"

She nodded. The dead, the murderers. All the mistakes she'd made.

"Antun Lončar?"

"Him too."

"I've got a different problem when I think," Ben said. "I start asking myself questions."

"Such as?"

"What prospects do we have? The two of us?"

She stopped. *Those* sorts of questions. She nodded. "Questions to you or me?"

"Me." Ben turned to her. In the darkness she could no longer see the lines around his eyes, which unsettled her for some reason. A shudder ran down her spine. No luck with men, Bonì, a voice in her head said. Always has been that way and always will be.

But the delight he showed when she turned up hadn't been put on.

"Let me summarise," she said. "You move to Freiburg because of me and then you wonder whether we should split up."

"No," Ben said.

"Good."

They went on. Questioning their future prospects, she thought reluctantly. No wonder given all those hours spent alone, with the darkness outside, and nothing to look at apart from an almost empty car park. In those circumstances you couldn't help asking yourself such questions. Is there life beyond the car park? A life in the light?

"I like your summaries," Ben said, pulling her towards him. "Just the bare essentials."

"Isn't that the point of summaries?" She shut her umbrella as it had stopped raining. "Well? Do any answers materialise when you ask yourself those sorts of questions?"

"Yes. I realise that I'd love it if we had prospects."

She sighed. "Now everything's in the conditional."

Having completed their first lap they now embarked on a second.

"How can you be so stupid as to ask about our prospects. I mean, either it's going to last or it won't. I thought we were both in agreement on this."

"We are. Don't get worked up, Louise."

"Prospects. Really, Ben." She shook her head.

"Don't get worked up."

"You need another job. Where you work and don't have time to think."

"I'm always thinking."

"But what's the problem, Ben? I mean, if the job isn't the problem, what is it?"

"It's got nothing to do with you."

"That's what my arsehole of an ex-husband said too."

Ben sighed. "Calm down, Louise. It's about me, not you. I'm not happy. I'm *never* happy. That's it."

"Not happy with me?"

"I said it wasn't about you."

"Could you just say whether you're happy with me? Whether you like me?"

"I really like you."

"Good. I really like you too. Problem solved."

"Yes," Ben said, laughing.

But the security guard wasn't going to get away that easily. "Why are you never happy?"

"It's just how I am."

"Not happy with what then."

"Leave it, Bonì."

"Out with it, Benno."

Ben groaned.

"Ben", if you want to stay alive, Ilic had told her.

"Don't ever call me that again, please."

She laughed. "Then talk."

"Look at me. What am I? *Who* am I?"

"I don't get it."

"You see? Could we leave this for another time?"

"Let me summarise. You don't like yourself."

Ben shrugged.

Achieved nothing, never felt at home anywhere, never started a family, drifted from city to city. Chucked in the career he'd once enjoyed because he was burnt out. And always the sense that he didn't deserve it if he ever felt happy somewhere, even for a while.

Because he was nothing. Nobody.

That's how it was.

Louise kept quiet. She could have said all manner of things. Three foreign languages, years of experience abroad, a good reputation with a number of police forces, teaching experience, an ability to settle and get along in foreign countries, and building up police structures in the post-war period. Was all of that nothing? What about making an impression on an eccentric colleague who hadn't been impressed by colleagues for years? Making this colleague feel that from nowhere a life had burst into her stagnant chaos. *Prospects?*

Prospects she hadn't counted on.

But everyone had their own criteria. People who didn't like themselves didn't like themselves to the very core, no matter what anyone else said.

"We'll leave the rest for another time," Ben said.

"Till tomorrow night."

Ben smiled.

She pulled him towards her and gave him a kiss. Beginning with love again at the age of forty . . . All the shadows, the baggage. So much was in the past, it couldn't now be shared with a partner who hadn't been part of your world for half a lifetime.

Louise moved away. "Another thing, Ben. Have you got a bright torch in your pretty office?"

A third lap, followed by a few passionate clinches, then she left Ben in his brightly lit cabin, and walked back to her car carrying a heavy torch that bore the sticker of a Freiburg security firm which had the job of keeping guard over empty car parks.

She drove to Grezhausen. Josepha Ettinger and her strange words.

Josepha Ettinger, who'd seen nothing and knew nothing. Who'd walked past the barn on Saturday, not Sunday. That was the beginning.

You don't even know where to look, do you?

Bonì understood that.

Who *to look for.*

She basically understood that too, apart from the stress on *who.* As if the person she was after was . . . somehow special. But how did Josepha know this?

And if you did get him, there would still be the others.

This is what she didn't understand. *The others.* In her resentment of the world was Josepha talking about people who'd done terrible things to her sixty years ago? Would they catch *one* criminal, but not those from the past? Or was she talking generally about the endless criminals who were never caught? *Oh, the police are useless anyway.* Was it so banal?

In a sudden fit of rage she slapped the radio. The symbols lit up, music started blaring. French cars, now *they* understood her.

She wound down the window and the breeze blew cool raindrops onto her arm.

Are you straying into hunches and speculation again, Bonì?

No hunches, she thought. Just a few oddities.

11

Louise drove slowly through Grezhausen. There wasn't a soul on the streets. She thought of Ben, who at that moment would be staring into the still night too.

A light was on at the Holzners'. In one of the windows on the first floor she saw Eddie's mother wandering around. A young woman appeared, then vanished again. Offering comfort at one in the morning.

Son and husband lost on the same day.

She turned around.

No lights were on at Dennis's house. She now knew that his mother was alone. The father wasn't even on his birth certificate.

Dennis and his mother were staying with relatives in Karlsruhe.

Louise turned again, drove past the Holzners' and sped away on the road to Hartheim.

In the darkness she couldn't make out the barn. The police vehicles would return at dawn and the search would resume.

Eddie and Nadine. Nadine and Eddie.

In Bermann's office earlier that evening Bruckner had said, What if it was the girl? What if he shagged her and she took her revenge? Drowned him?

But they didn't even know if Nadine was still alive.

She stopped by the side of the road, put the window down and gazed into the darkness. The air was damp and musty. Louise got out and stood there yawning for a while in the cool rain. She had to keep focused; she *did* have something.

There could be three explanations for Nadine's disappearance from the barn.

First: The person who'd abused her had gone looking for Nadine and discovered her whereabouts. Which meant she wouldn't be easy to find. She might not even be alive.

Second: She'd left the barn by herself. Which meant she had to be somewhere nearby. Somewhere here. But then she would probably have called her parents.

Unless Bruckner was right and Eddie had died because he'd "looked at" her and "touched" her in the barn.

What about the other person? Who'd laid her on the ground as Dennis had described. Would he be dead too?

The other person, she thought.

And if you did get him, there would still be the others.

She felt a tingling in her arms. The thought was becoming more concrete. That thing she'd overlooked in the afternoon.

Third: Someone else had found Nadine and was looking after her.

But then that person would have rung her parents. Or the police. Unless they were afraid of the police.

Or Nadine didn't want them to.

Just a dog this time.

No light, no woman's voice telling the dog to be quiet. Just barking and the patter of rain.

In the glow of the streetlamp she could see a few metres of gravel and puddles. The house lay in darkness. She rang again. The dog barked hysterically, the chain rattled and knocked against wood.

No light. No voices.

Louise switched on the torch. She couldn't see the dog. Nothing appeared to be moving in the house, but she had only a hazy view of the windows. The red car had gone.

She called Josepha's name. No answer.

Only now did she remember the business card. It was no longer wedged between the gates.

Louise returned to her car and looked for a telephone number in the photocopied documents. Mobile to her ear, she went back to the property. In the distance she could hear a telephone ringing. Nobody picked up.

Just as she had in the afternoon, she placed her hands on the railings and looked up. Raindrops fell onto her face. She would make it to the top, but climbing over the spikes would be more difficult. The railings were wet.

Louise closed her eyes. One o'clock. Public prosecutors and magistrates would be asleep. But even during the day she wouldn't have got a search warrant just because an elderly lady had said funny things and a car had gone.

What have you become obsessed by, Frau Bonì?

A hope.

So wait, she thought, and went back to her car.

Louise slept for a few hours and was woken at 5 a.m. by the alarm on her mobile. To the east she could see some light; to the west, above the property and the Rhine, lay darkness. Louise got out and breathed in the cool, damp air. It had stopped raining.

When she rang at the gate, again it was only the dog who responded.

The mobile ringing at her ear, the sound of the telephone in the distance. Freezing, she stared into the darkness and saw two old ladies with earplugs in a large bed. At the foot lay two old, practically deaf dogs, dreaming of better days.

She couldn't trespass on private property.

A few years ago she would have done, she thought. Putting her hunches above all else she would have climbed over the gate. But several dreadful incidents lay between then and now. Deaths for which she felt partially responsible. Wrong decisions, crass mistakes.

She followed the wall towards the edge of the village. It ran along the street for about fifty or sixty metres, then angled sharply southwards at a meadow. As Louise trudged through the tall grass her trainers and trousers became quickly soaked. To the rear of the property she unbuttoned her trousers, squatted and took a pee.

Ten minutes later she was back at the gate. No back entrance, no tree to help her get over the wall. But as she was walking a thought had occurred to her.

Cars.

The old woman was already awake. She stood facing Louise in a pink dressing gown, with an ironed napkin tucked into her neckline. From inside the house came music: "Liebe ist" by Nena.

"Oh, the woman from the police."

"I have another question."

A red car? The woman nodded. Yes, Josepha and Maria Ettinger's car. She'd seen it outside the barn at some point over the weekend.

"Outside the barn? Are you sure?"

"Yes, yes, it was outside the barn."

On Sunday, the same day she'd seen the blue car with the spare tyre on the back. She was on her way home from Bible class, and there it was outside the Ettingers' barn. When she looked out of the window later it was gone.

"Did you see the Ettingers with their car? Or anyone else for that matter?"

"No, just the car, and later, when I looked out of the window it was gone." She sounded apologetic. The old woman's eyes had grown large. I hope I've been able to help you, they were saying. "Has it got anything to do with young Eddie?"

"Did you know him?"

"*Such* a nice boy."

Louise nodded. Nobody liked Eddie, not even this woman. The headlines were announced on the radio. Brazil had won the Confederations Cup. Germany secured third place with its victory over Mexico. She thought of Holzner and Eddie, and how a football match was all that a father had left of his murdered son.

"Just one more question. Are there any shops here? In Grezhausen?"

"No, you have to go over to Oberrimsingen."

We were coming back from the Rhine and then did some shopping in the village. So it must've been Saturday.

Josepha Ettinger's lies.

Louise thanked the old woman.

"If there's anything else you want to know," she said, "I'm always here."

Yes, Louise thought on the way to her car, there was something else she wanted to know, but the old woman wouldn't be able to give her the answer.

Why hadn't the Ettingers contacted the police?

The outline of the house peeled away from the grey morning light. Bonì called again and rang the bell. The dog barked and was answered by a couple of others in the village.

Three possible explanations, she thought, for why Nadine was no longer in the barn. Number three: The Ettingers found her and brought her here. We need to call the police, they said. No, Nadine whispered. But why not, my child?

Indeed, why not?

Had the Ettingers had a reason not to call the police, then Josepha wouldn't have said what she did. *And if you did get him, there would still be the others. You don't even know where to look, do you?* Who *to look for.*

The others. Were there several of them? Did Nadine know one of them?

Was that the reason?

She grabbed the railings, put a foot on a crossbar and pulled herself up. The gates moved and something rattled. The dog barked like crazy.

The next crossbar, a bit further up. She grabbed a spike. One foot over, then down on the other side and she'd done it.

Now she could see the animal. A fully grown Alsatian, tied up outside a kennel to the left of the front door. He leaped forwards and reared up on his hind legs. As she approached the house Louise took the pistol from her bag. In summer 2003 she'd been attacked by a dog, escaping to the car just in time. As back then, now there were bared teeth, widened eyes, barking and that deep, menacing growl which scared her more than anything else.

But the chain held.

There was still no light in any of the windows, no sign that anyone was there. She approached the house from the side in a broad arc. She couldn't get as far as the door; the dog was in the way.

No windows tilted open, no balcony, the kitchen door at the back locked. Louise held her gun by the barrel. To everything else, now she could add burglary and criminal damage. She briefly wondered why she was doing all of this. Why she was risking her career, the life she was living, her life for this career that satisfied her like nothing else, even though she hated it at times. Why did she keep putting her job on the line every year? It was all she had.

Bonì told herself that she was doing it for Nadine. For people like her. Somebody had to.

But that wasn't true, of course. Nobody *had* to do it. So why?

She struck the glass, it shattered, and the barking became more and more frenzied. A thud, as if the dog on the other side of the house had thrown itself against the door.

Then she was in the kitchen. Stone floor, white wood, enamel glinting in the beam of the torch. She called Josepha's name, but got no answer.

She kept going without switching on the light. A long, narrow corridor with steps leading up, the smell of damp wood and flowers. A small loo, a sitting room with a dining room off it, stone flooring and dark, old wood throughout. In the sitting room, a dark-brown carpet, cream upholstery, reams of books, vases with flowers, a sideboard and a grandfather clock that ticked very loudly. The beam of the torch swept framed black-and-white photographs of four girls. The similarity between them was striking. Four sisters.

When Louise went back to the stairs something crashed against the front door beside her. She froze in shock. Only a couple of centimetres of wood separated her from the raging dog. Silently she inserted the safety chain into the metal track on the door.

The stairs creaked.

Upstairs a bathroom, a bedroom, both tidy and empty. The double bed was made and covered with a bedspread.

Bonì proceeded along the hallway to a closed door. Even before she'd opened it she detected the tang of iodine ointment and knew what to expect.

The room was in darkness, the shutters closed. Louise felt for the light switch. Another bedroom, the bed unmade and traces of dried blood on the sheets. On the bedside table was shrink-wrapped bandaging. A folded red blanket lay in a corner of the room.

One kilometre beyond Grezhausen, she stopped at the side of the road. She couldn't see the sun, but it was already light. To her right flowed the Möhlin, ahead lay Hausen, and on the other side of the motorway rose the slopes of the southern Black Forest, all the way up to Schauinsland. No mistakes now, she thought.

What about your sister?

She'd tell you the same as me. We didn't see anything. What happens outside these walls has not been of any interest to us for a long time.

No mistakes, Bonì. There is a reason for everything.

The sisters had found Nadine. They'd taken her home and looked after her. Three days later a policewoman had turned up and asked questions. Josepha Ettinger had lied.

And told the truth.

And if you did get him, there would still be the others. You don't even know where to look, do you? Who to look for.

Her mobile tore Louise from her thoughts.

"You're not home," Ben said.

She cursed. She'd forgotten Ben . . .

"The torch. You were going to shine it somewhere, then leave again, weren't you?" He gave a strained laugh.

"Ben, I can't right now."

"I should have known you'd get yourself into trouble."

"Me? Never."

"*Are* you in trouble?"

"No."

"O.K."

"You do trust me, don't you?"

"Yes," Ben said.

"I've got to hang up now."

"Come over to my place later. Whenever you have a spare few minutes."

"Maybe around lunchtime."

She ended the conversation and closed her eyes. The Ettinger sisters had found Nadine in the barn and looked after her. But they hadn't taken her to hospital or called the police. When a policewoman came to her door, Josepha lied. Nobody should know that Nadine was with them. Not even the police.

Louise got goosebumps.

Especially not the police?

Assuming the Ettingers and Nadine hadn't done anything wrong, there was only one possibility.

Louise drove on. She had to talk to someone, but not Ben. Not Bermann, nor Ilic.

She needed to speak to someone before what Josepha had concealed from her appeared in the case file.

Because there was a reason for everything.

12

Retirement was good for some people. Christian Almenbroich was not one of them. She found him wearier, greyer and more depressive than ever.

One wrong decision could change your life dramatically. Kripo chiefs shouldn't make mistakes that cost lives. She knew Almenbroich would never get over it, knew that in summer 2003 he'd trusted a man he should not have trusted. At the time Louise had backed him and he'd taken the wrong decision partly on the basis of her judgement.

She sat at a breakfast table on a bare balcony, watching an old man eat a boiled egg with a shaky hand. Once Almenbroich had put her on sick leave because of her alcohol addiction. When she returned, his severity had been superseded by respect and trust. Then came the episode with the terrorist hunters and the decision to back the false Marcel, which turned Almenbroich into a doddery old man who struggled to eat a boiled egg without making a mess.

But his mind was still working. "At least don't let it show," he said.

"I'm sorry."

"Another slice?" He offered her the breadbasket. "Try the quince jelly. I made it myself."

"You make quince jelly?"

"Of course. What else am I supposed to do?"

They ate in silence.

"Old people are wicked, Louise," Almenbroich said. "They hate the world. The world keeps turning – young, fresh and unwrinkled – while they themselves are slumbering towards the end. Some can't deal with it and pop off early. Others take their revenge." He took a sip of camomile tea. "Have the Ettingers checked out, that's my advice. Who knows what you'll unearth."

She nodded. "Do you still have any contacts in public prosecution?"

"Why?"

"I need a search warrant."

Almenbroich sighed. "You mean to officially make up for what you've already done unofficially? Not to mention illegally?"

"You could put it that way."

"You haven't changed, Louise."

"I have, a bit. I spent a long time considering whether I ought to do it."

"What fantastic progress."

They laughed.

"I'll talk to Hennemann," Almenbroich said.

"Thank you."

She stood up and went to the balustrade. Almenbroich lived in Ehrenkirchen, to the south of Freiburg. Lots of new buildings, lots of families, very green, probably very quiet at night. She'd been lucky to catch him at home; half an hour later and he would have set off on his daily walk. Up the hillside vineyards, then a rest on a bench by the Ölberg chapel or amongst the vines, with a view of the Black Forest. He'd told her he still went over in his mind, every day, what had happened back then, why he'd decided on one route rather than the other.

"If the sisters had something to hide, Josepha would have behaved differently," she said.

Almenbroich didn't respond.

Turning to him, she added, "Maybe Nadine didn't want us to be informed."

"What are you getting at?"

Louise stared at him. He looked up briefly, then focused again on his egg. Yolk was running over the shell, the eggcup and his fingers.

He put the spoon down and wiped them on a napkin. "Sometimes rape victims don't contact us because they feel shame."

"That's true," she said.

He looked at her. "A rich, innocent, naïve girl who's only known the beautiful and comfortable aspects of life. Then something . . . like *that* happens. The girl is ashamed, thinks she's somehow responsible. How can she mention the disgrace to her parents? Their unspoiled family world would crumble. It's happened before." He cleared his throat. "But you're thinking something else, aren't you?"

"Yes."

"Don't say it. I'd like to preserve the few illusions I still have, as I make my quince jelly."

Louise sat down. "She knows the identity of one of the culprits."

"If there *were* more than one of them."

"It's what we have to assume."

"Let's say your interpretation of what Josepha Ettinger said is correct. Don't you think you're attaching too much importance to it?" He stood. "Will you walk some of the way with me? It's really beautiful up there."

Louise shook her head; she had to get back to H.Q.

Almenbroich went into the sitting room and came out shortly afterwards wearing his shoes and a jacket.

She made no move to get up. "I have to get it off my chest."

"Would you like to take some jelly?"

"I—"

"*No*," Almenbroich interrupted. "Not in this apartment. Not in my presence. I don't want to hear it. Please respect that." His eyes had narrowed, his cheeks were tensed. There it was again, the severity she'd so feared and had such regard for.

He accompanied Bonì to her car.

"Get Rolf to ring Hennemann at the public prosecution department." Almenbroich pointed in the direction of the vineyards. He said he would phone from one of his benches. Have a little chat about

114

life before and after retirement. Extend an invitation to a glass of red wine. Ask a favour. He smiled. Something approaching life glistened in his eyes, and the grey face with its hollow eye sockets and cheeks was now slightly flushed.

As she had once before – two years ago – she felt the sudden urge to put a hand on his cheek. Widowed ex-Kripo bosses who'd ended up as failures needed warmth and comfort.

His face was cold and the skin felt unpleasantly soft.

"This is almost becoming a habit," he said, looking happy for a moment.

"Hold off a while with Hennemann. I need to think."

He gave her a long stare.

She got into the car.

"I don't know if you understood what I was getting at earlier, Louise," he said, resting a hand on the roof. "*Never* mention it. Not to anybody. Don't let anyone find out what's going through your head. If it does the rounds, then that's the end of your career with Freiburg police. For ever."

"I'll help you make quince jelly, then."

"I don't want your help. I want you to stay there. After all, you're what I've left behind. The one good thing." He smiled grimly. "Well, it's true to say that good things sometimes take the strangest forms."

She smiled to hide the fact that tears were welling in her eyes. Dear old Almenbroich.

He took a step back. "And if you're right . . ." He turned and left without finishing his sentence.

She watched him go. A short, crooked old man on the streets of Ehrenkirchen. The best and most human boss that Freiburg Kripo had ever had.

And if you're right . . .

Louise knew what he was trying to say: if he were prepared to entertain such a possibility, then he thought it was possible.

*

On the drive back to Freiburg she kept playing the conversation with Josepha over in her head. Three sentences which seemed unremarkable at the time, and assumed significance only when it became clear that Josepha had lied.

She and her sister had found Nadine and taken her back to their house. They'd spoken to her. Nadine had told Josepha what had happened. That's why she said: *And if you did get him, there would still be the others. You don't even know where to look, do you?* Who *to look for.*

The others.

Louise had mentioned *one* culprit.

This was the only way in which Josepha's words had made sense.

But they may have contained something else too: a terrifying clue, if no plausible answer could be found, as to why neither the sisters nor Nadine had contacted the police.

Nadine might be racked with shame, as Almenbroich had said. Maybe she'd opted for revenge, as Bruckner suggested. It was all possible. But then Nadine wouldn't have told the Ettingers and Josepha couldn't have spoken of "the others".

What reason could the sisters have? That their being checked out would lead to the discovery of something which must not come to light? Almenbroich's theory.

Not hers.

Back to the very beginning.

They found a girl who'd been abused, took her home and looked after her. They didn't call the police. But then the police were at their door. It could have all been very simple; they didn't even have to phone.

But they lied instead.

Why?

She recalled how she'd introduced herself, as she always did: *Louise Boní, Freiburg Kripo.*

Louise suddenly felt sick.

At the same moment she realised where she was: Hexentalstrasse, Merzhausen. Another girl came to mind. A girl who had died here in Merzhausen, eight months ago, because of her.

Louise Bonì, Freiburg Kripo, she thought.

She parked at a bus stop and staggered out of the car. The last thing she wanted was to throw up all over the new synthetic upholstery.

Bonì vomited over a bush behind the bus stop.

A few of the people waiting there watched. Most had turned away again. "You shouldn't drink and drive," an elderly man said. A pregnant Turkish woman gave a knowing smile. Expectant mothers in it together?

She went back to the car, washed her face and hands with mineral water and rinsed out her mouth. Then she stood there at the open passenger door, her gaze fixed on the Schönberg, at the foot of which the girl who'd died because of her had lived until Heinrich Schwarzer, alias Antun Lončar, burned the house down.

But her mind was on Nadine and Josepha Ettinger.

If you've got one of them, the others will still be at large.

Which meant three culprits at least.

One of whom was a policeman. A Kripo officer.

II

The Policeman and the Killer

II.

13

She'd wanted to have a word with Bermann, but arrived too late. The task force meeting had begun twenty minutes earlier. At least she was showered and wearing fresh clothes, and feeling feminine and beautiful, albeit tired and old.

A couple of dozen pairs of eyes looked at her as she entered the task force room. Her gaze scanned the assembled company: Bermann, Bruckner, Hans Meirich, Alfons Hoffmann, Sandy, Ilic, Reinhard Graeve, colleagues from D11 and Meirich's D23, two people she only knew by sight, and Marianne Andrele, the public prosecutor.

Ilic pointed to an empty chair between himself and Hoffmann. There was silence until she sat, then Bermann said, "Keep going, Andi."

In a croaky voice Bruckner relayed his conversation with Serge, who he'd gone to see the previous evening with Sandy.

Ilic scribbled something on a piece of paper and pushed it over to her.

D.N.A. test back. Cigarette was Holzner's. Interrogation to follow.

It took her a while to understand. The cigarette butt Lubowitz had found in the barn. She nodded mechanically. So Holzner had been inside the barn.

Blood on fibres is Nadine's, Ilic wrote.

The synthetic red blanket in the Ettingers' guest room. Sixty per cent cotton, forty per cent acrylic, no brand. She'd checked.

"A real cissy. No balls. But a heartthrob, I'd say."

Ilic wrote.

At 5 a.m. on Sun. Serge asks N. to come to Martinstor. Taxi driver sees both. Serge: problems with new gf. Wants advice from N. 30 mins later S. goes to gf (alibi O.K.). N. goes to taxi rank.

"What about Inge Rovak and Rudi?" she whispered.

At Kagan with N. Don't know anything, Ilic wrote.

"It's irrelevant now," Bruckner said.

Now that we've got Holzner, she finished in her head.

Holzner number one, the policeman number two.

Where were you? Ilic wrote.

"Later," she whispered, then turned to Bruckner. "Has Serge got a car?"

"Old, light-blue Daimler. Gorgeous set of wheels. His parents are pumping him so full of cash it's coming out of his arse."

"That thing with the jeep," Bermann said to her.

"Yes?"

"Holzner hasn't got a jeep. He hasn't got a car."

"I know."

"Are we forgetting the jeep?"

"How did Nadine get from Freiburg to Grezhausen, then?"

Nobody replied.

"And what if it wasn't just *one* attacker?"

"You think there might have been more than one?" Bermann said.

She returned his gaze. At least three, Rolf, one of whom is a policeman, maybe even Kripo. Freiburg Kripo, Rolf, a colleague of *Louise Boni, Freiburg Kripo.*

Louise needed time to think, time to make decisions. To answer questions. Questions like: What was the key thing to do now?

Protect Nadine.

She had to find her, but unofficially. She had to find out what Nadine knew about her attackers, but nobody else must get wind of this. Any of her Kripo colleagues could have access to the case file and keep themselves up to date with the investigation. But lie to her colleagues? Bermann, Illi, Hoffmann, Meirich?

Was Nadine safe where she was? Was she O.K.?

How about Claus Rohmueller? Shouldn't he be informed, at least?

She remembered Almenbroich's advice. Check out the Ettingers. Who knew what she'd stumble upon? What if he was right?

Questions about questions?

"Frau Bonì?" Reinhard Graeve said.

She turned to him. "There must have been at least two of them. Holzner doesn't have a car. Did he take Nadine to Grezhausen on foot? By train? Did he rent a car and then bring it back? Unlikely."

"I think she could be right," said a colleague she only vaguely knew. Chief Inspector Walter Scuma from Surveillance. Walrus moustache, strands of hair combed across his head to hide the bald patches, rimless spectacles and, behind these, distant eyes. From her colleagues' expressions she could reliably tell who knew about her and was hostile towards her. Scuma was one of those.

Which didn't necessarily mean he was a bad police officer.

She looked at Bermann. "Anyway, didn't we agree that Holzner was out of the frame? That the profile didn't fit?"

Someone gave a quiet sigh. Bermann grunted something unintelligible. But Marianne Andrele nodded and Reinhard Graeve signalled his agreement too. "On its own, a fag butt isn't evidence," he said. "Let's not make it too easy for ourselves."

"Yes," Louise said.

Ilic turned to her. "What about the Ettingers?"

"Sandy and I will take care of them," Bruckner grunted.

"Weren't you going to—" Ilic began.

"I was at theirs yesterday," she interrupted.

"Christ, who are the Ettingers now?" Scuma asked quietly. The corners of his mouth turned down as he pushed his glasses up the bridge of his nose, as if the movement irritated him.

The owners of the field and the barn, Louise explained. Two nice old ladies. Slightly eccentric. Drink tea from art nouveau cups, that sort of thing. They didn't know anything. Didn't want to either. Live in the past. Almost never leave their property.

"Are we going to forget the Ettingers, then?" Bermann said.

She nodded.

It was easier than she'd imagined.

Louise excused herself soon afterwards and left the room. She needed a few minutes to think, something she couldn't do amongst colleagues she'd just lied to.

She went to the loo, entered a cubicle with a window and opened it. The sun had risen and the city was glistening in the summer light.

What she was doing was arrogant and irresponsible, she thought.

But she was convinced too that she was doing the right thing, that many of her colleagues would do the same had they spoken to Josepha Ettinger and the old woman in the pink dressing gown.

On the way back to the task force room she realised she needed support. Somebody had to look for Nadine and the Ettinger sisters if she was busy with something else. Somebody who wouldn't scare them off if they found them.

And she needed support in house too. Someone inside H.Q. had to keep their eyes open. Someone on the case she trusted.

Louise opened the door and her gaze fell on Hoffmann. One of his hands was holding a chocolate croissant, the other picked crumbs off his voluminous belly, and he looked perfectly content.

She returned to her seat. Hoffmann, married to a dragon from Lower Bavaria, was usually the first to arrive and the last to leave, addicted to chocolate and compliments, an overweight, lonely man who only participated in life via case files and the internet. In his dreams the girls appeared, then Hoffmann would wake up, go to the fridge and eat chocolate. But the girls would still be inside his head and one night, rather than going to the fridge he would get dressed, head out to his car and . . .

"Fancy a bite?" Hoffmann whispered.

*

124

"You're joking . . ."

Hoffmann was sitting in his special, multifunctional office chair that was supposed to prevent back pain – or any other joint and muscle complaints for that matter – and looking at her wide-eyed.

She shrugged. "Am I being paranoid?"

"In a way, yes."

"But you'll help me?"

"Heavens! I've got to water my plants first." He rolled his chair to the sink, filled a watering can, rolled to the green jungle in one corner of his office and began watering. She heard him muttering to himself, though she couldn't make out any words. One sigh followed by another as his body slumped. Life wasn't kind to Alfons Hoffmann. It confronted him with decisions like this one.

"Alfons, I've got to go to the interrogation."

"Yes, yes, I'm nearly done." He rolled back. "Speak to Graeve. He's got to O.K. it first."

Louise groaned; she'd been expecting something like this. "Alright then. See you later."

"When?"

"This afternoon. Let's wait and see what Holzner says first."

Hoffmann nodded. "What do you need?"

She needed everything he could find out about Maria and Josepha Ettinger. He should focus on the property in Munich and their connection to the Cistercians. Had they ever been members of the order? Were any of the nuns friends or relatives of theirs? Did they have any other properties? A cabin in the Black Forest, or a holiday home in France? Anything that might give them a clue as to where the sisters had taken Nadine.

"Their past?"

Louise recalled Almenbroich's advice and nodded. "But nobody must find out. *Nobody.*"

"I'll tell my yucca. And maybe the cutting from my mother-in-law."

"Alfons!"

"I get it. And you talk to Graeve."

"I promise."

"I don't want to know whatever else you get up to. If you break in anywhere, and all that."

"I understand."

"Do you know why I'm helping you?"

"Because you're a good copper."

"I'm two good coppers," Hoffmann said, patting his enormous midriff. "Because you came to me rather than Illi or Rolf or whoever else. You trust me."

"I do."

He gave a satisfied grin. "Now say thank you and let me get going on this."

Holzner and Richard C. Müller. Bermann, Bruckner, Meirich. In the background a secretary at a laptop, but she wasn't typing. Nobody was saying a word.

Louise closed the door. From Müller's red face and Bermann's stony expression she could tell what had just happened. Bermann had added suspected murder to the charge sheet. Müller had become enraged.

Holzner sat motionless on the same chair as the day before. He was unshaven and looked tired. His listless eyes watched her sit down. "The police tart who likes football," he muttered.

A faint clattering on the keyboard.

"Don't say anything," Müller growled, today in light blue with a lilac handkerchief in his breast pocket, white trainers.

"Some game, wasn't it?" Holzner said.

"Yes," Louise said.

"We won against the fucking Mexican dwarves." Holzner's eyes flitted across the wall behind her, before fixing on something.

She caught Meirich's gaze. Where Holzner's fist had hit his cheek the skin beneath his grey beard was glowing a bluish-red. A dark

126

ointment had been rubbed into his lips and fresh plasters had been applied. He tried to laugh, but aborted it. Laughing probably hurt.

"What's wrong with his face, did he fall out of bed?" Holzner asked grinning, as if he'd only just noticed Meirich.

Meirich rolled his eyes.

"Say nothing," Müller snarled.

"I didn't think we were going to win," Holzner said. "The boy did, though."

Louise nodded. "Do you understand what this is about, Herr Holzner?"

"You think I killed him."

"Precisely," Bruckner said, keeping a tense eye on Holzner.

But Holzner remained calm. "Do you believe this crap too?" he asked her.

"She does," Bermann said.

Louise said nothing.

"She doesn't. She's smarter than the rest of you, even though she's a woman."

"The barn," Bermann said. "Do you want to say anything about that?"

"No," Müller said.

Holzner stared at Bermann. "What sort of barn?"

"Don't say *anything*," Müller ordered.

"Keep your trap shut, you shitty brief."

Müller grinned. "Clients with a sense of humour – my favourites."

"The Ettingers' barn."

Holzner nodded. "Is that where it happened?"

"No. By the river."

Holzner rubbed his thighs. "By the river. Right. So what was he doing by the river?"

Bermann's mobile rang. He stared at it for a moment but didn't take the call. When the ringing stopped he said, "The barn, Herr Holzner."

"Dunno. Not this year. Last year, maybe."

"What cigarettes do you smoke?"

"Now he's getting all matey with me." Holzner gave a fleeting grin.

"Say nothing," Müller said.

"Marlboro. Got one for me? I'm fine with Camel too."

Bermann held up the bag with the cigarette butt. "We found this in the barn. Marlboro. One of yours."

"No," Holzner said.

Bermann's phone rang again, and again he waited for it to stop. "We did a D.N.A. test."

"Bollocks to your D.N.A. crap," Holzner said.

Müller stood. "I wish to have a word with my client in private."

"Say what you've got to say, then shut it."

Müller sat down. "You're getting yourself deeper and deeper in this."

"Right, you've said it now." Holzner looked at Louise. "What was he doing by the river?"

"We don't know."

"You don't know, I see." Holzner coughed.

"Do you know?" Bermann said.

"No idea, maybe he wanted to go swimming." He shrugged, then started rubbing his thighs again. "Us Holzners swim like fish. I chucked him into the river when he was four, that's how he learned. When he was nine we swam to the island for the first time. Later he wanted to swim from the island to the Frogs, but I told him no. Too dangerous with all those boats about. You're a wuss, he said, so I slapped him one and said, Don't you dare talk to me like that. You're going to learn the difference between being a wuss and being sensible, and if I catch you trying to swim over there I swear I'll drown you like a kitten."

Müller had crossed his arms; he looked grim and was shaking his head. Bruckner raised his hands as if to say, What else do we need? Bermann rubbed his eyes then looked at Louise. What now? his face said. What am I going to do with him?

At that moment his mobile rang for the third time. Seconds later her telephone started to vibrate.

They both answered at the same time.

Hoffmann. "We've got a body. A murder."

"What?" Bermann barked.

"Not Nadine . . ." Louise said desperately. Her gaze met Bermann's.

"No, a man," Hoffmann said.

"Shit!" Bermann cursed into his phone without taking his eyes off her. "Where?"

"The Katzental," Hoffmann said in her ear.

Bermann turned to Meirich. "They've found a body in the Katzental."

"Nadine?"

"A man."

"I suppose my client is responsible for this one too," Müller said scornfully.

"Shut it," Holzner hissed.

Not Nadine, Louise thought with a deep sense of relief.

"Brace yourselves," Hoffmann said.

14

The drive passed in silence. Bermann at the wheel, Meirich beside him, Louise and Ilic in the back. Colleagues' voices crackled from the police radio. More patrol cars were being sent to the Katzental; the road had to be blocked off at Horben and at Au. The emergency services were already there and the coroner was on his way. At one point Lubowitz's grating smoker's voice could be heard: Bring me a fag, I've forgotten mine. And don't forget your rubber boots, people.

Günterstal, with the archway of the former Cistercian convent, then narrow, winding roads up to Horben, a rapid change of light and shadows in the rhythm of curves, trees and hills. Nadine and Eddie, she thought, and now another murder – what a week. Brace yourselves, Hoffmann had said: a bloodbath according to their colleagues who were first at the crime scene.

"Where were you first thing this morning?" Ilic said.

"I overslept."

He nodded. "Ben called."

"So?"

"One of you could have told me."

"Yes. I'm sorry. The opportunity just never . . . came up."

"Oh well," Ilic said.

Her favourite colleague offended. She stroked his arm. "Sorry, Illi."

Louise felt Bermann's gaze on her and caught his dark eyes in the rear-view mirror. He'd known Boni long enough to detect changes in her, in all aspects of her life. Her reticence during the task force meeting, during Holzner's interrogation. And he knew she'd never oversleep if there were a task force meeting.

When they got to Horben, Bermann steered past two patrol cars into the Katzental, then for several minutes they traversed hillsides on narrow roads. The roads became even narrower and the bends more frequent as they headed steeply downwards before parking behind another patrol car. By the side of the road were more police vehicles, unmarked cars and two ambulances. They got out. A uniformed officer pointed at two lines of police tape that formed a narrow path into the forest. Their shoes immediately sank into the wet ground. Wet feet again, she thought, and damp trouser hems, like that morning at the Ettingers'. Where the sunlight hit the earth a thin layer of vapour hovered above the ground. They slid down into a hollow then struggled up the other side, Bermann in front. He seemed to summon mysterious energies whenever a task force determined the rhythm of his life. She followed close behind. Ilic and Meirich had fallen slightly back. In other circumstances they would have given the impression of a touching couple. The young man helping the elder, the traumatised one helping the battered one.

Bermann turned around briefly. "Is there anything I should know?"

"No."

He stopped abruptly and she crashed into him. When she staggered backwards he grabbed her arm until she'd regained her balance. His eyes were glowing with anger. "Don't take me for a fool, alright? You're hatching something, aren't you?"

"O.K., O.K. I'm pregnant. How did you know?"

He stared at her in horror. "Crap. Who'd want to have a child with you? You as a *mother*?"

"Fuck off, Rolf."

Bermann burst out laughing. "That Ben chap? Who is he, anyway? Another oriental freak?"

"None of your business."

"Kiss my arse."

"Not in a million years, Rolf."

Bermann grinned. The anger had dissipated. Bermann loved that sort of banter.

Having caught up with them, Ilic and Meirich now stopped, panting. Louise set off again and Bermann followed quickly, reaching for her arm again. "This is your last chance, Louise."

She wondered whether she was being unfair on him. If there ever was a dedicated police officer, someone who put his heart and soul into the job, it was Rolf Bermann. Even if he'd only fallen into the camp of the good guys by chance, it didn't mean that he acted out his dark sides like *this*. None of her colleagues was so defined by their job as he was. By the power that police law and the criminal code lent him. The kudos that being head of a section and the pecking order brought him. Manipulation, bullying, ruthlessness, machismo, intimidation – in his position Bermann found enough opportunity to act out his dark sides in quasi-legal ways. He didn't have to torture women.

All the same she felt it was still too early. What if he didn't believe her?

"You know that Holzner's got nothing to do with it?" she said.

"I don't know anything."

"And that we've got multiple perps. There are others."

"Tell me more, Louise."

"Nothing more."

"What other perps? Is there any evidence?"

Lubowitz's body, clad in white, emerged from between the trees. They waited outside the cordoned-off area around the crime scene until they could have a first look without being distracted by C.S.I. officers, evidence markers or commentaries.

"We'll talk later."

Bermann let go of her arm. "Don't play with fire."

"Is that what you are, the fire?"

"A warning, disciplinary proceedings," Bermann said calmly.

She laughed. Every year she faced the same threats of disciplinary proceedings. "You really know how to motivate your colleagues."

"Nothing's changed, has it? Like when you used to get pissed up."

Louise took a deep breath and didn't rise to the bait. Keep calm, Boni.

"Stubborn, wilful and fucking irrational," Bermann said. "You just can't work in a team."

"We'll talk later, Rolf."

"Are you drinking again, is that it?"

She said nothing.

"And who's this Ben guy? Is he a pisshead too? Some loser from A.A.?"

"Arsehole."

"*You're* the arsehole. Almenbroich called me."

"Shit," Louise groaned.

"Yes," Bermann said, walking past her.

"Non-smoker." Lubowitz grunted sadly, putting a hand to his brow in greeting.

Banishing the thought of Almenbroich, the disappointment, she ducked under the police tape and went to stand beside Bermann.

Five metres away a pair of legs in suit trousers, the feet in black shoes, the body in a supine position. A tree shielded the torso and head. Faint traces of blood and drag marks leading to the road. Otherwise nothing remarkable.

"I.D.? Mobile? Keys?" Bermann asked.

"No," Lubowitz replied from behind them.

"Anything at all?"

"Not even a tissue. Shit, they don't smoke either . . ."

Ilic and Meirich joined them.

"Who found him?" Ilic said.

"A dogwalker," Bermann said.

"Three cheers for dogwalkers," Meirich slurred.

Louise thought of Meirich's fighting dog, Andi Bruckner, and wondered where he was. She couldn't imagine him missing out on a body.

They kept going, one behind the other.

Suit jacket, torn, bloody white shirt, shreds of flesh, gaping stab wounds. She forced herself not to avert her eyes from the gruesomely savaged body. First impressions were important.

Stabbed in blind fury. A killer with no restraint. Two stabs would have sufficed, whereas he must have put the knife in a dozen times.

"Fucking hell," Bermann said.

Out of the corner of her eye she could see Ilic turning and walking away. She heard him throw up. Someone laughed, clapped and said, "Hey ho!". Lubowitz.

The hand that she could see was red with blood. Louise smelled excrement and urine. Only now did she look at the man's face. Mid-thirties, a round, unremarkable, horrified father's face, one arm of the rimless spectacles hanging from an ear, the lenses beneath his chin. Streaks of blood on his cheek, mouth, forehead, where he'd touched himself in panic and in pain.

Rays of sunshine slanted onto the face.

"Well?" Bermann said.

Meirich shrugged.

Nobody said anything.

Bermann kneeled beside the body. "The same person who killed Eddie?"

"What do you mean?" Meirich asked.

Louise looked away from the father's face. "One with his bare hands, the other with a knife?"

Bermann gave a curt nod.

The brutality was the same, as was the lack of inhibition. Add to this the fact that two murders and an abduction within a few days was incredibly unusual for this area. But serial killers don't as a rule change the way they murder. They have their favourite weapons.

Unless one of the killings was planned and the other wasn't.

"He didn't have a weapon with Eddie," she said. "He didn't plan to kill him. This time he did."

Meirich mumbled something unintelligible and Bermann said, "But let's not rule out other possibilities."

Ilic came back to them with Andi Bruckner. "Shit," Bruckner said. He bent over the body. A few years back in Karlsruhe, he said, they'd had a Russian who looked similar. "Perforated like a sieve, I tell you, with a Japanese vegetable knife."

"Who was it?" Meirich said.

Bruckner gave them all a meaningful look before answering.

A woman who'd been abused.

On the way back to the road Bermann got a call from Hoffmann. A person had been reported missing early that morning. A woman from Horben rang to say her husband had left the house around midnight and hadn't come home. Bermann rattled off the details as he walked: Dietmar Haberle, thirty-four, G.P. with a practice in Freiburg, married, one daughter.

Men who disappeared for a few hours weren't anything unusual. But now there was a body in the woods near Horben.

"You and me," Bermann said to Louise.

She nodded.

Decisions were looming.

The dogwalker was waiting in a patrol car on the road. A small old man, a small old dog, both of them trembling. Bermann spoke with him; Louise and the others listened, but there wasn't much to hear. The man and the dog – "we" – lived half a kilometre away on the Horben road. They went walking every morning, always the same route. The dog – "he" – darted into the woods, then barked like mad

135

for minutes on end. The old man followed him and found the corpse.

No, he'd never seen the man before and "he" didn't know him either.

The dog whined, the old man pressed him to his chest. Only Louise seemed to notice the dark stains on his suit jacket.

Bermann got out. Uniformed officers took the old man and his dog home.

"The little bitch," Bruckner said in a tone of both disgust and admiration.

It took her a moment to understand who he meant. "You're off your rocker."

"Only women kill like that."

"Maybe where you come from," said Ilic, who seemed to have recovered. "Not in our neck of the woods."

"You mean Croatia?"

"Freiburg."

"A monster at any rate," Meirich said, still finding it hard to talk intelligibly.

Bermann shot Louise a glance. "Let's go."

She nodded. "Let's go" meant "Let's talk."

"What did he say?"

"That I should keep an eye on you."

"Is that all?"

"It's enough for my gastric ulcer."

"Men like you get prostate cancer, not gastric ulcers."

Bermann gave a weary grin. "Christ, Louise, you're really hard work."

They were sitting in his car, driving back along the narrow, serpentine roads they'd taken an hour earlier. Keep an eye on me, Louise thought with a mixture of anger and disappointment. Of course this wasn't Almenbroich's only concern. He was worried about making another mistake. He was privy to the case and keeping his mouth shut, so was partially responsible for the consequences of her behaviour.

He'd called Bermann.

She ought to have known that he wouldn't be able to deal with it. That she'd asked too much of him.

But Almenbroich's call to Bermann meant something else: he trusted him.

Although he'd trusted the false Marcel too.

"Well?" Bermann said.

So she told him a little more.

The conversation with Josepha Ettinger, the strange behaviour that Louise hadn't noticed at first, but then couldn't get out of her head. The old woman who'd seen the sisters' red estate car outside the barn. The shopping lie. Her second "visit" to the Ettingers'. The guest room.

Louise didn't say any more. She would tell him the facts, but Bermann would have to draw his own conclusions.

A policeman, Rolf, maybe a Kripo officer.

Bermann was frowning and his face reflected fury, confusion and bafflement. Hoarsely he said, "You can't just break into a house like a common—"

"Yes I can. If circumstances dictate."

Having arrived at Horben, they turned into the street where they would have a conversation with a woman who'd been made a widow just a few hours earlier. Bermann parked and switched off the engine. She sensed he was trying hard to remain calm.

"Let's leave the formalities for later, O.K.?"

"Formalities?" he said. "You're a *police* officer. You don't just enter people's houses without a search warrant."

"Get one, then."

He thought about this for a moment, then took out his mobile and asked for Marianne Andrele, the public prosecutor. Strong suspicion against the Ettingers, possible involvement in an abduction. Evidence that Nadine had been held there against her will. He tried his very best and five minutes later was given the O.K. "So then you went to see Almenbroich?"

"Yes."

"Why? To get you out of the mess?"

"Rubbish."

"What are you hatching in your pisshead brain? And why didn't you say anything during the meeting? You *lied* to us. You're obstructing the fucking investigation! Are you out of your mind?" He'd talked himself into a rage; his voice was loud and aggressive. Sort of paranoid, Hoffmann had said. Pisshead brain, Bermann said. A paranoid pisshead brain.

"Are you drinking again? Is that why I've got to keep an eye on you?"

"Do I look as if I am?"

"What would I know?"

Bonì blocked out the sudden anger, the shame, the memories. She couldn't blame Bermann for finding other reasons to account for her behaviour. "The Ettingers, Rolf."

He rubbed his brow. "O.K. They found Nadine in the barn and took her back to theirs. They lied to you. Now they've gone. So?"

Louise turned away and looked down the street. A few metres further on was number 23. Thuja bushes hid the ground-floor windows. On the first floor was a balcony with open doors, yellow curtains wafting in the breeze. In the carport stood a silver Mercedes. Something was preventing her from confiding in Bermann. A vague feeling. Maybe the fear of making a mistake. Maybe a hunch.

"And the thing with Holzner," she said.

"Holzner," Bermann said, making no effort to conceal his anger. But he played along. "A car. The guy's got to have a car. Holzner doesn't have one. But he was in the barn – we've got the fag butt. So he lied. Why? Because he's up to his neck in this. Pure and simple."

"Rubbish."

"Rubbish, of course. How could I forget? You think everything that's logical is rubbish."

As she held his gaze she asked herself for the first time why Holzner had lied. Had he used the barn for his extra-marital activities? His wife had left him. He no longer had to lie for her sake.

"There are at least two of them," Bermann said. "Holzner is one. But he didn't kill Eddie. He's not the sort to do that. So it was the other guy . . . Surely you don't think it was Rohmueller?"

"Come on!"

"I don't want to play these fucking guessing games. I don't have the *time!*" Now Bermann was shouting.

Louise sighed. She understood him. Working with Louise Bonì must be pure torture sometimes.

Living with Louise Bonì too.

"Calm down, Rolf."

"The Ettingers and Nadine? Avenging Nadine? Two old battle-axes and a princess? How loopy are you? For fuck's sake!" Bermann opened the door and got out.

Good old blinkered Bermann. She'd expected too much of Almenbroich and had done the same with Bermann.

Bermann pointed to the house with the yellow curtains and snapped, "You're doing this one."

15

A sitting room all in white, soft, dust-free, silent. Walls without pictures, a bookcase behind glossy white doors. Two white flokati rugs muffled all sounds. An association nagged away at Louise's mind, one she couldn't immediately get. The room.

Then it dawned on her. White like a doctor's surgery.

They waited there, sunk into plump cushions, having taken off their mud-caked shoes. Brigitte Haberle had gone upstairs into the bathroom. On the other side of the room, Emily, the daughter, was drawing at the dining table. Louise guessed she was around eleven. A strikingly thin, shy angel with dark-brown hair. Tights, sweatshirt, pink hairclip, the child was the only dash of colour in the entire room.

They'd said Hello, but Emily hadn't looked up.

Always lost in thought, Brigitte said.

As they described the body, Brigitte had begun to cry silently. Emily didn't look over, didn't listen. She didn't yet know.

Then Frau Haberle stood up and went upstairs.

"I really hate this," Bermann said.

Louise nodded. Her eyes were still on Emily; she noticed the hand holding the pencil stop momentarily when Bermann spoke. Then she went on drawing. No sound, no clearing of the throat, no involuntary gasp, no shifting around on the seat. If Louise had her back turned she wouldn't know that Emily was there. Peculiar child, she thought. A child who was there, but also not there, locked in her own world and yet quite alert.

Bermann got to his feet and went over to her. "What are you drawing?"

The hand holding the pencil stopped again. Emily didn't look up this time either.

"Hey, a horse," Bermann said softly. "That's pretty. My daughters have real horses. Icelandic ponies. They always throw me off."

Rolf Bermann, with between four and six children – at some point she'd given up counting. A good policeman and a good father, so far as she was able to judge. But like Almenbroich he was a policeman who could only think as far as the double doors in police H.Q.

"Have you got a horse too?"

No reply. The hand holding the pencil froze above the paper. Emily had pulled her head in very slightly and now her face was in the shadow cast by Bermann's body.

"I bet it's really good riding up here. All these meadows and forest paths." Bermann waited another moment before turning to Louise. He looked pale.

The hand came down and Emily resumed her drawing.

A few minutes later Brigitte Haberle came back into the room. Her tears had been wiped away. She'd changed and was now wearing a brown skirt and blue blouse in place of the grey housecoat. She sat in an armchair, her knees pressed together, waiting for questions. When they didn't come immediately she said, "Somebody called. Last night. That's why he went out."

"When?" Louise said.

"Around midnight."

She nodded. At that time she'd been standing beside Ben and his guard cabin. While Dietmar Haberle was going to meet his killer, she was talking of the shadows that came when her mind began to churn, the shadows of the dead and of the killers. At that very time two more shadows were on the move in the Katzental. A murderer and his victim.

"And he didn't come back."

Frau Haberle shook her head.

They spoke softly so that Emily couldn't hear. She hadn't moved;

141

she was still drawing at the dining table. Bermann struggled out of the upholstery and shuffled forwards. "Who called?"

"A friend, he said."

"Which friend?"

"He just said a friend." Brigitte smiled uncertainly.

"Does he have a mobile on him?"

Frau Haberle nodded. "It's switched off."

"Did he have many friends?" Louise asked.

"Two or three."

"We need a list."

"I only know . . . know their first names. Once, a few months back, someone came to pick him up. Our car wasn't working. I don't know the others." Again that uncertain smile. I realise I'm no help, the smile said. I'm so stupid. I'm sorry.

No more tears, no more grief, Louise thought.

"How's the surgery going?" Bermann asked.

"The surgery? Oh, very well, I think."

"Did your husband have any debts?"

"Debts . . . I don't know. No, I don't think so. A few years ago he inherited an apartment from his father and sold it. Debts . . . the loan on the house, perhaps. But why—"

"And the surgery? Equipment? Machinery?"

"I don't know. We never talked about financial matters. Money. He wanted to shield us from all that. Everyday worries."

Frau Haberle looked over at her daughter. Nobody said anything for several seconds.

"Why's she at home, actually?" Louise asked. "Shouldn't she be at school?"

"He takes . . . he always took her. To school. But this morning . . ." Brigitte lowered her gaze. "I can't drive."

Another silent pause.

"I must learn how to," Brigitte said. "There are a lot of things I've got to learn now. I don't know if I'm up to it."

Louise leaned forwards and laid a hand on her arm. Frau Haberle gave a sheepish smile. Tears were shimmering in her eyes again.

"Did he pick Emily up from school too?"

Frau Haberle blew her nose. "Yes, he did."

"Every day?"

"Yes. From school, from swimming, from ballet. We're very remote here."

Louise glanced at the window behind Emily. She could see a few neighbouring houses and beyond these a steeple. Buses came to Horben. Remote was something different.

"So he took your daughter everywhere and picked her up again?" Bermann said.

Frau Haberle nodded. For a moment Louise got the impression that she was ashamed. "The bus . . ." she said apologetically. "Something might happen. He didn't want her to take the bus. *We* didn't want her to."

"And that worked? I mean, he had patients . . ." Bermann said.

Brigitte shrugged. "It was never a problem. He liked doing it. It was important to him. He wanted to be a . . . a good father."

"And was he?" Louise asked.

"Yes, of course. The best father a child could wish for."

Silence descended on the white room. Brigitte Haberle turned to the dining table.

Emily had gone.

Frau Haberle had got up to check on Emily. Louise could hear her footsteps on the stairs and a door being closed. For the first time since they'd entered this house she thought of Dietmar Haberle's body. The gentle, horrified, father's face, the stabbed torso. She pictured the three of them sitting together here, in this white prison of dependency and control. The father taking the daughter to school, swimming or ballet, and picking her up later. The best father a child could wish for. A child drawing silently at a table, living in her own world, there and

143

yet not there, disappearing without a sound. Frightened of men.

Three people with an unmentionable secret.

Bermann went to the dining table and picked up Emily's picture. "She's afraid of me."

"Yes."

"You know what's been going on here?"

"I think so."

"It's a good thing the bastard's dead."

Louise said nothing.

"Let's notify the child welfare office."

"Not right away, Rolf. Don't take her mother away just at this moment."

"The mother let it happen. May even have joined in."

"We don't know that."

Bermann put the picture back. "Yes we do."

"We'll get Katrin here. She can deal with the two of them. Everything else . . ." She didn't finish her sentence.

"Who's that again?"

Katrin Rein, lecturer at the police academy and former therapist to both Louise Boni and her Kripo colleague Günter, who'd persuaded himself he had bowel cancer, which turned out to be just a silly old neurosis. For policewomen of her ilk Katrin Rein was too young and inexperienced. But one of her specialisms was child abuse.

"The pretty one from the academy with the nice tits, Rolf."

Bermann snorted. "Oh, you mean the psycho woman?" A fleeting grin. He remembered the tits.

Louise stood up. Through the window behind the sofa she could see a neat little garden. Mown lawn, clipped hedges, weeded beds. People like Dietmar Haberle needed an impeccable façade to hide what they did. From others and from themselves.

Assuming it was as they suspected.

"Holzner and the killer and Haberle," Bermann said from the other end of the room.

Louise said nothing. Haberle might have been killed by the same person who murdered Eddie. Someone without restraint, who got a kick out of torturing and killing people. If this was the case and Haberle had abused his daughter, he could be one of the men who had abused Nadine.

"Not Holzner, Rolf. Another man."

"So why did Holzner lie?"

The key question.

But had Holzner really lied?

Brigitte Haberle came back. Everything's fine, she said. Emily had gone to lie down; she must suspect something was up. The girl was scared and clearly worried, Brigitte said, that Papa hadn't come home. She'd calmed her down and hadn't told her anything yet; she had to wait for the right moment. Frau Haberle wrung her hands and her eyes darted between the two of them. She looked confused, helpless, distraught. No, Louise thought, she hadn't joined in. But she had looked away, ignored it, been in denial.

Frau Haberle offered them tea. Bermann declined, Louise nodded.

The kitchen was white too. Base cabinets and wall cabinets, glossy backsplash, the table alone was made out of an agreeably warm brown wood.

They didn't sit.

"Did your husband seem different recently?"

"Different?"

"Unsettled, worried. Not his usual self."

Frau Haberle filled a kettle and tipped some tea into an infuser. Half of it spilled – dark leaves on white veneer. She wiped them away with a cloth. "He was . . . he seemed . . . Yes, he *did* seem worried."

"How did that show?"

He'd been sleeping badly, Brigitte said, the past few nights. He came home later than usual. He looked stressed, even agitated sometimes.

Wasn't so loving with Emily. Yes, thinking back on it now, it struck her that he seemed *very* worried.

Nadine, who had disappeared. Eddie, who had been killed. If her suspicions were correct, Louise thought, Herr Haberle had every reason to be worried. "But you don't know why?"

"No, we didn't talk about things like that . . . his everyday worries. He wanted to spare us all that. Problems at the surgery, those sorts of things." Brigitte gave a coy smile. No more tears, no more grief. Perhaps, Louise thought, grief and relief were balancing each other out, the result being irritation and helplessness.

"Right," Bermann said. His arms were folded in front of his chest and he was standing in the doorway as if to say to Frau Haberle, You're not getting out of here. You're not getting past me. I'm not going to let you get away with it.

"Where was your husband at the weekend?" Louise asked.

"At the weekend . . . On Saturday he was at a friend's. They played cards and—"

"Just the two of them?" Bermann said.

"I . . . I don't know."

"When did he come home?"

"Not until Sunday evening."

"That was a long game of cards," Bermann said.

"Yes. No . . . he went on from there, he had to do a house call."

"Where? Don't you know?" Louise asked.

"No."

"Right," Bermann said again. He took his wallet from his jacket, slid out a photograph and laid it on the table. Nadine. "Ever seen her before?"

Frau Haberle leaned forwards. "I . . . no."

"Are you sure?"

"I don't think so, no. Who is it?"

"Another child." Bermann put the photograph away.

"I don't understand . . ."

The kettle switched itself off with a click.

"The kettle," Bermann said.

Brigitte moved swiftly and poured boiling water onto the infuser.

"Did you hear what your husband said on the phone yesterday evening?" Louise asked.

"No, he went out of the room." Brigitte put the cup on the table. Her hands were shaking. She was deathly pale.

"*Green* tea," Bermann said.

"Yes," Frau Haberle said, looking at Louise.

"I thought you'd only drink white tea."

"I . . . No, we don't have white tea."

"I just thought," Bermann said.

Nobody spoke for several moments. Louise caught the look on Bermann's face and raised her eyebrows. She remembered Pham, who she'd come across at the Kanzan-an, the Zen monastery in Alsace. A four-year-old boy from Vietnam, earmarked for sale to adoptive European parents. Now Pham was a part of Bermann's family.

Bermann and children.

"What happens now?" Brigitte asked. "Do I have to . . .?"

"Yes, you do," Bermann replied.

"And his things?"

"You can pick them up from police H.Q."

Frau Haberle nodded. "And . . . the car? Could you bring me the car? I mean, I can't . . . drive."

"It's in the carport," Louise said.

"The other car. He took the other one."

"The other one?"

"We've got two cars. There was something wrong with the first one. He bought a second one straightaway."

"What sort of car, Frau Haberle?"

"I don't know, I haven't a clue about cars."

"A jeep?"

She nodded.

A blue jeep.

147

16

Uniformed officers found the blue jeep with the spare tyre on the back: a three-door Toyota Land Cruiser. It was parked on a forest path, not far from where they'd found Dietmar Haberle's body. Louise assumed Forensics would find traces of the Haberles as well as Nadine and at least two other people. Fingerprints, hair, skin particles, clothing fibres. Exactly what you would expect to find in a car that had transported an abductor and his victim.

The body had been removed. Forensic scientists and investigators were on their way back to H.Q.

Now they knew that Haberle had been killed right on the edge of the woods, barely twenty metres from the police tape Lubowitz had used to demarcate the path to where the body had been found. The Forensics team had found faded residues of blood, tyre prints and footprints. Two cars and at least two people. The jeep and another car. Haberle and his killer.

Louise stood with Bermann at the crime scene. Both of them stared down at the prints. A few more hours of rain and they wouldn't have found anything.

A call around midnight. A friend. Haberle goes out of the room. Soon afterwards he gets into his jeep and drives to the Katzental. A strategy talk between rapists? Panic?

What had they known at that time?

Eddie's body had been found, Nadine had been missing for days, and was possibly safe. They would have found this out from the media. If she'd been in their shoes, Louise would have kept quiet, got on with her life and waited. The killer hadn't waited. He'd murdered Haberle. But why?

If they had access to information in the case file, at midnight they would have known that the police were working on the basis of multiple culprits, weren't convinced that Holzner was guilty and that they were looking for a blue jeep – Haberle's car. This could have been enough to throw someone like him into a panic. A man who carried a dreadful family secret and kept his wife and daughter captive in a net of control. The façade threatened to collapse. What was unravelling couldn't be controlled.

An accomplice who panicked was dangerous, and so Haberle had to die.

"But what I don't get is why they're killing each other," Bermann said, more to himself than to her.

"Panic," she said.

"Haberle?"

She nodded. "We were looking for his car."

"He didn't know that."

Louise said nothing.

Bermann looked up. "He didn't know that, Louise," he repeated patiently, as if speaking to a child. Or to a crazy pisshead.

"Why, then?"

"Like I said, I don't get it."

And yet it was so simple. So simple and unimaginable.

Bermann called Hoffmann, made preparations for the search of the Ettingers' property and had an alert put out for their red estate. Louise had turned away and was gazing over the sunlit hillsides. Gabled roofs hidden behind trees and hilltops, cows in the meadows, a tractor slowly working its way around a field. Back at H.Q. Hoffmann was making notes in a dossier. Red estate car. Search of the Ettingers' property. Whatever they might find at the Ettingers' would also appear in the file. Maybe clues as to Nadine's whereabouts.

The policeman would make a phone call, the third man would set off.

149

"No," Bermann said behind her. "But we do have his laptop."

The laptop was locked with a password, which Brigitte Haberle didn't know. They'd spent a few minutes trying to guess it. Not "Emily" or "Brigitte", of course, not "Dietmar" or "Horben", and of course no dates of birth.

The I.T. specialists would crack it.

Frau Haberle had also given them three first names: Markus, Bert and Micha, the "friends". Her husband had never mentioned surnames. Nor did she have any idea where he knew the three of them from, whether they were colleagues or friends from school or university.

"Come on," Bermann said.

She turned around. They looked at each other. Another thought she couldn't pin down. Something Bermann had said or done. Something that had come to her.

Bermann spoke, but she wasn't listening. The thought was becoming more concrete. The search of the property.

Then it hit her. What if they got there first?

Now that a search warrant had been issued, the policeman must suspect that there might be something to find at the Ettingers'. What if he'd already made the call and someone was on their way?

"Send a car to Grezhausen, Rolf."

"There are enough of them already."

"To the Ettingers'. In case they've come back."

Bermann grunted and called Hoffmann.

This time they drove along the narrow road towards Au. Sharp bends flanked by trees wound their way upwards, with the odd building here and there. Louise thought of the house on the hill, number 23. She saw Emily sitting at the dining table and Brigitte Haberle in a white armchair. Their old life was over, a new one had to begin. But it was still too early for that. The abysses would open up first. They had to learn how to deal with the shame, the hatred, the grief and the hurt.

"You check out the surgery with Illi," Bermann said. "The others will come with me to the Ettingers.'"

"I've left fingerprints. Please tell Lubowitz."

Bermann nodded.

"And take someone from the canine unit. They've got an Alsatian."

"What did you do with it?"

She smiled darkly. "Chained it up."

In Au they passed the house where the Niemanns had stayed after Antun Lončar, alias Heinrich Schwarzer, had burned down the house in Merzhausen. Bermann glanced at it too for a moment and she wondered what was going through his mind. They'd failed so miserably.

Her mobile pinged: a text. Hoffmann.

Call me.

She dialled his number.

"Colmar," Hoffmann said, his voice bristling with excitement. "They've got an apartment there." He gave her an address, talking quietly as if this would make his treachery less serious.

She thought of her conversation with Josepha Ettinger, the Alsatian accent.

"Will you go?"

"Yes. Later."

"Before the conversation with Graeve or afterwards?"

She hesitated. "Afterwards."

"Fine," Hoffmann said, sounding hurried. "Let's move on to Markus, Bert and Micha. I assume you want me to draw up a list of all police officers with these names?"

"Yes."

"The whole of H.Q. or just Kripo?"

She didn't answer.

"I get it. Everyone?"

"No."

"Just Kripo."

"Yes. Is that it?"

"Wait," Hoffmann said. "If he's a Kripo officer ... I mean, if you're right, which I don't believe. But if you *are* right ..."

"Yes?"

"He could be on the task force too, couldn't he?"

Merzhausen flew past, and Vauban with its colourful houses, she saw it all without registering anything. Her mind kept chewing over Hoffmann's last words. On the task force. She felt herself baulk at this idea. Task forces were the centre, the holy of holies. The heart of the organism that was Kripo. Only the best officers, or at least the most reliable ones, were appointed to task forces. Colleagues you could trust.

It was unimaginable that he could be on the task force.

She glanced at Bermann and suddenly she understood him and Almenbroich. They just defined the holy of holies slightly differently.

Unimaginable that he was a policeman.

Not far from H.Q. Bermann stopped at a petrol station and got out. In the wing mirror she saw him insert the nozzle.

On the task force.

Rolf Bermann, Thomas Ilic, Alfons Hoffmann and other men from D11: Horst Riemann, Jörg Seibold, Thomas Breutle.

From D23: Hans Meirich, Andi Bruckner and a couple of others.

Walter Scuma from Surveillance.

A colleague she couldn't place.

Reinhard Graeve, head of Kripo.

Unimaginable.

A few hundred metres further on the skyline was dominated by the Solar Tower, whose top floor housed the Kagan Club. In her head Louise saw Nadine descend in the glass lift, a depressed but laughing girl on her way to hell. At Martinstor a kiss for Serge, her ex-boyfriend.

A blue jeep, three men at least, and the ordeal begins: three or more men and a girl. Several hours later the girl lies in a barn in Grezhausen, more dead than alive.

Two boys, two elderly ladies, and the girl disappears.

Two murders.

One of the culprits panics: Dietmar Haberle, a child abuser but not a hardened professional. The whole thing gets out of control. Because it hasn't been planned, perhaps? A few men, a spur-of-the-moment decision early on Sunday morning and a chance victim. Nadine escapes, a frantic search begins, leading to two deaths which didn't have to happen, which ought not to have happened. The policeman must know this. Haberle in particular ought not to have died. His death provides dozens of new leads. Now they're onto the perpetrators. They've got names, other details.

The policeman must know all of this.

The Kripo officer who could be on the task force.

Bermann came back from paying. His eyes skimmed over her. Something wasn't right between them, hadn't been for years. Something remained unspoken. Occasionally she sensed that a fondness lay behind his aggression. Some days he wouldn't miss an opportunity to touch Louise even as he bawled her out. Then he would be more distant again, as if disgusted by her and even more by himself. How many times could he have dispatched her to some provincial police force as punishment? But he never did.

Bermann had stopped. He was looking at a car that had pulled up at one of the other pumps. A patrol car. A constable got out and waved at Bonì. She waved back.

As he turned to Louise, Bermann was frowning. She could see his thoughts crystallise into a grim realisation.

A policeman.

*

They stood beside the low wall separating the petrol station forecourt from the pavement. The morning traffic roared past and a tram screeched as it took a bend. Bermann suddenly looked tired, his tanned face grey. He waited until the screeching had passed, then said, "That's why you went to see Almenbroich."

She nodded.

"But what makes you so sure?"

"I'm not sure, Rolf."

"The fact that Josepha Ettinger didn't say anything about Nadine?"

"Not just that. They looked after her for three days without telling anyone. Not even her parents. Then they simply vanished and took her with them."

Bermann nodded and mechanically stroked his moustache with a thumb and forefinger. He was frowning again, or still. "Maybe they're after money?"

"Rubbish. They took her to safety."

"Safety from a police officer."

"Yes."

Bermann groaned and rubbed his eyes with both hands. For a moment he looked like a tired little child.

Then Dietmar Haberle, Louise said, he'd evidently become a disruptive element. The killer had been armed with a stabbing weapon. He'd planned the murder. Was it because Haberle had panicked and was now a risk? But why? Because the perpetrators had known more than they should have. What other plausible option was there? They no longer had Nadine so it couldn't be about ransom money. Or an argument about what they should do with her.

Bermann was looking away. He nodded again. "All this is just between us, O.K.? If you're wrong I might as well give up."

She smiled, disappointed. "If *we're* wrong."

Bermann looked at her. "Yes."

"I've spoken to Alfons."

"Oh, really?" He gave a twisted smile. "To everyone apart from me."

"To Almenbroich and Alfons, Rolf. Not to *everyone*."

"Certainly not to me."

She shrugged. Whingeing men – unbearable.

"Don't you trust me, or what?"

"Leave it, Rolf."

They went back to the car.

"Do you suspect anyone in particular?"

"No. But we have to assume he's on the task force."

Bermann stopped. "On the *task* force? He commits a crime and is then coincidentally appointed to the task force that's meant to solve the case? No. Too much of a coincidence."

"Who was appointed, in fact? Only the officers from D11, right?"

Bermann nodded.

"The others . . . were suddenly there. They offered to help because of the staff shortages in D11. We need to find out who Löbinger actually sent and who volunteered."

"Scuma volunteered."

Walter Scuma, Surveillance. The man with the comb-over, rimless spectacles perched on his nose. One of those who was hostile to her. Which didn't mean anything – many of them were hostile to her. "Others too."

Bermann kept walking, shaking his head, and hissed, "He *can't* be on the task force, Louise."

"It would be ideal for him. He would be right at the source."

"That simply cannot be the case. It would be a disaster for Freiburg Kripo, do you understand?"

"It is anyway."

They got in the car.

"Markus, Bert, Micha," Bermann said – Haberle's friends. "One of Meirich's men is called Michael and he's on the task force. Michael Ahlert . . . I think they call him Michi. Then Markus Hund from

National Security. Nasty piece of work, far-right sympathies, about to be transferred to Tuttlingen for disciplinary reasons."

"Not on the task force."

"No." Bermann slapped the steering wheel. "For fuck's sake. Michael Roninger, Information Management. Not on the task force either, but he's got access to everything anyone types into the computer. The thin one with the goggle eyes."

She nodded. A quiet officer with slim, fast fingers and sad eyes.

"Bertold Uhl," Bermann said. "One of Lubowitz's technicians."

"Stop it, Rolf."

"Michael, Michael . . . Michael Schönberg. Or is he Matthias? The baldie from Records?"

"Rolf."

"Fuck, fuck, fuck."

"Maybe Haberle's friends don't have anything to do with it."

"On the *task force*. This is doing my head in."

"Why don't you listen for a moment?" She told him about Colmar. Only a possibility; maybe the Ettingers had other properties and were somewhere else. But they had to check it out.

She decided to call Hugo Chervel. Chervel would be helpful without all the bureaucracy. He would position a few plain-clothed officers near the apartment in Colmar.

Bermann started the engine. As they drove they discussed how to proceed. Ilic would go to Haberle's surgery with one of Meirich's officers. Bermann would organise the search of the Ettingers' property, then go with the team to Grezhausen. Louise would head for Grezhausen right away, in case the policeman already knew that the house was being searched and had sent someone there.

"But in no circumstances are you to enter. I'll call you when we're on our way. Then you'll leave for Colmar."

"I can't promise that. If he's inside—"

"—you wait till he comes out. You'll have the patrol and we'll soon be there too."

"Whatever."

"How about Holzner?"

"Keep him in his cell. Make it clear to the others that you still suspect him. Can you put off the meeting with the judge?"

"Yes." He looked at her. "Shit, the cigarette butt . . ."

She understood. The cigarette butt which hadn't been stubbed out. Which had lain amongst dry grass and hay, but hadn't left a single scorch mark.

The policeman had called the others, one of whom had found the butt in the Holzners' front garden and chucked it into the barn. Holzner had already been there and was the chief suspect. She saw him standing, smoking, grinning at his front door. *You're not coming into this house. Piss off.* Flicking his cigarette butt away.

"Meirich was there when we arrested him. And he offered his services."

Bermann laughed in disgust. "Meirich's a poof."

"What?"

"Years ago some colleagues from Freiburg North saw him in a car with a young rent boy." Bermann turned into the carport at H.Q. and parked. "Andi Bruckner?"

"Stop, Rolf. It's not going to get us anywhere."

They got out.

"Right, then," Bermann said. "Be careful."

"I will."

She went to her car. As she opened the door she could see Bermann watching her. He gave a fleeting smile. Louise nodded and got in. She didn't want to smile.

Ilic was there too when they arrested Holzner.

17

Heavy traffic on the A5. Louise drove at 80 k.p.h. alongside the Tuniberg, which blocked the view of the Vosges. For the first time she realised how important it was to her to be close to France. To be able to enjoy the odd glimpse of the Vosges.

The French heritage.

Her French father lived in Kehl, newly married with a son he'd kept secret from her for seven years, perhaps because he'd christened him Germain, like his older son who'd died in a car accident in 1983. Louise's German mother lived in Provence, slightly lonely, selling baguettes part-time in a bakery and cultivating her general hatred of men, and of one or two of them in particular.

What a family.

"Would you like to meet my mother?"

"Oh," Ben said sleepily.

"Is that Bosnian for 'yes'?"

"No, for 'I'm surprised'."

"*Je comprends.*"

"French for 'I'm disappointed'?"

"No. For 'We'll drive down there next weekend'."

She heard Ben laugh quietly. "*D'accord.*"

"She hates men."

"Who doesn't?" Ben's bed creaked and groaned. "Are you on your way here?"

"Not right now." She told him about Grezhausen, Colmar, not all of it, only the essentials. Only so much that Ben wouldn't get worried.

He did worry. He wanted to get into the car and be with her, as he had been back in November in Bosnia and Croatia. There he'd been a help and a hindrance, she thought. He'd had a different rhythm to hers, different ideas, had felt duty-bound and authorised to keep an eye on her. Remnants of a social tradition in which women could do as they pleased, but in the end they always needed men for things to turn out well.

Ben was developing promisingly, however. He'd accepted her way of dealing with things, especially the idea that *she* made the decisions about her life and how she acted, not anybody else.

Certainly not a man.

"Go back to sleep, Ben."

"I could be there in half an hour."

"Don't be irritating."

Ben said nothing.

"You do your job and let me do mine. We'll see each other at midnight."

"Can I make a request?"

"No ... What?"

"Ćevapčići today, just for once?"

She laughed, and at that moment she'd passed the Tuniberg, giving her a full view of the Vosges, which stood silently in the sunlight on the other side of the Rhine. For a fraction of a second a peculiar feeling stirred in her stomach, an unfamiliar feeling, bulky, awkward, unpleasant. It happened so seldom, took hold so clumsily, only to dissipate again almost at once.

The Vosges and Ben Liebermann.

For a nanosecond she'd been happy.

Then everything returned to normal, and perhaps it was better that way. At least she was used to it.

When she left the motorway at Bad Krozlingen, Ilic rang. "Where are you?"

In his own way, Ilic could be irritating too.

She made do with a white lie. She was in Grezhausen, seeing what the search party was up to, trying to put together a few officers for the search of the Ettingers' house. That sort of thing.

"I see," Ilic said doubtfully.

"What about you?"

He was standing outside H.Q., waiting for Sandy. As soon as the search warrant came through he and Sandy would drive to Haberle's surgery.

Louise smiled. "Be nice to her. Say something nice about her plaits."

Ilic laughed half-heartedly. "Something's up. Rolf's behaving . . . weirdly."

"There have been two murders. Are you expecting him to be happy?"

"Sure, but . . ."

Illi, her favourite colleague – she'd asked so much of him over the past year. And she had so much to thank him for, including Ben Liebermann. Illi had put his career on the line to help her put her own career on the line. And now she was lying to him. Wondering whether *he* . . .

Unimaginable.

"Oh, Illi."

"You're *both* behaving weirdly."

Determination, she thought. If there was anything that marked her out from the others, then surely it was that. The determination to decide for herself what was sensible and necessary from all the clauses, guidelines, regulations, formalities, the rigid scheme of common sense and boundaries. Responding to people she dealt with differently from whatever was expected, given her function or job description.

"One of the perpetrators is one of us."

"One of *us*? A police officer?"

"Kripo."

There was silence for a moment, then Ilic said, "Wouldn't surprise me. I mean, just look at those guys."

"Which guys, Illi?"

"Just generally. All those moustaches, macho types, silly arses. Are you sure?"

"Pretty sure."

"Who knows? Rolf?"

"And Alfons and now you. And Almenbroich. I went to see him this morning. Silly arse Almenbroich, you remember."

"Oh, I see. When you 'overslept'."

They said nothing for a while.

Louise had passed Hausen an der Möhlin and now turned left onto the narrow road to Grezhausen. Before her, hidden by woodland, lay the Rhine Valley, and beyond it, at the foot of the Vosges, Colmar.

"Not a word to Sandy," she said. "Or anyone else."

"Do you suspect anyone in particular?"

"No. But I doubt it's someone from D11. He's probably on the task force."

"Andi Bruckner, if you ask me."

"Not so *loud*, Illi."

"Andi Bruckner," Ilic repeated softly. "I'll do a little research. I know someone in admin who'll let me have a peek at the personnel files."

"Not just Bruckner, Illi, the others too. Every man on the task force. Then we'll see."

"D11 too?"

"Yes. But watch out. Promise?"

"Here's Sandy."

"Promise, Illi?"

"Yes, yes, I promise. God, you can be irritating."

Sometimes, she thought, irritating might be rather a good thing.

18

Two constables from Breisach, one old and slim, the other young and fat. For a moment, memories were stirred: Hollerer and Niksch from Liebau in the Glottertal. Only there it had been the other way around: the old one fat, the young one slim. Two men who'd helped her, so often a dangerous endeavour. Hollerer had been seriously injured and Niksch shot dead. The other side of the coin. Those who engaged with her, her methods, put themselves in danger. It was important to know that.

The Breisach officers did seem to know. "Bonì," the old one drawled when she wandered over to their patrol car parked a few metres from the gate to the Ettingers' property. The constables were sitting inside with the doors half open. Now they got out.

"Nobody's arrived and nobody's left," said the older man, a sergeant.

They'd been there for half an hour. The young officer said he'd walked around the property "earlier".

"And?"

He shrugged, which in Breisach-speak no doubt meant: nothing.

They went to the gates. The small house stood there beneath the trees, and thanks to the sun now shining through the foliage it didn't appear quite so unwelcoming this time. They peered through the railings. Louise heard the wind rustling the leaves and branches knocking into one another. Suddenly she detected a strange whiff in the air; it took her a moment to realise where it was coming from. The old officer from Breisach smelled of tiredness, frailness, illness.

She looked at the name on his badge: P. Oertel. Normally only the surnames were printed. They must have several Oertels down at Breisach. "What does the 'P' stand for?" she said.

"Pensioner," the young colleague replied.

"Paul," Oertel said with a chuckle.

She turned to the younger officer: H. Barth. There must be several Barths at the police station on the Rhine too. "And the 'H'?"

"Heavens," Oertel said.

Now they were both chuckling.

"Fatty's name is Heinrich," Oertel said.

"H. and P.," Heinrich said. "Together we're H.P. Like horsepower." She could detect a certain pride in his voice.

They looked at the house again.

"Peaceful here, isn't it?" Oertel said.

Louise nodded.

Then it dawned on her. "The dog."

"What dog?" Barth said.

Bonì shook the gates, which scraped against each other and creaked at the hinges – no barking, no dog. She pressed the bell. Ringing in the distance. But the dog didn't start up even now.

"What dog?" Barth repeated.

"Bonì," Oertel sighed as she put her foot on the first crossbar.

"You two, stay here."

"Heavens," Barth said. "I wouldn't get over that anyway."

Louise jumped down on the other side and readied her gun. Oertel and Barth watched her silently through the railings.

Barth was the first to understand. "Is one of the suspects in there?"

Slowly she approached the house. Barth said something, but she didn't react. The wind in the leaves, branches knocking against branches, her quiet footsteps and nothing else, no barking, no movement.

The kennel to the left of the house. The taut chain running between the trees towards the wall. Now she saw the dog lying on the ground a dozen metres away.

The front door was closed, nothing moving behind the windows.

Under the cover of the trees she ran to the rear of the house. The kitchen door she'd gone through that morning was open. She knew she'd closed it.

Bonì sank to her knees behind a tree trunk. About an hour ago Bermann had called H.Q. regarding the search. The officers from Breisach had arrived about half an hour ago. They hadn't heard any barking, so the dog must already have been dead.

Maybe he was long gone. Maybe not.

Should she enter the house? She had to know if he'd found what he was looking for. If he was on his way to Colmar.

But Louise was scared. She thought of Eddie, of Haberle, of the lack of restraint. Eddie, who'd been beaten, strangled and finally drowned. Haberle, who'd been stabbed umpteen times.

The wrong thoughts.

She tried to think the right ones. If he was still in the house he was trapped. The Breisach officers were here and the squad would be arriving soon. She didn't have to go in. She had to go to Colmar. Colmar was important. And her fear was important too, somehow. Perhaps her fear was a hunch. Don't go in, her hunch said. Think of Eddie and Haberle.

The wrong thoughts.

Come on, come *on*, she thought.

Bermann and the others didn't come.

Louise stood up and walked back to the kennel. Oertel and Barth hadn't moved from the gate. She raised a hand: everything's fine, stay where you are. Oertel said something in a hushed voice, but she couldn't make it out. She kept her eye on the house and ran over to the dog. It was lying on its side, blood still trickling from a gaping bullet wound. The chain had cut deeply into its neck. But it wasn't yet dead and it stared at her with exhausted, terrified eyes.

For several seconds she couldn't tear her eyes away, then she ran to the wall.

Eddie drowned, Haberle stabbed, now a firearm. He used whatever was to hand.

The barbed wire on top of the wall had been cut. He'd taken a metre out of it.

Louise turned around. The dying dog amongst the trees, behind it the house in the sunlight. Was he still here?

You've got to go inside, she thought. But she couldn't. If he was still here he would already have noticed her. He would be waiting inside for her.

Come on.

They didn't come.

Louise went back to the dog. Again she was transfixed by the eyes. A faint, distressed howl came from its open mouth. Show determination, she thought. This was, after all, what set her apart from the others.

She raised her pistol and shot the dog in the head.

The trees swallowed the report.

Shouting from the gate: "Bonì!" Oertel's old voice. "Oh God! Oh God!" Barth screamed.

Not a sound from the house. Nothing stirred.

I don't *want* to go in.

She went to the kennel. Oertel was hanging from the gate, Barth holding one of his legs. "Just the dog!" she cried, and ran to the rear of the house. She stared at the open kitchen door and tried to order her thoughts. An intruder would close the door behind them to avoid giving themselves away. But when they left the house again perhaps they didn't care.

He'd left the dog lying there; he didn't care.

But what if she was mistaken?

Bonì didn't want to go inside. She had to go to Colmar.

Slowly she went back to the gate. Oertel was now on the ground and eyeing her sceptically. "Why did you shoot the dog?" Barth called out.

She asked him about the barbed wire on the other side of the house. Barth hadn't noticed it. He'd been looking out for a man, not barbed wire or a place to climb over.

"So why shoot the dog?"

"Because it was dying."

"Why was it dying?"

Without giving an answer she turned back to the house. What if the sisters had other properties, not just in Colmar?

Louise called Hoffmann. Oertel said something but she wasn't listening.

"Louise?" Hoffmann's familiar voice sent a shudder of relief down her spine.

No, only Colmar and Munich so far. He hadn't been able to find anything else.

That didn't mean they didn't exist, she thought.

She had to go inside.

This time she went the other way around the house.

The kitchen door, shards of glass on the threshold and stone floor, just as there had been that morning. Silently she crossed the room and peered into the hallway. Sunlight poured in from the sitting room to the left; to the right, where the loo and staircase were, it was dark.

If he was down here he would be in darkness.

She'd begun to sweat and stopped breathing. Breathe, for God's sake! Don't be like this! She stared for several seconds into the darkness and listened, but there was no sound apart from her breathing and the soft ticking of the grandfather clock in the sitting room.

She forced herself, step by step, into the blackness, her pistol at the ready. She knew that if he were down here he would have spotted her. So he *wasn't* down here, she thought, or at least not here in the darkness that was turning into a colourless grey the further she went, because he would have shot her, seeing as he was armed with a gun this time, but he really wasn't down here, as now she had a view of the rest of the hallway and he wasn't here. Bonì opened the loo door as quietly as she could and left it open once she'd ascertained the little room was empty.

As she went back to the kitchen she glanced at the stairs. No sound from above. Another shiver down her spine, but this time it was fear. She didn't want to go up.

Louise edged towards the sitting room and into the sunlight that was almost blinding. For a few moments all she could see were outlines – window frames, the arms of a chair – then her eyes were able to scan the room, the dark wood absorbing the light. Now the ticking of the grandfather clock sounded deafening, and, as she had that morning, Louise smelled flowers and wood. She made her way around the furniture, then froze in shock when she noticed the chaos by the sideboard. The doors were open and on the stone floor were spilled the contents of files and folders, documents and brochures. She knew what he'd been looking for.

For a moment her gaze alighted on black-and-white photographs of the four girls, four sisters, one of whom was Josepha. Their black frames looked like the borders on death notices.

In the dining room she went once around the table before going back to the sitting room. Kneeling by the sideboard she looked through two folders for Munich, statements detailing the partition of assets, ancient sales contracts, rental contracts, expenses allowances, one folder for the house in Grezhausen, no other properties, nothing on Colmar, no matter how hard she looked. Had he taken the documents?

As Louise was leafing through the papers she became aware of a new smell in the room, the fugitive scent, heavy and sweet, of a men's fragrance she hadn't noticed that morning.

She knew the scent. She knew a man who smelled like that but she couldn't place him. Not someone she worked with on a daily basis, that much she knew. Someone who'd once been important to her. A colleague?

Bonì went back to the hallway and her gaze lingered on the stairs.

The creaking staircase, again that terrible fear, the risk, no. She knew she wouldn't go up, even if she hadn't found what she wanted.

Outside in the yard the name came to her and she couldn't help smiling. Mick had smelled like that at the end of their marriage, for a year or two.

"Pasha" by Cartier, the killer's aftershave.

More police were now by the gates, blue lights were flashing, three or four patrol cars. It couldn't be Bermann's team. Oertel and Barth must have summoned officers from the search party by the Rhine.

"Bonì," Oertel said, shaking his head.

"Is he in there?" Barth asked.

"I don't know. He's not downstairs."

She clambered back over the gate with jittery limbs. Barth helped her down. She stayed by his warm, fat belly for a few seconds, just sticking to him, to his strength, his youthfulness, his wonderful awkwardness. When he recoiled in surprise she put her arms around him and it was almost as if she were embracing Hollerer, good, old, sad Johann Georg Hollerer, who two years ago she'd visited by Lake Constance, tearing him from his convalescence and his process of coping with the past.

A Heinrich from Breisach would do for the moment.

She heard and felt Barth clearing his throat. His stomach tensed and something rumbled inside. "Heavens," he said.

That must be Breisach-speak for "It's O.K., Bonì, it's all O.K. now," she thought.

19

The Tuniberg from the other side, to the left of the Rhine, which she would cross at Breisach. This thought unleashed an inexplicable sense of longing, although she wasn't able to say for what. A longing for France and her childhood perhaps, for her mother and father, maybe more generally for a place she could call home. Her existence seemed to have been thrown off course since she'd met Ben and had a proper private life again – the fear she'd just felt at the Ettingers', clunky feelings of happiness in her tummy and now a tiresome longing for an indefinable something.

But that wasn't completely true. Her life had never really been on course, and the question of her home had already surfaced the previous October. Perhaps Ben was a sort of answer to this, not the whole answer of course, merely part of it, like her new apartment and new car. And perhaps everything together – her new apartment, new car and new man – was just an awkward attempt to evade the fate of all people of her age: wondering how and where she wanted to spend the coming decades.

Then she focused on other questions again, other people. The police officer who'd telephoned. Nadine, who may no longer be safe. The man who could be on his way to Colmar, who might have arrived there some time ago.

Hugo Chervel sat in his office in Mulhouse, doing a number of things simultaneously – she heard him switch between chewing, drinking, yawning, puffing on a cigarette and chatting to colleagues. They were having a little drink. He'd turned forty-five.

"My commiserations."

Chervel gave a bitter laugh. "Someone who understands me. I'm heading for *fifty* . . . What can I do for you?"

She told him about Colmar, the Ettingers, Nadine. About the man who might be on his way there.

"*Bon*," Chervel said once she'd finished. "You'll have to make do with two, the rest are all drunk."

"Two's better than nothing."

"These are French officers, *ma chère*, not Germans. So *much* better than nothing."

She laughed.

"*Attends*," Chervel said, then gave instructions via a second telephone. "On their way."

"I'm impressed."

"It's the influence of American films on the French Kripo. In the films everything happens really fast. Boom, bing, bang. We want to be even quicker. We admire the Americans."

"Not that your lot ever wade in or shoot."

"No, no. In our hearts we're Japanese. Zen, remember? We sit and wait."

"But you do it really quickly."

"I can see you understand."

Having reached Breisach, Bonì drove over the Rhine bridge. The sense of longing was back, stronger than before. Speaking French with Chervel, the Vosges in the distance, Gérardmer and her French uncles and aunts. A life that was long in the past. She wondered why there were moments when this past life was so important.

"How will I recognise them?"

Chervel drank, drew on his cigarette and said, "They're wearing diving goggles."

"Richard Bohringer buttering a baguette in 'Diva'."

"*Mon Dieu*, you're a dream." She heard him laugh. "They'll

recognise *you*, Louise. The whole of France knows you. You're the Joan of Arc of the German Kripo."

Now that would be something, she thought.

"A phone call, at last!" Rohmueller said.

He was walking with Cesare along the Dreisam, as he had so often these past couple of days since arriving from Bonn, waiting for news, a telephone call, any information. One long walk along the Dreisam over the past two days, up the river, down it, by now they knew every tree and every stone on either bank, they knew every dog and dog-owner, and were regulars at the Dreisam-Ufercafé.

He laughed uneasily and went on talking, but she interrupted him. "I may have some good news."

Rohmueller cleared his throat and said breathily, "Is she *alive*?"

"I believe she is, yes. But—"

"Do you know where she is?"

"I have an inkling. But it's complicated."

"Complicated?"

"This case is complicated. More complicated than we thought."

"I . . . I don't understand."

"Why don't you blow your nose first, Herr Rohmueller."

There was a rustling, a clinking, then a sneeze, a clearing of the throat. "Excuse me."

"Do you know what happened to her?"

Rohmueller said he did. Reinhard Graeve had told him what state Nadine was in when she was found in the barn and that she'd vanished again. And he'd told him that they'd found Eddie's body. Since . . . well, since then they'd been wandering up and down the Dreisam, he and Cesare, trying to take their mind off things. "What's complicated?"

"I think there may be multiple men involved. At least three. Men who possibly . . . have connections."

Rohmueller was silent for a while.

171

Louise drove across flat, almost treeless country, passing Neuf-Brisach. The Vosges were about fifteen or twenty kilometres away, and before them lay Colmar. Suddenly her fear returned. If she was right, he had gone to Colmar. He'd been there for half an hour or forty-five minutes.

"Connections?"

"I can't tell you any more and I don't have time at the moment anyway. Go back to your hotel. A friend of mine will pick you up and—"

"A friend of yours?"

"He'll bring you to me and I'll bring you to Nadine."

"It all sounds very . . . mysterious."

"It is," Louise said.

"Colmar," Ben said.

"As fast as possible. Could you do that for me?"

The bed creaked and groaned. Of course he could.

"Bring your gun."

Ben didn't reply.

"Just in case."

"Do you know what you're doing?"

"Yes."

"Good. What's the dog called?"

20

The first houses in Colmar came into view around quarter past two. She'd been here as a child with her parents and Germain, and as a wife twice with Mick, both times for just a few hours, and both times she'd visited the Château du Hohlandsbourg, which stood somewhere among the green hills above the city. She saw two children running, two parents quarrelling and for a moment she had the aroma of Gugelhupf in her nostrils. Louise barely remembered the time she'd spent with Mick; the anger and disappointment had flushed most of it away. What remained were vague images of a sweet, colourful old town, jammed with people, narrow canals, planters by the railings, low awnings, half-timbered houses in the old town.

The Peugeot's satnav led her to one of these half-timbered houses.

It was on a small square with a fountain, from which the pedestrian zone led into a traffic-calmed street. An almost enchanted, pink building with pale-blue shutters, three storeys beneath a roof that looked like a witch's hat. On the ground floor was a clothes store. According to Hoffmann the apartment was on the second floor. Three windows at the front, four along the side facing the street.

Louise had spoken with Henri, one of Chervel's men from Mulhouse. The French had been observing the building for about ten minutes. The occasional customer in the shop, he'd said, but nobody had entered the house itself. Otherwise, on the square and the street, just tourists and locals ambling past. No old ladies with a young woman, no red estate car, no suspicious man.

But he *had* to be here, she thought.

Don't forget, Henri had said at the end, that you're in France. This isn't your territory.

She'd parked the car one street further on and walked back. Henri was sitting at the window on the first floor of a café opposite the pink house. There was a brief hand gesture as she headed towards it.

"What now?"

"We wait."

Henri gave a hesitant nod. He had a narrow, pale face, glasses with steel side arms, and looked more like a maths student than one of Chervel's officers. His French sounded as if he hailed from the south, the coast. Marseille, perhaps.

Not that she was an expert in dialects.

"Where's your colleague?"

"Noureddine? Here and there. He's wandering around." Henri shrugged. She thought he came across as a bit too easy-going. A bit too professional. A man who thought he was important. "They like doing that, the Algerians, wandering around the whole time. Fancy a drink? You're allowed that without having to file a request for mutual assistance."

She pointed at the bottle of Perrier in front of him.

"Same as you."

He motioned a waiter over and ordered.

"Second floor, right?"

"Yes." Louise looked at the house opposite. White curtains prevented anyone from being able to see in. Discreetly she allowed her gaze to roam across the square and the street. Nobody who looked suspicious.

Bonì wondered what she would do if she were in the killer's shoes. Would she try to get into the apartment? Would she wait? If she opted to wait, she wouldn't wait too long. She must know that at some point Kripo would hit upon the apartment in Colmar. But she wouldn't rush anything. There was still a bit of time. It would take a while, she would think, until the Germans got support from the French.

Maybe she would wait until nightfall before breaking in.

"I saw someone briefly at the window a few minutes ago," Henri said. "An old lady. She stood there for a couple of seconds, peering down at the street. Small. White hair tied back." Another excessively casual shrug of the shoulders.

She nodded. Josepha Ettinger, her sister? "Have you been inside the building?"

"No. Should we have gone in?"

"No."

"But I looked at the name plates. A few French names, a few German ones."

"Ettinger?"

"Yes."

She nodded again.

"We could ring the bell and see," Henri said. "Us French lot. They'd let us in, wouldn't they?"

"What if they didn't. A copper is a copper. We'll wait, Henri."

He rolled his eyes.

"What about you? Half French?"

"French father, German mother."

"You meet all sorts." Henri gave a dry laugh.

Her Perrier arrived. They drank in silence.

"What are we waiting for?" Henri asked.

"A dog."

Bermann rang soon afterwards. "Can you talk?"

"Yes," she said, getting up and moving a few metres away from Henri. Her eyes drifted mechanically across the customers in the café. Henri had chosen this place because it offered a good vantage point from which to watch the sisters' apartment. Perhaps the culprit had thought the same.

A few students, a few elderly people, two men on laptops, a group of women. Nobody who stood out.

Louise told Bermann where she was. That she was waiting for Claus Rohmueller with Chervel's men. Bermann understood at once. If anyone had a chance of getting to the Ettingers and Nadine, it was the girl's father.

The father, she thought, and the dog.

In Bermann's opinion it was risky to bring in a civilian, especially the father. And particularly a father like Rohmueller, an important man with influence and money.

Not just *one* civilian, Rolf. Two. "It's the only way."

"Yes," Bermann said. "Whatever. But don't forget that you're not at home. And we have to notify Kehl. Kehl, home to the Franco-German Joint Centre for Police and Customs Cooperation. Bermann promised to take care of this.

He was in Grezhausen with part of the task force and some uniformed officers. They'd searched the house and grounds. Lubowitz and his team had just shown up and were looking for any usable evidence. "What happened to the dog?"

"He shot it," she said. "The bullet in its side. I'm responsible for the one in its head."

"That explains that," Bermann said.

"Do you think I shoot dogs for fun?"

"I don't know what you consider fun, Louise," Bermann said. "Apart from Zen weirdos, of course."

It sounded conciliatory. A friendly joke, Rolf Bermann style.

When she was back in her seat, Louise remembered the other two dogs. The sisters had three dogs, one of which they'd left behind in Grezhausen. Where were the other two?

Henri nodded, frowning. An old lady with two dogs, yes, she'd gone into the shop shortly before Louise arrived and hadn't yet come out again. "*Merde!* You can access the stairs through the shop."

He narrowed his eyes. "Someone ought to have thought of that."

Louise looked again at the second-floor windows. They'd missed her by a few minutes.

But more importantly, he'd seen an elderly lady with two dogs. Finally they had concrete proof that the Ettingers were indeed in Colmar.

At around a quarter to three Ben arrived with Claus Rohmueller and the collie. She stood up and took Rohmueller into the corridor where the loos were. She wanted to avoid a scene at any cost. "Not a word," she said.

Rohmueller nodded.

He was wearing elegant clothes that fitted him perfectly, just as he had yesterday. But from his face she could see that he hadn't slept a wink since their conversation. His eyes were small and sat in dark hollows, his skin was pasty, white and greasy. He smelled of sweat, of unwashed man.

Bonì told him about the Ettingers and her suspicion that there were at least three perpetrators, one of whom was probably a Kripo officer. About the murder of Dietmar Haberle, the apartment in Colmar and that one of the culprits was possibly here, watching the apartment too. She explained that the Ettingers probably wouldn't open the door to a German Kripo officer, maybe not even to a French one. That's why he was here, she said. He and Cesare.

Louise waited for Rohmueller to respond, but he didn't say anything. He was standing close to her, leaning forward, his arm pressing on her shoulder, as if seeking comfort. The old collie lay at his feet.

"Would your daughter recognise Cesare by his bark?"

He nodded.

She glanced at the collie. People and their dogs. "Let's give it a try. You and the dog. But you have to promise me that you won't do anything. Assume that he can see you. He mustn't get suspicious. Will you manage that?"

Tears glistened in Rohmueller's eyes. Yet another nod; clearly he wasn't up to speaking. Of course not. She thought about the dreadful days he must have suffered ever since first being confronted with the idea that something might have happened to his daughter. Now she was possibly no more than fifty metres away from him, but he couldn't run over there and take her in his arms.

"Blow your nose first, Herr Rohmueller."

He took out a handkerchief and turned away.

Then they looked at each other again.

"Somehow you've got to make the dog bark. Play with him, do whatever you need to for a few minutes. Then come back here."

He cleared his throat. "Are you hoping that she calls me?"

"Well, she is an intelligent girl."

"What if she doesn't?"

"We'll think of something else."

"But if . . . if she's . . ."

"She isn't, Herr Rohmueller. She's alive, she's got two people looking after her and now we're here to protect her."

"Is this about my daughter or the . . . man who did it?"

"Your daughter. We'll deal with him afterwards."

"Do you swear?"

"Swearing is silly, Herr Rohmueller. Just believe me. All that matters to me right now is that we get Nadine to safety. O.K.?"

He nodded. More tears, more nose-blowing. "But do it now, Herr Rohmueller," she said quietly.

Ben was talking to Henri in English about Sarajevo. He was in civvies rather than his security guard uniform. Louise hadn't seen him in his own clothes for ages. The same coat and the same jeans he'd worn in Osijek that first day. She placed a hand on his shoulder. It was good to feel him, to have him here.

But now it was time for him to go home.

He broke off and returned her gaze.

"I'm very grateful."

He nodded.

"I don't know," Henri said in English, shaking his head sceptically. "Sarajevo. End of the world. *Barbares, tous les yougoslaves.*"

Ben was not paying attention. "What's happening now?" he asked Louise.

"You're driving home, Ben."

The waiter brought an espresso. Ben added some sugar and stirred. "In a minute," he said, looking at her.

She ran a hand through his hair and gave him a warning smile. She knew this look. The protector look. She nodded at his coffee. "Well?"

"Still too hot."

"Drink up, Benno."

Ben smiled and picked up the cup.

She informed Henri of the plan and asked him to call Noureddine to keep him in the loop. While he was on the phone Rohmueller appeared with Cesare in the street below. Where the pedestrian zone started, barely ten metres from the house, Rohmueller kneeled, put both hands on the dog's collar and spoke to him. Cesare began to bark, Rohmueller nodded with a laugh and got up. The dog jumped around him as best he could given his age, barking all the while.

Dogs and their people.

"Noureddine," Henri said quietly.

A man of Algerian extraction walked into the square from the pedestrian zone, stopped a few metres away from Rohmueller and took out a map.

"The old woman," Henri said.

Louise nodded. Josepha Ettinger was standing at the window of the second-floor apartment.

A few minutes later Rohmueller concluded the little performance.

Josepha had moved away from the window after a few seconds. Henri had left the café and gone into the shop. Noureddine had sat at a table in a different café at the beginning of the pedestrian zone. Ben was still slurping his espresso.

"The long journey," he said with a smile as she looked at him reproachfully. "My back."

Then Rohmueller came to the table and the waiting began.

Henri called. He was on the second floor of the pink house. No suspect. No old ladies with a young woman. Just silence, semi-darkness and a faintly musty smell of clothes.

Noureddine hadn't noticed anyone either.

What if the man wasn't in Colmar?

But he *was* here, she thought. He *had* to be here.

"Yes," he said sceptically. "What's the scene with you?"

She glanced at Rohmueller. He'd put his mobile on the table and was staring at his hands. "Nothing yet."

"So, what do we do now?"

"Stay where you are."

Louise hung up.

The waiter came to the table and set down a large bottle of Perrier in front of Ben.

"For Christ's sake, Ben."

He shrugged. Another smile, more sorrowful this time. Why don't you want me here? it said. Why are you sending me home?

"O.K. But you're not to get involved."

"I wouldn't dream of it."

"Maybe you can actually help," she said, discreetly indicating Rohmueller.

He nodded.

At that moment a mobile rang. But it wasn't Rohmueller's, it was hers.

She pulled it from her trouser pocket.

Josepha Ettinger.

21

"Your idea?"

"Yes."

"Have you come with Nadine's father?"

"Yes." Louise looked at Claus Rohmueller, who was on his feet. "How is she?"

"She'll recover. But it's going to take a long time."

Rohmueller held out his hand for the mobile, but she shook her head and asked, "Could I speak to her?"

"No. She was so badly abused she can barely utter a word."

"She needs a doctor, Frau Ettinger."

Rohmueller moved towards her in an attempt to grab the mobile. Ben got up, took his arm and said a few gentle words to him.

"Everything's fine," Louise whispered.

"We've taken her for an X-ray," Josepha said, "and now we have someone here. How did you know where we were?"

"We did our research."

"We?"

"Me and a colleague I trust."

Josepha paused before replying. "So you know."

"Yes."

"Do you know who it is?"

"Not yet."

"Why did you come, then?"

Louise took a few steps towards the window and gave a brief summary of the situation. One of the suspects was in Colmar but they didn't know where, or what he looked like. One was a Kripo officer, possibly in the task force, but they didn't have any further clues. Were there any more? They needed descriptions from Nadine to identify the men and they had to take her to safety. Because here in Colmar she wasn't safe any longer.

"How do you imagine you're going to bring her to safety?" Josepha asked.

"If we know who we're looking for, then we've got a chance. Please help us, Frau Ettinger."

Josepha was silent. Louise looked at Rohmueller, then at Ben, both of whom returned her gaze, both ready to go, one of them distraught, the other tense. Calm down, she gestured, even though she wasn't in the mood to calm people down. They urgently needed information, they had to find the man who was waiting somewhere nearby; he might not wait much longer. Perhaps he was already on his way to the pink house.

"Frau Ettinger?"

Hearing the rustling of paper, Bonì reached for her notebook and pen.

"There were three of them," Josepha said. "One around sixty, fat, with a beard. Blue Wrangler jeans, black leather jacket from Mangoon. Quiet, said little more than 'I'm sorry', but said it over and over again. A grandfatherly type. Erectile problems. Very . . . *tender*." She spat that last word out. "The second one about forty, broad, American chin, film-star type. Charming smile, friendly eyes, blond, light-blue Boss shirt. He was the most brutal of the three, wanted to cause her pain, and when she screamed he hurt her even more. He . . . hit her, kicked her, threw her against the bed and the wall. And he . . . But that doesn't matter now." Josepha broke off. Now her voice sounded even colder and more distant than during their conversation in Grezhausen.

"What about the third?"

"The driver. Round moon face, rimless spectacles, conservative type, off-the-peg suit. A pervert and paedophile if you ask me. He wanted her to call him 'Papa'. 'Papa, make love to me.' They forced her to say it. And when she did it turned him on. He lost his self-control."

"He's dead, we found his body this morning."

"Divine justice, I should say. How did it happen?"

"One of the other two killed him."

"The beasts are slaughtering each other."

Louise fell silent. She turned to the window and looked at the narrow house opposite. One with a beard, a grandfatherly type, and a blond one who looked like a film star. One of them the policeman, the other the killer. One in Freiburg, the other here in Colmar.

"Which of the two is the policeman?"

"I'm afraid I can't tell you that. On the ground was a brass, oval badge with the word KRIMINALPOLIZEI and an engraved star. But she doesn't know who it belonged to."

"Did she see the number on it?"

"No."

"Could the badge have been there before—"

"No," Josepha interrupted her.

Louise nodded. A brief flicker of hope that passed as quickly as it had come.

"Where did they take her to from Freiburg?"

"A basement. Oberrimsingen, I suspect."

So many gaps remained and there was so little time. Noureddine was at a café table in the shade. Henri was waiting for instructions in the building. And somewhere was the man they were looking for.

A grandfather with a beard; a blond film star.

These descriptions ruled out Bermann, Ilic and Hoffmann, although she'd never seriously suspected any of them. Likewise Walter Scuma, who she didn't like. And Reinhard Graeve, of course, the Kripo boss.

Holzner, but he hadn't been involved anyway.

Was Andi Bruckner a film star? And was gay Hans Meirich in fact a grandfatherly type with a weakness for young girls? Jörg Seibold was older and had a beard. Thomas Breutle was blond and handsome.

If the Kripo officer wasn't on the task force, then others were in the frame too.

She checked her notes. Wranglers, black Mangoon leather jacket. Light-blue Boss shirt. Fashion and brands, a girl who knew her stuff. Maybe scents too. "Did she notice an aftershave?"

"Well, she didn't mention it. Should I ask her?"

"Yes. Ask her if one of the men smelled of 'Pasha' by Cartier."

The film star.

She called Henri and passed on the description. Blond, broad American chin, around forty. Charming smile, friendly eyes, maybe a light-blue Boss shirt. Extremely brutal, enjoys torture, impulsive. Watch out, Henri, he's killed two people.

Henri would stay in the building opposite; Noureddine would begin the search. His scepticism seemed to have vanished. They would request support from the Commissariat Central de Colmar as well as the Brigade de Recherche et d'Intervention and Task Force Command in Stuttgart. A killer in Colmar . . . They would get the support.

"And please notify Chervel," she said to finish.

Ben wanted to come with her, as did Rohmueller. Louise shook her head, no civilians, for God's sake. Drink your water, your espresso, she said to Ben. Don't get involved. Look after Rohmueller. She gave him a peck on the cheek.

"Do you really think you'll find him, Louise?"

She paused. Did he realise he'd asked her the same question in Osijek?

He smiled grimly; he had realised.

As back then, her answer was merely a shrug.

The street, cafés and shops were full of people. Water-soaked children played by the fountain in the middle of the square while mothers stood around. A nightmare, she thought, if you were trying to apprehend a killer. But she didn't want to arrest him, she wanted to flush him out, scare him off so that they could get Nadine away. They would catch him later.

First the police officer, then the killer.

Everything was moving, faces everywhere, men everywhere. Children laughing and shouting, sunlight reflecting brightly off windows. Noureddine moving watchfully amongst café tables.

Bonì began on the opposite side of the square, went into a bakery, eyed a dozen faces, then hurried out. Police sirens wailed in the distance, coming closer, while two gendarmes approached from the pedestrian zone. Noureddine beckoned them over. Louise opened a door and made her way pushing and shoving along the narrow aisles of a chemist's. She saw two blond men, but neither was handsome or had a striking chin.

A police car had stopped in the square, blue lights flashing. Gendarmes got out and children stared open-mouthed. Beyond the fountain stood the Ettingers' house in the sunlight, and behind one of the curtains the outline of a slim body, maybe Josepha.

Louise carried on.

Another building, the door closed. She pressed the handle and entered a silent stairwell. Grezhausen came to mind, the Ettingers' hallway with the staircase up to the first floor, where she could never have gone; she was too scared. This time she forced herself up the stairs, three storeys. Luckily the corridors were wide with no blind spots. He wasn't here either, of course he wasn't – how could he have kept watch on the pink house from here?

Outside there were even more police officers now. Noureddine had disappeared, Ben was standing at the open window of the café, one hand on the upper frame. She suppressed the impulse to wave and turned away.

Was the man here at all?

Bonì thought she would be here if she were him. If she'd found documents with the Colmar address in the Ettingers' house, she would be here. She would try to kill Nadine. She would have killed Eddie and Haberle because they could have identified her, now she would kill Nadine too.

And she would do it *right now*.

Louise hurried towards an antiques shop. Noureddine appeared and kept on running. The square and the pedestrian zone were teeming with gendarmes. The street had been blocked off. A killer in Colmar . . .

Now, she thought, now he *had* to act, or it would be too late. He had to make a decision now.

Flee, or try to kill Nadine.

As she walked she dialled Henri's number. No answer. She kept on the line for an eternity, but it just rang and rang. Disconcerted, Louise turned to look at the Ettingers' house. She dialled again, but again it just kept ringing.

She'd stopped. The sounds around her fell silent, the movements all blurred into one. The windows on the second floor. The slim body was gone.

Had he been waiting inside the house? In one of the other apartments?

She became aware of shouting. Noureddine, a few metres away. What? he called out. What is it? Pointing at the pink house, she broke free from her paralysis and set off at a run. "Henri!" she cried to Noureddine, who followed her, pistol in hand. From the corner of her eye she saw Ben come storming out of the café, behind him Rohmueller and the collie, and now she reached the entrance of the clothes shop on the ground floor, squeezed her way past customers to the emergency exit and opened a heavy metal door.

Beyond it a dim hallway with stairs leading up into the darkness. Fear shot into her limbs like a piercing pain. Boni hesitated for a moment, found a light switch and was just putting her foot onto the first step when dogs started barking furiously. Then she heard a shot, a monstrous noise that reverberated powerfully like an explosion. Yanking the gun from her handbag, Louise rushed upstairs, Noureddine right behind her. Another shot, louder than the first, and the unrelenting hysterical barking of the two dogs.

Seconds later she was on the first floor, glimpsed Ben at the foot of the stairs, shouted, "No, Ben! No!" and kept running. Footsteps and voices echoed around the stairwell, and suddenly two high-pitched commands, like those she'd heard in Grezhausen: Maria Ettinger giving orders to the dogs. On the second-floor landing a body, bent double like a foetus: Henri, his skull bludgeoned, a pool of blood around his head, countless rivulets trickling across the floor. In falling he'd lost his glasses which lay undamaged before him. His arm was moving, his hand feeling for them, to no avail.

"Help will be here any minute," Louise whispered, forcing herself on towards an open door. "Josepha!" she shouted, over and over again as she hurtled into the apartment, a narrow hallway smelling of lavender, garlic and coffee. She turned right, Noureddine left, the barking started up again, again the high-pitched shouts, but the dogs didn't obey; they kept barking, now very close. At the end of the narrow hallway a door, where Bonì stopped abruptly. Two fist-sized holes in the wood at chest height, splinters of wood on the floor and a few drops of blood.

"Josepha?"

"Careful, the dogs," Josepha said calmly.

"Is anyone hurt?"

"No."

The high-pitched command again, and this time the dogs did obey.

"Do you know where he is?"

"No."

Noureddine's voice from one of the other rooms: everything fine, he's not here, he must have got out, maybe he ran upstairs. Then Noureddine was standing before her, a lean, pockmarked man with a serious expression. He put a hand on her forearm. "*Tout bien?*"

Bonì nodded.

He left the apartment. She heard his soft voice as he spoke to Ben, then Ben's voice in English: He's going to make it, everything O.K. in there?

"*Oui*," Noureddine answered.

Louise went to the damaged door. "I'm coming in now."

"Yes," Josepha said.

A small bedroom, by the bed two dogs and three elderly ladies. Josepha was standing, a huge revolver in her hand; her sister was kneeling between the dogs, holding their collars; and the third woman, in a nun's habit, was sitting on the bed. One hand wiped tears from her cheeks, the other stroked a body that was hidden beneath the duvet. In spite of the duvet Louise could see the trembling and hear a muffled whimpering.

She was overcome by sheer relief.

Sheer exhaustion.

She sank into a chair and began to cry.

"Everything's alright now, my child," Josepha said, maybe to her, maybe to Nadine. What did it matter? They had found Nadine.

22

Ten, fifteen minutes had passed. Louise was still sitting on the chair, watching the people around her as if through a veil, rapid movements, soft footsteps, hushed women's voices. The door was closed again. She'd been vaguely aware that Josepha had stopped anyone else from entering the room: Ben, the French policeman, even Rohmueller. Give her a few more minutes, don't you understand, she *can't* yet, and again she didn't know who Josepha was referring to. Maria Ettinger handed her a glass of water and Louise held it without taking a sip. Yes, she thought, everything is fine now, and for ten or fifteen minutes she allowed herself the luxury of believing this.

"Gérardmer," Ben said slowly.

"Write it down."

"I'll remember it. And when?"

"As soon as she's recovered. Take her there, then drive back to Freiburg. You'll make it by nine."

Ben nodded.

She'd just called Gérardmer. At first her uncle Pierre asked, Which Louise? Gradually in Gérardmer she was being forgotten. But Pierre would get the guest room ready.

What about you, Louise? Will you come too?

Maybe later. Maybe in the next few days. Maybe.

She sat close to Ben at a large oak table in the kitchen. On the table were three white cups with the dregs of coffee, a glass of milk, three plates with half-eaten slices of apple cake and a bowl of broth. Three elderly women and a young one having afternoon coffee, then the collie barked.

Josepha at the window, describing the dog and the man.

There was a ghostly silence inside the building. Henri had been taken to hospital; Noureddine and the gendarmes were searching for the man who'd made it as far as the bedroom door, only to be driven back by Josepha. A British revolver from the Second World War. Family heirloom, she said. Extraordinary that it still worked . . .

Bonì had informed Bermann a few minutes earlier. Who is it, Louise? he asked. She didn't know. Not yet. Maybe when she'd had a chance to talk to Nadine.

A tender grandfather with a beard.

Markus, Bert, Micha, Bermann muttered, his angry mantra. She'd never seen him so shocked, so grimly determined. Bertold Uhl from Forensics, didn't he have a beard? Michael Ahlert from Meirich's department, wasn't he the grandfatherly type? And when the hell was Hoffmann going to have that list of first names ready?

For Christ's sake, who *is* it, Louise?

He's going to disappear, she said. Now he knows we'll get him. It'll be the one who disappears.

Nobody's disappeared, Bermann said.

It won't be long. When he knows we've found Nadine he'll disappear.

How did Nadine realise he was a policeman?

Louise told him about the Kripo badge. Another brief flicker of hope, this time for Bermann. All Kripo badges were identical on the front; only the backs differed, showing the name of the *Land* and the individual number. So he could just as easily be with Stuttgart or Cologne Kripo, even Berlin. A rapist on holiday.

But this didn't fit. He knew too much.

Markus, Bert, Micha. *Shit*, Bermann muttered.

Louise took Ben's left hand and gently stroked it. She didn't know if getting him involved was right or wrong. Rohmueller had begged her and she'd agreed, irrespective of Ben's own feelings. Both of the perpetrators – the police officer and the man in Colmar – now had better things to do than look for Nadine again. Besides, there was no longer any point in shutting her up.

But she had to anticipate every eventuality.

"Don't tell anyone about this."

"About Gérardmer?" Ben said.

"Yes."

"Not even the French?"

"They can know. I don't think our man's got such good contacts in France that he can simply make a call."

"It's far too late anyway. Why would they still be interested in Nadine?"

She nodded, reached for one of the plates with half a slice of apple cake with flan topping, began eating and was glad to see the grin on Ben's face.

She'd called Hugo Chervel too. He was up to date and on his way. Yes, he'd give her a few officers to escort them to Gérardmer. Yes, the manhunt was up and running. Yes, checks at the border were in place.

He'd sounded brusque and monosyllabic.

Mon Dieu, it's always the same with you, isn't it? Bringing your killers over here. That was just a joke, Louise, forgive me. I've been drinking. It's my birthday. I'm fifty. And now I've got a killer giving me the runaround.

"Come with us to Gérardmer, Louise," Ben said.

"No." She stared at him, the pale lines in the darker skin around his tired, anxious-looking eyes; she had to get him out of this habit of feeling anxious. But right now he looked calm and focused, totally composed. That's how he was when they met, calm, focused and composed. He'd been like this in Croatia and Bosnia, but not since.

"Come with us," he said again.

She ran a hand through his short hair. "See you at midnight."

He shrugged. "Remember the ćevapčići."

"I haven't forgotten."

Ben smiled, nestled his head beneath her chin, and that's how they stayed until footsteps rang out in the hall and Josepha came to take her to Nadine.

One swollen eye, the other half open. Brown and green ointments covered the cuts on her cheeks and forehead, and her broken nose was taped with some sort of support bandage. On her neck were blue strangulation marks, and the rest was beneath the duvet. Nadine sat hunched on the bed leaning against the wall, pillows behind her neck and back, the collie on her left, Josepha to her right. Her distraught eyes darted back and forth between Louise and her father, who was on a chair by the window. He sat there stiffly, battling the tears, an alien element in the room, as was Louise, perched on a chair in the middle, feeling as if she were in the dock.

The silence dragged on.

"They'll leave you alone now," Bonì said finally.

Nadine and Josepha looked at her, mistrust and a single accusation writ large across their faces. It should never have happened, where were you when it *did* happen, how is it possible that such a thing *could* happen? In pretty, cosy, sweet old Freiburg? Why don't you ensure that this sort of thing *can't* happen? Why do you work with men who do this sort of thing?

She understood the accusation. Who wouldn't?

"The police officer," she said. "We still don't know who it is. Help me identify him."

"You've got a very precise description," Josepha answered in Nadine's place. "And you're not going to expect her to describe his . . . *body*."

"Of course not—"

"There wasn't much light," Nadine whispered faintly and with great effort. "At first it was bright, but then there wasn't much light."

192

"You can't do this," Rohmueller said to Louise, his voice cracking. "She can't cope with this." His eyes said, "*I* can't cope."

Louise turned back to Nadine.

They'll leave you alone now . . .

Not for a long time, she thought. They'll come back again and again in Nadine's dreams, her thoughts, her feelings. She wondered if Nadine would endure this life. If she would endure the process. If more medicines would be added to those in the mirrored cabinet in her apartment.

She hoped that somewhere a spark of life was glowing. That the three men hadn't destroyed her will to live too.

"It wasn't dark," Nadine said. "But it wasn't light either."

Louise nodded. "His voice. What did his voice sound like?"

"Nice," Nadine said, starting to cry. "Really, really nice."

23

Soon afterwards Bonì was on her way again, but making slow progress in the rush-hour traffic on the long arterial road out of Colmar. In her rear-view mirror the odd glimpse of the Vosges, from a bridge a view of the Kaiserstuhl to the east. How lovely they were, she thought – Colmar, Alsace, Freiburg and the Breisgau – and what people they were home to. Individuals like Haberle and the two other men who snatched a girl in Freiburg at five o'clock in the morning. In her mind she kept seeing Nadine's terrified, ill-treated face, Rohmueller's despair, and she heard the unspoken accusations. That's just how it was, she thought, that's how this society was too: lovely, friendly and peaceful on the outside, but rotten on the inside, a quagmire of desire, lust for power and lack of restraint, which found endorsement everywhere, sometimes in the most horrific way.

Hiding behind a nice voice.

The voice. Now she had a hunch as to who the policeman was.

No. She knew.

Then Breisach Minster, looming darkly a few kilometres ahead of her on the other side of the Rhine. One day she'd love to show Ben this beautiful country between the Black Forest and the Vosges. That was how it should be, her life away from work, looking at beautiful things with a man like him without always seeing the other, ugly side. It occurred to her that time and again Ben had spoken of war, politics and destruction whenever he'd shown her a city or landscape in Croatia. Maybe this was something they had in common, always seeing the ugliness in the beautiful.

And perhaps he'd come before her to the realisation that they were part of this ugliness, because they were part of this society.

Twenty minutes later Hoffmann called.

"Where are you?"

"Almost in Freiburg."

"Haberle had an apartment in Oberrimsingen."

Hoffmann had stumbled upon it by chance when ringing around. A property tax debit from an account, an entry in the land register, an apartment inherited from his father who'd died four years earlier. Louise thought of her conversation with Brigitte Haberle, who said her husband had sold it.

A double life over the course of several years.

"Are you sure?"

"Yes, I am."

I suspect Oberrimsingen, Josepha had said.

Oberrimsingen to Grezhausen was a couple of kilometres. A narrow road with maize fields on either side, which crossed the main road, if she remembered rightly. Nadine must have dragged herself across the fields and the main road. Another field of maize, then a few houses, the Möhlin, two hundred metres further on the Ettingers' fallow field with its barn. On Sunday morning or early afternoon, a naked girl wrapped in a red blanket, barely able to stand up. Nobody had seen her. Perhaps she'd used the tall maize to hide. Perhaps because the three men were after her.

"Has someone already gone there?"

"No. I'll chase down the caretaker if you like."

"Send me Illi too, and get me a search warrant from Andrele."

"Consider it done. Are you going to call again? I've got more."

She turned off at St Georgen, drove across the main road and continued on to the southern motorway slip road.

A few minutes' respite for her colleagues.

*

"Rolf was here," Hoffmann said a few minutes later. "My God, you found them."

"Yes."

"Officially?"

"Officially. We found them, she's alive, she gave a description of the men and now she's on the way to a secret destination with her father. We have to get her out of the line of fire, Alfons. Graeve and the public prosecutor should hold a press conference as—"

"They *should*?"

"Correct."

She heard Hoffmann giggle excitedly.

"O.K., they *should*."

"And as quickly as possible."

"That's going to be tight."

"Yes."

"You don't happen to know who it is, do you?"

"There are several possibilities."

Hoffmann was quiet for a moment. She knew what he was thinking: you couldn't wring things out of her.

"Did Nadine describe him?"

"She did. Is there anything new at your end?"

Hoffmann chuntered sulkily. It sounded like a "Yes".

The I.T. people had hacked into Haberle's laptop. There was nothing objectionable on it, no pornographic videos or anything like that, just tax files, addresses, appointments, holiday photographs, spreadsheets of overheads, lists of expenditure, etc. And hundreds of photos of his daughter. Not a single one showing her as a baby or a small child; in all of them she was at least eight or nine. "As if he was in love with her or something," Hoffmann said.

Louise nodded. She'd been expecting child pornography, but perhaps that wasn't Haberle's style. A control-freak, who'd also controlled his sick urges by directing them towards a single object.

Then, when it came to Nadine, he lost control. Let himself go. Was that because other like-minded men had been there?

Hoffmann was still chuntering. "Markus, Bert, Micha." There were several men with those names amongst Haberle's addresses. If the surnames were right, then none of them were Kripo officers.

"Forget them," Louise said.

"No Markus, Bert or Micha?"

"I think it's unlikely."

"Unlikely, Louise?"

"Yes. Did Illi go to Haberle's surgery?"

A disappointed chunter. Yes, he did. And he found a diary there. On Saturday it said: "Micha". They'd telephoned all the Michas in Haberle's address list. On Saturday evening a Michael Engele had held his stag do. He said that Haberle had been there, along with twenty-five other friends – all men, obviously. "Sandy and Andi Bruckner are with him now. With Michael Engele, I mean."

"The cards night."

"Yes."

"We need a list of all the guests. Then we'll have them. Both of them."

She left the motorway at the Bad Krozingen exit. This time she didn't turn left to Grezhausen, but right towards Oberrimsingen. Another view of the Tuniberg, the Kaiserstuhl, and the Vosges far off to the west. She wondered what the man who almost succeeded in killing Nadine in Colmar was looking at now. Where he was. What his plan was.

The French hadn't called. Which meant they hadn't got him.

He'd killed Eddie because the boy may have seen or known too much. He'd killed Haberle because the doctor had clearly become a risk. He'd tried to kill Nadine to stop her from talking. Was he now planning to kill the policeman before he was arrested? Or Michael Engele, who'd probably invited him to his stag party?

"Louise?"

"Sorry."

Hoffmann cleared his throat. "Who is it?"

She sighed. What if she told him, and then the door opened and he was standing there? How would you react, Alfons?

"Oh God," Hoffmann said.

"You see? Have you got hold of Illi?"

"He's not answering. Should I send someone else?"

"No."

She hung up.

A stag do.

Mick had a stag do. Rolf Bermann too, if she remembered rightly. Other friends and colleagues. If she asked, the most she ever got by way of an answer was a grin. Allegedly wild and yet just ridiculous memories that lasted all one's life – men in the company of men. Alcohol, inappropriate jokes, plenty of half-naked women. Dancers, strippers, prostitutes. She'd heard of porn nights, group masturbation and even rape. Many stag dos were now held in eastern Europe – Bratislava, Prague, Budapest, where the beer and the women were cheaper.

The crown of all creation, boozing and bellowing amongst others of their ilk, penis in hand.

There were some traditions she would never understand.

Everything was fine over in Alsace. They'd set off a few minutes earlier, Ben and Rohmueller in one car, the three ladies and Nadine in the second, and the two French officers in the third – a small convoy on its way to the mountains. Once again she wondered if it had been wrong to get Ben involved, possibly putting his life in danger. Rohmueller had wanted him to stay in Colmar and come to Gérardmer later, a kind of personal bodyguard, and Ben finally felt needed again. But she couldn't use that as an excuse; she'd got him involved.

"Be careful, Ben."

"You too."

"I still need you."

"Me too."

"Tell me, did you have a stag do before you got married?"

Ben laughed gently. "No."

There were other men, too, thank goodness, she thought.

There was Ben Liebermann, who was on his way to her family, who would meet her uncles and aunts in Gérardmer. It felt weird that someone was there again. Comforting, in a way.

If only she weren't hounded by the worry that behind his face was ugliness too, and that it would reveal itself to her somehow, at a time she was least expecting it.

24

A plain white house at the edge of the village, two floors, standing at an angle to the street, the maize fields just a few metres beyond. Waiting in the drive was an old man in a grey apron, his hands in the pocket with just his thumbs visible. "It's high time I got back to work," he said by way of a greeting, squinting in the sunlight.

"You're telling me," Louise said.

Along the front of the house was a grille set in the tarmac, beneath which she could see narrow windows.

A basement in Oberrimsingen.

They climbed the steps to the front door. Four name plates, and on the ground floor: EDGAR HABERLE.

"I don't know why he never changed the plate," the caretaker said. "I don't care either." He pointed at her Peugeot. "Can't you afford proper cars anymore?"

She stared at his hand, which was missing all its digits except the thumb.

"The German police ought to drive German cars."

"Yes," Louise said. "Do you live here?"

"Why should I live here?" He took a key out of the pocket of his apron and unlocked the door.

In the hallway it smelled of disinfectant.

He pointed to a door. "Don't touch anything in there."

"I wouldn't dream of it."

"How do I know what the police dream of?"

"What happened to your hand?"

He shrugged. "The war for Alsace-Lorraine."

"The one sixty years ago?"

"I wasn't around for the others."

"Are you telling me you fought in the Second World War?"

"Of course I did. I threw stones. The French wanted to chop my hands off. They almost succeeded." From his pocket he took another key with a name on the fob and handed it to her.

"As she was nearing the door she checked herself. They'd found no I.D., no money and no keys on Haberle's body. The killer had taken everything. Including a key to this apartment?

Had he come here from Colmar?

She half closed her eyes and tried to concentrate, but her fear wouldn't allow it. The same fear she'd felt in Grezhausen, and in Colmar. The fear of meeting this man.

No sound came from inside the apartment.

"Well, what are you wait—"

Bonì swiftly put a finger to her lips. She took out her gun and put the key in the lock, but it only went in halfway. She tried a second time, without success. Still nothing to be heard on the other side of the door.

Louise carefully ran the side of her hand across the surface of the door. If he were here he couldn't help but be aware of her presence. The door was made of thin wood.

He's not here, Bonì.

Her fear gradually subsided.

"Haberle changed the lock," she said.

"Unlucky for the police. Or are you going to shoot it open?"

"Yes," Bonì said, aiming her gun at the lock.

"Crazy woman."

"No, a half-French woman."

"Oh well, that explains everything. Your German's not bad, though."

She ought to feel sympathy for him because of his hand, she thought, but she didn't want to feel sympathy. "A perfectly normal, unpleasant day in Oberrimsingen," she said, "and then you meet a madwoman with a French car and a pistol. Life isn't what it used to be."

The caretaker shrugged. "At least the pistol's German."

She turned around. He was staring at her, and she thought he looked more friendly than before. Maybe he'd noticed her fear. "Go back to work."

"What, now that it's getting interesting?"

She put her pistol away. "It's not that interesting."

"How do I know what you're going to get up to when I've gone?"

"I'm going to kick the door in."

He nodded. "I wouldn't want to miss that."

"I've got to get inside, Herr . . ."

"Derfflinger."

"Bonì," she said, offering him her left hand. He took it.

"Marry a Frenchman, did you?"

"A German, and that was bad enough."

"So why do you have to get in there, Madame Bonì?"

She told him. Because the man who used to own the apartment had been murdered. Because on Sunday he and two other men had raped a girl in a basement room of this house.

Derfflinger frowned. "Dietmar Haberle?"

She nodded.

"Well, then, you really do have to get in there."

"How?"

He raised his eyebrows. "Herr Derfflinger and Frau Bonì are going to use a little force."

"That's my preferred method anyway."

Derfflinger laughed croakily.

"But it's illegal, Herr Derfflinger."

"Then you'd better look away."

She turned away and heard Derfflinger throw himself at the door, which crashed open on the second attempt.

A dark, narrow hallway lay ahead. Two things immediately struck her. First, the pungent smell of disinfectant and other detergents. And second, Emily – wherever you went and looked. On the walls in the hallway, in frames on the bathroom shelves, poster-size pictures in the sitting room and bedroom. Emily everywhere: portraits, whole body shots, Emily playing, drawing, doing ballet, swimming, sleeping, in the bath, restrained laughter, restrained tears, restrained anger, thoughtful, sometimes dressed, sometimes naked, sometimes alone, sometimes with her father, never with her mother or anyone else, and never as a baby or toddler but, as Hoffmann had already noted, always eight, nine or ten years of age.

As if he was in love with her or something, Hoffmann had said. The photographs conveyed something else, too: you're mine, you're mine, you're mine for ever.

"To think that someone like him lived in this house," Derfflinger said.

They were in the sitting room, which like everywhere else in the apartment gleamed with cleanliness and order. No fluff, no specks of dust, no smears on the windows, not a single object which wasn't perfectly centred or aligned or exactly where it was supposed to be.

"Don't touch anything, Herr Derfflinger."

"I wouldn't dream of it."

She went into the hallway and closed the front door. The latch didn't click into place, but the door stayed in its frame.

"Is that the girl?" Derfflinger said when she came back to the sitting room.

"No, that's his daughter."

"He had a daughter? I never saw a child here."

In her mind Louise saw Haberle on his knees, cleaning, mopping, drying. Maybe this was how he'd been able to control his feelings of guilt. Maybe the order within this apartment had been a sort of perfection where he'd felt at home. Everything how he wanted it, everything in hand, everything under control. Nobody messing anything up.

The very opposite of life outside. The façade that had kept everything together, the inside and the outside.

Then, all of a sudden, there was another smell in the air, and with it the fear came rushing back.

"Can you smell that?"

"What?"

"'Pasha' by Cartier."

25

So he had been here at some point in the past few hours, after killing Haberle and before the break-in at the Ettingers' house in Grezhausen. She sent Derfflinger back to his office, put on a pair of disposable gloves and went through the apartment again. He must have left some trace behind in this perfect order.

And Bonì found it.

A kitchen chair slightly out of place, blades of grass and a few specks of mud on the floor. The loo seat up, drops of water in the sink. On a windowpane in the sitting room she saw a faint mark that could have come from a sweaty hand.

She was just about to look for the basement key when she heard footsteps on the stairs outside. They stopped by the door to the apartment.

Louise grabbed the pistol from her handbag and ran into the hallway.

Someone rang the bell.

A man's voice, loud and clear: "Freiburg Kripo, open the door!"

She waited, holding the gun with both hands.

The jangling of keys, then the door was pushed slowly open. Walter Scuma from Surveillance stood facing her, holding a pistol.

"Bonì, for God's sake!" he said in shock.

They put their weapons away.

"So this is where you are," Scuma said. "People back at H.Q. are wondering where you've got to." He nervously ran a hand over his partially bald head and adjusted his rimless spectacles. Beads of sweat had collected on his moustache. "Christ, that could have gone horribly wrong!"

"Why don't you just come in."

Scuma closed the door behind him, sighed in relief and stroked his head again. "I'm beginning to understand my colleagues."

"What do they say?"

"That anyone who works with you needs strong nerves and a good heart."

She forced a smile. "Only the slow ones."

"I thought I was fast." His gaze fell on the photographs of Emily. Then he looked at Louise, but said nothing.

No mistakes, now, Bonì, she thought. Don't fix on one man only to discover it's someone else in the end.

"Where did you get the key?" he said. "Assuming you didn't smash another window. My God, have you noticed how *clean* it is here?"

She told him about Hoffmann's phone call, Derfflinger, the changed lock.

"Poor coordination," Scuma said, wiping the sweat from his moustache with finger and thumb. "I've been thinking this all afternoon. Your Bermann doesn't talk to anybody, your Alfons Hoffmann doesn't leave his office, your Thomas Ilic is always looking glum, as if he had bowel cancer. Don't you like each other anymore in D11?"

Her eyes were still on Scuma's walrus moustache. A grandfather with a beard. Had Scuma ever worn a beard? Louise tried to recall the times they'd met in the past, at a Christmas party, in the canteen, in the lift. She couldn't remember.

She shrugged. "We can't take the heat."

Scuma just stared at her.

"Bad joke, I'm sorry. You know what our colleagues say."

"What do they say?"

"That anyone who works with me needs a thick skin."

Scuma smiled. The grey, expressionless face acquired a few lines, looking friendly all of a sudden. With a bit of imagination you could call that grandfatherly. But Scuma had a whiny voice.

Although what was "nice", she thought, was a matter of personal preference.

Scuma went into the bathroom, bedroom and came back. He was wearing gloves now too. When he looked at her there was a certain distance in his eyes again, as if he held her responsible for what he was seeing here. "His refuge," he said. "His place to dream."

She nodded. "How did you get hold of the key, by the way?"

"The key, shit!" Scuma went into the hall and opened the door. He'd left the key in the lock. "The shock," he said when he was back.

He'd been to Haberle's apartment with Meirich from D23. That's where they found the key. Brigitte Haberle didn't recognise it, so they took it with them. Then Hoffmann found out about the apartment in Oberrimsingen and he'd set off because there was no-one around to give him another task, precisely because of the lack of communication or coordination. He'd dropped Meirich off at the doctor's and driven on to Oberrimsingen.

"To do what?"

"To do something."

"It's half past six. You could have knocked off."

"When I'm on a task force I never knock off."

"A task force you couldn't find."

"I thought I'd look for it here."

She smiled. "How's Meirich?"

"Not good. He's lost a filling and one of his teeth is wobbly. Looks like death warmed up. Shall we take a snoop around?"

"No." She told him about the basement room. If everything was as she suspected, they'd taken Nadine there, to the basement in this house.

There was no third key on the ring that Scuma had. They found another in a kitchen drawer, attached to a resin locket in the shape of a heart, inside which was a photograph of Emily. In love or something like that, she thought, shaking her head; obsessed was a better way of putting it. Dietmar Haberle had been obsessed by his daughter, and even her limited experience with such people told her it was a good thing he was no longer alive. For in a few years perhaps, when the urge and the obsession had become overwhelming, he might have brought Emily here.

Would have locked her in the basement and lived with her here.

Scuma went ahead. When they got to the basement door he took out his pistol; Louise followed suit. They went down a staircase and found themselves in a vault with several doors off it. Spiders' webs spanned the corners of the walls to the ceiling and it smelled of damp concrete. Unlike in Haberle's apartment, down here it was dirty, dusty and mouldy. Louise tried the key with the heart on various doors, and had success on her fourth attempt, at the far end of the vault. She opened the door and beyond it was another, which had clearly been built subsequently. Scuma handed her the ring with two keys, one of which fitted. The door opened inwards and Louise gave it a push. Behind it lay a small, windowless room – a single bed with bedspread, a wardrobe and dressing table. Here too was the acrid stench of disinfectant and other detergents. Louise registered this only fleetingly as her mind suddenly turned to Scuma. He would only need to give her a shove, she thought, and she'd be a prisoner here like Nadine, if she were wrong and *he* was the grandfather, even though he had a whiny voice, even though she couldn't remember him ever having had a beard . . .

Bonì turned and looked at him intently.

"You were right," he said, making to step past her into the room.

She touched him on the shoulder. "Wait until Forensics have been."

Louise found a light switch beside the door. A bulb on the ceiling bathed the room in bright light. The two of them peered in. Despite the furniture the room looked empty. It took Louise a moment to realise why: there wasn't a single object on the dressing table, bedside table or floor. And certainly no clue as to what had happened here on Sunday morning.

Three men and a girl.

She bet the wardrobe was empty too. A room waiting for someone.

And yet Louise was sure that Haberle and the two other men had brought Nadine here at six o'clock on Sunday morning. At some point, by early afternoon, she'd managed to escape. Haberle might have gone looking for her with the other two, but then he must have returned to remove all traces of evidence. To turn the place where they had abused Nadine back into a room that was waiting for someone.

Emily's room.

"Christ, it's creepy," Scuma said.

They were back in the apartment, sitting at the kitchen table and looking at Emily's smiling face on the wall opposite.

"When you think what the girl had to go through. What Nadine had to go through." With his index finger Scuma pushed his glasses up the bridge of his nose, the corners of his mouth were turned down and his eyes wide open. A bizarre sight. For a brief moment his face was contorted into an ugly mask.

She stared at him. Not a grandfather, not a nice voice. Even if that wasn't much to base decisions on – what didn't tally didn't tally.

Time to get the team behind her, she thought. "We found her."

"Nadine?"

She nodded and told him about Colmar. They'd found her, she was safe, on her way to a secret destination.

"*Who* found her?"

Bonì shrugged. "We did."

"We. You." Scuma shook his head. There was irritation in his voice. "What's really going on here, Bonì?"

"What do you mean?"

"A team inside the team?"

"One of them is a police officer, Scuma. A colleague. Nadine saw a Kripo badge."

Scuma said nothing for a while, just stared at her with those clear, distant eyes that seemed to lump her with the responsibility for everything that had happened and would happen. "Did she see the number?"

"No."

"But you've got your suspicions?"

"Yes."

"Who?"

She shook her head. "Too early."

"Have you got clues? Proof?"

"Just an inkling."

"Careful, Bonì, this isn't a game." Scuma ran a hand over his head. "Was I on your list?"

"To begin with, yes."

He shook his head in disbelief. "You thought *I* could do something like that."

"I don't know you."

"You've got a really pitiful insight into other people."

"Maybe."

"Why am I now off the list?"

"No beard and you're not a grandfatherly type. And your voice isn't right. Nadine said he's got a nice, soft, deep voice. Yours is . . . well." She gave him an apologetic smile.

Louise waited. She suspected he'd come to the same conclusion as her.

He shook his head slowly. "Two years ago Lederle, then Almenbroich, now . . ."

"What?"

His face became animated. The corners of his mouth and eyes arched downwards, signalling hatred. "You're clearing us out, are you? Getting—"

"Stop talking rubbish, Scuma."

"Getting long-standing colleagues into trouble because with their plain old legal methods they've made it further than you, with your hysterical behaviour."

"Are you mad?"

"What are you after? Section head, then A13 perhaps? Or is it just because you hate men?"

"You're such an arsehole."

"Yes," Scuma said. "And the booze has screwed your brain."

They stared at each other.

"I want two things from you," Louise said finally.

Scuma raised a hand defensively as he got up. "Let me out of here."

"First, you're not going to call him."

He laughed scornfully. "Are you giving me orders?"

"I am."

"It's about time someone put you in your place, Bonì."

"Second, and this is a plea, stay here in Haberle's apartment for a few hours. I don't think the third man's going to come here, but anything's possible."

Scuma sat down. "Not anything, Bonì."

"No? You must know better than me, then."

"None of us would do something like that."

"*You* wouldn't."

Scuma didn't respond.

Louise stood up. A final word to Scuma, the idealist or ostrich. She thought he might prefer it if someone like her told him. Someone he didn't respect. "Police officers lie, deceive, manipulate, assault, drink, commit adultery, rape, abuse children, steal, embezzle and kill. Not you, Scuma, but others. Colleagues of ours. Police officers are no different from anyone else. Do I really have to spell that out?"

He looked at her silently. The hatred had disappeared and now he appeared simply exhausted. "Bonì, even if he . . ." Scuma took off his glasses and placed them on the table. She wondered what he could see without them on. If he could see anything at all. "There are other options apart from putting him in the dock. Putting *us* in the dock.

211

Us, Kripo, Louise, which you've been working for all these years. Which is all you've got, which didn't leave *you* in the lurch. Kripo took you back under its wing when you fucked up, and not just once. Is this how you show your gratitude?"

Louise snorted. "What sort of options are you talking about. Early retirement?"

"That sort of thing. Or a transfer. Even straight dismissal, if you like. But not a public procedure. That would destroy people's confidence in us."

Louise didn't reply. Sometimes there was nothing to say. When things got so curiously mixed up, silence was all that was left. She wondered why so many people found it difficult to be consistent when events took an unpleasant turn. People like Scuma, but not just him, Louise too, of course. When events took an unpleasant turn people sought refuge in comfort.

Allowed things to get mixed up.

Scuma must have realised that she wouldn't entertain his suggestion. He put his glasses back on and pushed them up with his finger. "You're going to see this madness through to the end, then?"

"Yes."

"Just like that? Without any proof?"

"With proof," she said, and left.

26

On the A5 towards Freiburg she called Ilic. The several hours he'd had must have been enough time. The personnel files weren't that fat, especially if you knew what you were looking for.

It took six rings for him to pick up.

"Alfons says he can't get hold of you."

"I'm not answering the phone."

She paused before continuing. She was not the only one to have been seized by paranoia. "Have you finished?"

"Only just. I had to start again from the beginning, you see." The information from Colmar had come in late, Bermann had rung – grandfatherly type, beard. Ilic hadn't only checked the files of the task force members, but those of all the older Kripo officers too, and he'd been through them twice.

"And?"

"Three possibilities. Two are on the task force. Jörg Seibold . . . Actually, I'd rather not do this over the phone, Louise."

"I'll be there in ten."

"Come to Admin, I'll wait."

Louise thought of Walter Scuma. She wondered if he would let the things that had been set in motion roll on without intervening. Or would he make some telephone calls to protect Freiburg Kripo from Louise Bonì? Call Anselm Löbinger, the relevant section head? Spin some intrigues to prevent the madness?

Keep calm, Bonì.

"Scuma knows," she said.

"Rolf, Alfons, Scuma. Anyone else?"

"No. And don't speak to anybody about it. Where's Rolf?"

"With Michael Engele."

The bachelor with the names of three rapists on his guest list. An abuser of children, a criminal policeman and a killer. What an illustrious guest list, she thought.

"How about Löbinger?"

Ilic didn't reply. Anselm Löbinger, head of section 23.

"Now you know," she said.

"No. Yes. Him or . . . the other one. I don't think Seibold."

"Where is Löbinger?"

"No idea. Should I call him?"

"No, that can wait."

"And are you . . . sure?"

"Pretty sure."

The only officer who ticked all the boxes: grandfatherly type, beard, nice, soft voice. He'd volunteered for the task force rather than having been assigned to it.

And she'd accepted. Taken him on the team.

Ben thought Gérardmer was rather lovely. The mountains, the lake, the uncles and aunts. Slightly quirky and emotional with a propensity for hysteria, but he'd been prepared for that. After all, he'd known one member of the family for a while now.

"What's that supposed to mean?"

He laughed.

They'd arrived a quarter of an hour ago. Nadine, the Ettingers and the nun doctor had withdrawn to one of the guest rooms, one of the two gendarmes had driven to the local police station to fetch some more officers, while the other was on the telephone in the car. Rohmueller was pacing around her relatives' two houses. He wasn't being allowed in to see Nadine yet; she wasn't letting anyone near her apart from the three old women and Cesare. Ben himself was sitting in the garden with a glass of . . . He cleared his throat. Tap water.

Louise sighed. She knew her family. "Tap water with absinthe."

"Oh, that's why it tastes so funny."

"You can drink what you want, Benno."

"And I do, occasionally, Bonì."

"But don't forget to keep your eyes open." She didn't know what the man in Colmar was planning once he'd got himself to safety. Maybe this wasn't over yet. Maybe he'd disappear, maybe he was out for revenge. If he'd followed them . . .

"He didn't, I kept an eye out."

"All the same. Have another look around before you drive home. You've got the description."

"In a bit. When my glass is empty, otherwise I'll offend the person sitting with me."

"Which person?"

"If it *is* a person. He looks like a small, gnarled olive tree with lots of hair. A mistrustful olive tree – he hasn't let me out of his sight for a second."

"Uncle Pierre! He's checking to see whether you're good enough for the family."

"Oh," Ben said. "How do you say 'cheers' in French?"

"*À votre santé.*"

"*À votre santé,*" Ben said loudly. "Now the olive tree's laughing. I've passed the test." She heard the clinking of glasses.

"Uncle Pierre is the family absinthe expert."

"It took him five minutes just to prepare it. With the spoon, sugar and all that."

"He takes it very seriously."

"And drinks it very fast."

It was good to know that Ben felt at ease with her family, and in Gérardmer too. For a while at least he wouldn't be thinking about the past, St Georgen, the future. About prospects and all that. But she would be concerned until they got the man from Colmar.

"Can you receive MMSs?"

"Yes."

"I'll send you a photograph in twenty minutes max. Stay in Gérardmer until you get it."

"The policeman?"

"Yes. If Nadine identifies him we'll have our proof."

"O.K. How are things your end?"

She told him about Oberrimsingen, the stag do, but – as always – not everything, to avoid making him unduly anxious. She could always sense when he was anxious. But he said nothing.

"I'll see you at midnight. With tap water and ćevapčići."

"Looking forward to it," he said.

"Me too."

"*À votre santé,*" Ben said loudly.

The clink of glasses.

Yes, a man she might be able to love one day, in the very distant future.

By the entrance to police H.Q. stood another man, a man she'd never understand and never like – at best she might feel sorry for him. He was wearing jeans, a light-blue T-shirt and a black cowboy hat. In one hand he held an overnight bag, in the other a cigarette. He looked left, right, then set off slowly, as if he had all the time in the world.

He didn't notice her as she drove past him.

Louise parked in the carport and, following an impulse, walked through the building to the entrance and outside. A few minutes' respite for her colleague, she thought, but that wasn't quite true. She sensed she wanted to put off the moment when she confronted him.

Holzner had turned around and was coming back along the pavement; he must mean to go the other way. When he noticed her, he stopped. "The police slapper who likes football."

"Would you like me to drive you home?"

"Some game, wasn't it? We beat the Mexican dwarves." His

unshaven face formed an empty grin. He flicked his cigarette butt away. "I didn't see that coming. The boy did, though."

"Come on, Herr Holzner."

He laughed. "*Herr Holzner.*"

Bonì took him by the arm and escorted him to the carport. He plodded stiffly beside her; the bed in his cell was hard.

"So what was he doing down by the river?"

"He'd been in the barn shortly before. I assume he wanted to go to the river to be safe."

"That's what you assume, is it? Safe from who?"

"The man who killed him."

Holzner nodded. "He was up to something again, wasn't he? Yes, that was him, he always had to be up to something. Just like his old man." He laughed softly, but now it sounded put on. "That's what us Holzners are like. One's lucky and pulls through. The other is unlucky and doesn't. Such is life when you're a Holzner."

Louise didn't respond and Holzner said nothing else either. He didn't ask who had done it, or about how or why his son had been killed, or if they'd got the man. Such was life for the Holzners. It just happened, and the details seemed irrelevant.

In the carport she asked a colleague from Freiburg South to organise a patrol car to take Holzner back to Grezhausen. As they waited Holzner lit a cigarette, flicked it away when he'd smoked only half, and lit another.

A patrol car stopped beside them.

"Copper taxi," Holzner said.

She opened the rear door for him.

Holzner took off his dreadful hat, but made no move to get into the car. He stood there motionless, staring at her. For the first time she thought she could see a trace of sadness in his expression.

"Will you come to the funeral?"

"If I can."

"It'll only be a small do. Not that you'd be expecting anything big."

"No problem."

"Me, Gabi, Dennis, you, a few kids from school and that's it. Us Holzners aren't much liked."

She nodded. "I wish you all the best."

"Then it'll happen, the best," Holzner said, and got into the car.

27

Ilic was sitting on the floor of a little room in Admin. In front of him were three personnel files with red covers.

A young, fidgety Rhinelander with laceless trainers had brought them to him. "Do you still need them?" he asked.

"Only one," Louise said.

Ilic took the middle file and stood up. He looked exhausted, she thought, and somehow out of place in this room, in this case, maybe even in this profession since his return from sick leave. Somehow he'd never fully returned. He'd become too distant, changed too much, which no-one could blame him for, but it needed to be acknowledged all the same. For the first time she wondered whether these changes would ever be compatible with his work. Whether he would ever come back to them, to her.

Suddenly she knew that she didn't want to take him with her, later. She should never have taken him up the Rappeneck and she shouldn't take him along to see Hans Meirich.

"*Meirich!*" Hoffmann said, horrified.

Louise and Ilic said nothing. They were standing in Hoffmann's office; he had a large cup of tea in one hand and a chocolate croissant in the other. I'm nervous, he'd said with a shrug when they entered. She'd put the personnel file in front of him, open at the page with the photograph.

All three of them looked at it, already with a beard, already grand-fatherly at the time, even though he looked far younger in the photo than now.

Hans Meirich, Freiburg Kripo.

Unimaginable, Louise thought.

"We ought to wait until Rolf's done with Engerle," Ilic said. "Maybe."

"No," she said.

"Not Hans Meirich ... surely not," Hoffmann muttered.

She didn't have to wait; she was certain. The expressions on Meirich's face, his behaviour, his cautious questions, his joviality, his reserve towards her. A man who'd wormed his way into the team with a strategy.

Your case. What can I do?

And the fact that after Holzner had punched him he hadn't wanted to be signed off work, but had stayed on the task force and been present everywhere – on the hunt for Nadine in Grezhausen, during Holzner's interrogation, in the Katzental, after Haberle's body had been found, with Scuma at Haberle's apartment in Horben.

The desperation in his eyes that hadn't merely been due to Holzner's punch. The doctor's visits which would have given him the opportunity to meet Haberle or the killer. Holzner's cigarette – Meirich was present when Holzner was arrested. Who apart from him would have hit on the idea of taking a half-smoked cigarette from Holzner's front garden to the Ettingers' barn?

His fear of Holzner after he'd knocked him to the ground, and the shame he felt on account of this fear. A veteran, experienced, armed Kripo chief inspector afraid of an oik in front of half a dozen colleagues? Meirich evidently wasn't what he pretended to be, had pretended to be all these years. Not a hard, outstanding old copper with no weaknesses ... Meirich hid behind a façade too.

She ought to have seen it earlier.

"Konstantin Hilpert from Surveillance has an entry for suspected sexual harassment of a trainee policewoman," Ilic said. "There was an investigation, but the accusation couldn't be proved, which meant it was his word against hers. The evidence was thin and the process was halted.

"When was this?" asked Hoffmann, a note of hope in his voice.

"1993. He was on a training course at the police academy, while she was training to become a middle-ranking constable. She went to the female staff rep and said he'd groped her."

"There you go," Hoffmann said.

"It's Meirich," Louise asserted.

Ilic rocked his head back and forth. "Ah, I'm not sure."

"But Meirich's supposed to be gay," Hoffmann said.

She nodded. This was the only thing that didn't tally. Perhaps it was a façade too.

They would get certainty.

Hoffmann scanned the photo of Meirich from the personnel file and transferred it to Louise's mobile using a U.S.B. She called Ben and sent him the image. For investigative purposes it was wrong to show Nadine Meirich's photo alone; she ought to have been shown seven or eight different men. But this wasn't about an identification that could be used in court. Louise just wanted to be sure. She was convinced that Meirich would confess.

Tog it, Ben texted.

She smiled. Did Ben have a problem spelling? Or just a problem with absinthe?

Then the waiting began.

Bonì leafed through Meirich's file and browsed his personnel record. He'd spent a long time at the Criminal Investigation Bureau in Stuttgart, then transferred to Ulm Kripo, before moving to Freiburg twelve years ago. Heaps of praise for his analytical skills, an exceptionally friendly colleague, but also repeated mention of his "indecision" and "reluctance to take risks". Someone who liked "hiding" within a team, but who performed "valuable work". "An alcohol problem" towards the end of his time in Stuttgart, but he'd "clearly got to grips with this". No children, never married, had lived in Herdern for the last twelve years.

Out in the corridor there was now a flurry of activity. Voices and footsteps could be heard, doors opened and slammed shut. Noises she'd loved from the day she started. Things were in motion. A crime on the verge of being solved. A case about to close.

A gruff voice rose above the others: "Nobody's going home, got that?" Bermann, who'd returned with the other officers questioning Engerle and those on his guest list.

"Rolf," Ilic said. He sounded slightly relieved. The section head who would take the decision out of their hands.

She went to the door.

Bermann was in the corridor, beside him Anselm Löbinger, whose expression spoke volumes. Hans Meirich's name was on the guest list and Löbinger knew.

"Rolf?"

Bermann turned to her. "I was just about to call you."

She went up to them.

"Tell me," he said grimly. "Just for fun."

She told him.

"Yes." There was anger in his eyes. "*Yes.*"

With his usual self-assurance, as if God himself had ordained this gaze, Löbinger, barely taller than Louise and roughly the same age, glanced first at her breasts and then looked her in the eye. "Where is he?" he asked calmly.

"Scuma said he dropped him off at the doctor's. That must have been around quarter past six."

"The bastard's trying to do a runner," Bermann said.

No, she thought. Not him. He knows the game's up. "Have you got the other man's name?"

"Not yet." They'd checked out fifteen other guests and their alibis, either in person or on the phone, Bermann said. Ten left to do. According to what Michael Engerle had said, they could exclude four of these on the grounds that they were too young, according to Nadine's description. One had dreadlocks, one was in a wheelchair, which left four. Four names, four addresses – two from Freiburg, one from Kaiserslauten, one from Rostock. They would organise teams to deal with them. He and Löbinger would go to see Meirich.

Of course: Meirich was a job for the bosses.

"Do you want to come along?"

"Yes."

"Rolf?" Jörg Seibold had come out into the corridor. "We're ready." His gaze met hers. Chief Inspector Jörg Seibold, member of the task force, bearded, grandfatherly type. Nice voice when he spoke loudly. He'd been on the shortlist.

He smiled and she returned his smile.

"See you back here in ten." Bermann disappeared into an office.

The double doors swung open at the end of the corridor and Marianne Andrele came bustling in. The public prosecutor was wearing jeans and a sweatshirt, and her grey-blonde hair, styled up with too much mousse, quivered with every step. She must have gone home and then been summoned back.

Andrele gave a curt wave then went into the same office as Bermann.

Search warrant and arrest warrant. This time Andrele wouldn't cause any difficulties as she had with Holzner. This time they had the right man.

"When did you know?"

"A few hours ago. When Nadine described his voice."

He nodded thoughtfully. As calm and supercilious as he was pretending to be, he took the Meirich thing personally and she could see this in his demeanour. A hint of doubt, incomprehension, disappointment had crept into his face. A man from his section was an abductor and a rapist.

"And the thing about him being gay?"

Löbinger shrugged. "I'd heard about it. Maybe it was just tittle-tattle. Maybe he likes fucking young arses when he's not fucking young pussies."

Bonì didn't react. Löbinger and his provocative comments. She bet he only spoke to her like that, and only when there was no-one else around. Language that went hand in hand with his ogling.

"We ought to take a look at his office," she said.

"Some colleagues are already downstairs."

At that moment her mobile vibrated in her hand.

Ben. *It's him. Congratulations.*

"Nadine has identified him."

Löbinger nodded again.

She walked away, leaving him alone with his doubts, incomprehension, disappointment. As she wandered down the corridor she felt his eyes on the back of her neck, on her bottom.

"You can't do this to me," Ilic said. Incomprehension and disappointment were all over his face too.

"You know you mustn't, Illi. You're not fit."

"I may not be fit, but I feel fine. I'm *fine* again, Louise."

She shook her head. "I don't want you to come with us."

"It's not your decision."

"I know."

They were standing in the office they shared, waiting for the espresso machine. Ilic's gaze roamed the wall opposite, alighting on the poster with the laughing Asian children in monks' habits. He hadn't been on that investigation team, on the "Liebau" task force. The first time they'd worked closely together was a few months later, on the "Weapons" task force. The hay shed in Kirchzarten that had exploded, the weapons cache, the Marcel case. She pictured Ilic when it had all begun, standing smoking outside police H.Q., shaven head, pale, expressionless face. An unremarkable, quiet man in the shadows. Then came Heuweiler – in a forest clearing a S.W.A.T. officer was killed a couple of metres away from him. The drive to the Rappeneck, the ascent, the dead Pakistani terrorist. Ilic had a breakdown and was signed off work. More than a year later, still on sick leave, he'd helped her on her journey into the land between the Sava and the Drava, arranging for Ben Liebermann to act as her translator, accomplice and arms provider.

Ilic, her favourite colleague.

Louise felt dreadful, but she'd made her decision. She wasn't going to make another mistake like the one at the Rappeneck – who could say how Meirich would react, or whether the third man would turn up? Bermann's scepticism had already been spot on. How's Illi bearing up? Not a stupid question; at most an unpleasant one, but perfectly justified. She just hadn't wanted to acknowledge it till now.

"I'm sorry, Illi."

She gave him a long, hard look. Five hours poring over personnel files in a tiny room in Admin while his colleagues were carrying out searches, questioning witnesses, while a catastrophe had almost taken place in Colmar, and four of those hours without Nadine's description of the policeman. What was that other than a retreat? It was highly unlikely that you would find key clues in a personnel file.

The red light on the espresso machine came on.

"After all this time," Ilic said.

"You've changed. What happened in Heuweiler changed you."

Ilic snorted. "Of course."

"Is this still your job, Illi? Do you still want all of this?"

He didn't reply.

Louise took two espresso cups, filled them and put a spoonful of sugar into each. "Here."

Ilic turned and took one of the cups without looking at her. They stirred their coffees in silence and drank, avoiding eye contact as the aroma of espresso became ever more intense, while out in the corridor came the sounds of more footsteps, voices, shouting. Louise Bonì and her favourite colleague: a farewell. And they both knew it.

III

The Magic Moment

28

L ouise drove, with Löbinger in the passenger seat and Bermann in the back. Whenever she glanced at him in the rear-view mirror, he was looking out the window.

Löbinger on the other hand, who never said much, was talking incessantly.

"A brilliant career, in fact," he said. "But when it came to leadership . . . I mean, he never wanted to head up a task force. I asked him a few times but he always declined. He liked being in his own space with no responsibility. Twice he worked undercover for several months, but that's a long time ago now, fifteen, maybe twenty years. He talked about it occasionally, and it always sounded like he was doing desk work. All the fuss they make about undercover work, he would say. The only problem is not knowing who you are anymore, but you don't know that before either."

"Did you find anything in his office?"

"No."

"His pistol?"

"He's probably got it on him. But he won't use it. Never has. He had to be forced to do shooting practice."

"That's true of everyone," Louise said.

"Andi Bruckner once went with Hans . . . with Meirich to the cinematic shooting range, and afterwards said that he shut his eyes. That his biggest problem with a weapon was that he automatically closed his eyes. They laughed about it a lot, Andi said, Meirich included. Watch now, Meirich said, lifting his gun and putting his finger on the trigger. Click, and his eyes were closed again."

"Is he scared of guns?"

"And pretty women."

"Who isn't?" Louise said.

Löbinger sniggered. "He always lost his tongue. Once we had this cute secretary, Steffi she was called. Jesus, what a thoroughbred, she had everything a man could want in a woman. He couldn't open his mouth when she was around."

"Josepha Ettinger talked of erectile problems."

Löbinger looked at her. "How did he get it in, then?"

She shrugged.

"It's not easy, you know." He gave a friendly smile.

"Grow up!" Bermann said.

She shot him a glance in the rear-view mirror. Sections heads together, men together – they fought over everything, her included.

Hans Meirich lived in Herdern, in an ugly, seven-storey blockhouse on busy Stefan-Meier-Strasse, with tiny windows and low covered balconies, to the rear a view of the railway tracks and perhaps across Stühlinger district and the city up to the Kaiserstuhl.

Löbinger didn't know of any police officer who'd ever visited Meirich at home. In fact they knew very little about him, very little about his private life. Unmarried, no children, no affairs, the occasional beer with colleagues after work, when he would come across as an introvert, but he'd joined in, drinking, talking and laughing with the others. He was smart, Löbinger said, an analytical thinker, tenacious when he had a hunch. I don't want to say it, but . . . a good investigator.

They were standing at a kiosk by the railway underpass. Some way down Stefan-Meier-Strasse two patrol cars were waiting with four uniformed officers from Freiburg North. As Meirich lived on the seventh floor one man was enough to keep watch on the entrance to the building. The others in the stairwell would see to it that no bystanders came to any harm.

As a police officer, Meirich knew the procedure. Cops ringing at the door, shouting warnings and threats, then he would either open up or not. He knew at what stage they would break down the door, how they would storm in, where in the apartment he had to wait if he fancied chancing a skirmish.

Assuming he was in fact home.

The only thing he didn't know was how many they would be. Whether Löbinger had called for the S.W.A.T. team from Umkirch or whether he was going to try to solve the problem himself.

Shoot or talk.

"So?"

Löbinger frowned. "I'm thinking."

"Think faster then."

Clouds had gathered and a gentle rain had set in. Eight o'clock. Ben would already be on his way back to St Georgen; after all the day's excitement and beautiful Gérardmer, his lonely, night-time car park duty now awaited him. She was desperate to touch him, talk to him about things that had nothing to do with the case. To leave all this behind her, enjoy another lie-in with Ben, chat about things that concerned them rather than anything else. The past had to be untangled, questions about their prospects answered.

Maybe they should go to see her mother in Provence. Even though she knew what her mother would say.

Watch out, Louise. They're all the same. You've got first-hand experience of that.

There are other kinds of men, too, Mama.

And you think he's one of them?

Maybe. Isn't it worth trying to find out?

Yes, they would go to Provence at some point. When Hans Meirich and the man from Colmar had been arrested. When Nadine had returned to Bonn with her father. And the Ettingers to Grezhausen. When the case was closed and had been passed to the public prosecutor.

Maybe then it would be time for her other life.

"I wonder how desperate he is?" she said.

"Indeed," Löbinger said.

"How ashamed."

"Why should he be ashamed?"

She told him what Josepha had said. That the grandfatherly one kept apologising. Having been a police officer for decades, Meirich had now become a criminal.

Of course he was ashamed. Of course he was desperate.

But was he so desperate that he would pull the trigger in spite of his fear of guns? Or take his life when they were at the door?

"You speak to him," Löbinger said. "Tell him you're alone. When he opens the door, we'll nab him."

Louise looked at Bermann. There was barely concealed fury in his eyes. He could have done it simply – Meirich was in Löbinger's section. But he wasn't doing it simply. Meirich was a Kripo officer and he was on Bermann's task force. He was everyone's responsibility.

He nodded.

The caretaker let them in. They took the lift and uniformed officers from Freiburg North stood at different points on the stairs.

They waited outside Meirich's door for a moment, then Löbinger and Bermann took up position to the left.

Louise rang the bell. Nothing happened.

"Meirich," she said, knocking at the door. "It's me, Louise Bonì."

Nothing.

"Open up. There's no point pretending any longer."

The door opened slightly, as far as the security chain would allow. It was dark inside the apartment, but in the light from the stairwell she could make out Meirich's bearded face and the two plasters on his lips.

"Louise, thank God!" he whispered indistinctly. He closed the door, she heard the security chain being unfastened, the door opened, she pushed it and moved aside to make way for Löbinger and Bermann. Meirich cried out in shock, she saw movement, bodies entwined, heard the click of handcuffs, a dull blow, another, a body fell, a gleaming white vase toppled to the floor and shattered with a crash.

Then she was inside the apartment and switched on the light.

Meirich was lying on his side, his hands behind his back, gasping for air.

A small, square hallway, coats and jackets hanging on hooks, on the floor, everywhere, shoes, a pile of pizza boxes that had collapsed. Three open doors – bathroom, tiny kitchen, bedroom – but only the hall light was on. An unpleasant odour hung in the air: stale food, musty clothes, unventilated rooms.

Bermann bent down to retrieve a pistol that was lying by the door to the kitchen.

"What was that for?" Löbinger asked calmly.

"What do you mean?" Bermann replied.

Löbinger didn't answer.

"Help me," Louise said, kneeling beside Meirich.

They'd put Meirich on a sofa that clearly served as his bed. He sat there, sunk into his duvet, staring into space. His top lip had burst open again, the plaster had come away and blood was gathering in his grey beard.

Löbinger had read him his rights. A bizarre moment. Words that Meirich had uttered himself for decades.

"The arsehole is a hoarder," Bermann said.

In the sink and on the tiny kitchen table stood heaps of crockery with encrusted food residues, and there were dirty pots and pans on the cooker. In the bathroom was a pile of dirty washing, filthy towels hung from plastic hooks, and the sink and bath were yellowed with deposits of limescale. The floor in the bedroom-cum-living room was littered with shoes, newspapers, a few books, bags, more pizza boxes, D.V.D.s, C.D.s and a shrivelled plant by the window. The television, D.V.D. player and hi-fi stood at random on the floor, with a tangle of cables in-between. There was no other furniture apart from the bed. One large mess, and clearly it hadn't just been like this since Sunday morning. Meirich must have lived this way for years.

In the midst of the chaos stood Anselm Löbinger, frowning, his hands clasped behind his back as if terrified of touching something by accident and sullying himself. When the realisation of how Meirich lived sank in, his face registered a mixture of astonishment and disgust. A veteran investigator he'd known for years, but who he'd only really got to know that evening.

"For God's sake, Hans, why?" Louise said. She was now next to Meirich and was gazing down at him.

"I thought . . ." Meirich broke off. Tears ran down his cheeks and vanished into his beard, where they mingled with the blood.

"Do you know his name?"

"Only his first name. Frank."

"Do you think he's going to come here? To see you?"

Meirich nodded.

"But why? He'd just put himself in danger."

Meirich shrugged. "He's unpredictable."

"Do you think he's going to kill you?"

Another nod.

"'Scrooged'," Löbinger said.

Bermann came into the room holding a list.

"Frank Nicolai?"

Another shrug.

"One of the four men we haven't yet checked out. Frank Nicolai, works for a management consultancy, mid-forties, married, no children."

Bermann left the room clutching his mobile. She heard him talking in the kitchen. Frank Nicolai. Wait till I get there. He came back. "I'm off. Have you got a phone number?"

Meirich nodded in the direction of a mobile that was on the floor by the sofa. Bermann picked it up.

Nobody said a word until he'd left the apartment.

"What do you mean unpredictable?" Louise said.

"Because he killed the boy, then Haberle."

"Were you present?"

"Not with the boy, but with Haberle."

The jeep had been the tipping point.

Meirich called Haberle around midnight and told him to go to the Katzental. Haberle panicked when he heard that the blue jeep had been spotted in Grezhausen. They'd tried their best to reassure him. A jeep, there were lots of blue jeeps, don't get worked up. They had a man on the police task force, he'd ensure the finger was pointed in a different direction.

But there was no appeasing Haberle. It was all over, why did we do it, what's going to happen to my child if I go to prison? We have to turn ourselves in before it gets even worse, I mean, it's not so bad at the moment, I haven't killed anyone and nor have you, Hans, and the girl's alive, it'll be fine.

Is that what you think? Frank had said, and before he, Meirich, was able to intervene, Frank had a knife in his hand and he stabbed Haberle, once, twice, three times, a dozen times, saying, So, it'll be fine, will it? It'll be fine? I don't think anything's going to be fine, not for you, you fucker, not for you.

Still holding the knife dripping with blood, he turned to Meirich. Do you think it's going to be fine?

No, Meirich said.

No? Is that really what you think?

Yes.

Do you believe in one for all and all for one? No betrayals because we're in it together? What we started as a team we're going to finish as a team? Is that what you think?

Yes, Meirich said.

Together they'd dragged the body from the side of the road into the forest. Together, they'd rapidly erased the evidence. Together they'd wondered what to do next.

"I still don't understand why you think he's going to kill you now," Louise said.

"Because he thinks I betrayed him after all. That Colmar was a trap."

"Did he say that?"

"Yes."

Löbinger took a step forwards. "He called you?"

"An hour ago."

"Where from?"

"He was on his way somewhere. From a telephone box I think."

"On his way to Freiburg?"

"I assume so."

"From France?"

"Germany."

"And what did he say?" Louise asked.

"'You were trying to get rid of me in Colmar, weren't you, Hans? You think it's all going to be fine,'" Meirich whispered.

But Frank had said more than that.

Your pretty colleague was there in Colmar too, Hans, she's really getting on my wick. What's her name again, where does she live again?

"What?" Löbinger said stridently.

Louise waited, feeling tense, but Meirich kept quiet. All of a sudden the fear had returned, the fear she'd first felt so clearly in Grezhausen on the Ettingers' land and then in the house when she saw the darkness in the hallway and on the stairs to the first floor. In Colmar, as she ran up the stairs of the pink house, and then late that afternoon in Oberrimsingen, in Haberle's apartment. The fear that crept over her when she was close to the killer. When she arrived somewhere he'd recently been.

Meirich had lowered his eyes and was still silent.

"Did you tell him?" she asked in disbelief.

"You fucking arsehole," Löbinger said.

"Did you tell him where I live?" she screamed. She took a step forwards and slapped him in the face as hard as she could, then again, repeatedly, alternating between her right and left hand. He didn't resist, his eyes closed, his head flopping to the left, then the right. The palms of her hands felt his beard soaked with tears and blood, and this made it worse; in some strange way this almost intimate contact made everything far worse, and she slapped him harder and harder. Over the past hours and days she'd been able to remain fairly distant, but now no longer. This sudden proximity destroyed the distance, Meirich's beard, tears, blood on her hands dragged her into the filth, into the abyss, and she kept hitting him, even though she knew that with each blow she was sliding further into the abyss.

At some point, when her energy was spent, she stopped, panting.

Meirich didn't make a sound. His head hung to the side. His cheeks were a fiery-red, his eyebrows split, his temples bruised and blood trickled from his nose, which she must have hit too.

"So now the three of us have got a little secret, haven't we, Hans," Löbinger said.

Meirich gave the slightest of nods.

She looked at Löbinger who hadn't moved.

"Wash your hands," he said calmly.

No soap in the bathroom, but on the side of the bath she found some cheap shower gel. She could hardly believe the bright-red colour of the water that sluiced down the plughole. In the mirror she saw a face distorted by disgust and loathing, glistening with sweat, and hair that had loosened from the band. She washed her face too.

As she dried herself with loo paper, the feeling returned: Meirich's damp, scratchy beard on the palms of her hands.

29

When Louise came back Löbinger had already undone the hand-cuffs and was taking Meirich to the bathroom too. She pulled up the blind and opened the tiny window. Across the railway lines it was getting dark; in the distance she saw a streak of light above the Kaiserstuhl. The rain was falling more heavily. She didn't try to persuade herself that she'd done it for Nadine or out of disappointment that Meirich was one of them. She'd done it only for herself.

Louise heard Löbinger and Meirich coming back into the room. Löbinger made calls, first to Bermann, then to Surveillance. He asked her for a spare key to her apartment – with a neighbour, the caretaker? She shook her head. "In the desk in my office, top left-hand drawer."

"Thanks," Löbinger said, and passed the information to Surveillance. "And now, Hans, you're going to do some talking."

Although Meirich was in pain and found it difficult to talk, he did so willingly, as if a detailed confession could undo what he had done, or at least make it comprehensible to himself. Löbinger asked the occasional question and Louise listened as she watched it grow ever darker outside. She wished it were early morning and getting brighter; in the sunlight, she thought, it was easier to cope with what others had done and what you'd done yourself. The smell of the rain helped, but the darkness didn't.

One of the villas on the Oberwiehre hillside – the largest apartment Meirich had ever seen, around 250 square metres, he reckoned, six tall rooms styled by an interior designer, view of the city woods, an ostentatious display of wealth, power and success. He'd invited twenty-five or so men from all over Germany, friends from college, military service, sport, his wild Freiburg days all those years ago. Estate agents like Michael Engerle, the host, bankers, doctors, a handball player, a couple of eternal students. Hans, the police officer, Dietmar, the G.P., and Frank the management consultant. This is where they'd met.

"What? Are you saying you didn't know each other before?"

"No."

"You mean you'd never met, but then you went out and grabbed a girl?"

Meirich didn't answer.

A moment later he went on talking.

An evening with a programme: the guests moved from room to room at hourly intervals. They took their aperitifs in the first room; in the second, from 6 p.m., the Germany–Brazil game was shown on a large screen with beer and hors d'oeuvres; after the game, dinner in the third room; dessert by the fire in the fourth. In the fifth was a bar with every spirit you could imagine. At some point Engerle unlocked the door to the sixth room, which had been blacked out. Loud disco music started up, coloured lights, strobe, a porn film playing on a T.V. screen, and in the middle of the room, in a column of red light, stood a large cage, in which a no-longer-quite-so-young stripper was dancing.

Most of the men were drunk by now. Those who weren't, and who didn't want to watch porn or the stripper, gradually left.

"What about you? Haberle, Frank and you?"

Meirich hesitated. "We stayed."

"And got turned on."

No answer.

"You'd met by now?"

"Yes."

They'd been chatting since the football match, the three of them united by their lack of interest in the sport. During the game they took the mick out of the German players and the passion with which the other men in the room were following the action – Meirich and Haberle discreetly, Frank provocatively and loud. They were rounded upon and asked to leave, at which Frank just scoffed. Haberle went back to the aperitifs, Meirich kept watching the game quietly, while Frank continued to laugh. All of a sudden one of the other men was towering over him, his fists clenched. Frank leaped up, but Meirich and Engerle managed to intervene just in time.

Meirich dragged Frank into the first room, where Haberle was sitting with a drink. Frank turned the conversation to the topic of women, and talked of the penchant he'd had for young twenty-year-olds ever since he'd hit thirty. Firm, fresh bodies – not yet saggy like those ten or twenty years older – that he scooped up at the university, student bars and discos. He bragged about how they liked him, his experience, fatherliness and because he made them explore beyond their boundaries. Meirich and Haberle said nothing – you've got nothing to tell, Frank said, laughing, and clearly he was right.

Meirich stopped talking.

"Keep going."

"Not with—"

"She's staying," Löbinger said.

As they sat in the first room, isolated from the others, Frank described with relish how easy he found it with young women: all it needed was a smile, a touch of charm. How willing they were, open to everything, really, really open, he said, laughing again, an aggressive, self-satisfied, scornful laugh. I wanted to smash his face in, Meirich said, because he wouldn't stop laughing and being provocative . . .

Frank continued in the same vein. He asked Haberle when he'd last fucked a woman apart from his wife. Haberle said nothing, Frank giggled. Then he asked Meirich when he'd last had any sort of fuck – Come on, old man, can you still get any apart from when you have to pay for it? So I made up some stories, colleagues, secretaries, a neighbour. Ah, a real womaniser, Frank said, laughing. It was obvious he didn't believe a word of it.

And so it went on until dinner, when the three of them sat together again. The other men talked about football, weighing up Germany's chances against Mexico, while Frank kept going on about women. We'll get ourselves some pussy this evening, he said, pointing at the door to the next room. I hear there's some to be had in there.

At around two in the morning fifteen or so guests were left. Discussions began about how the night would proceed from there, most of them revolving around the stripper. Frank wanted to get her out of the cage, but the little door was locked and the key was dangling from the stripper's G-string. Others talked about fetching whores, but Engerle didn't want any prostitutes in the apartment he would soon be sharing with his wife. So no women, just more porn films and the naked lady in the cage. Until the discussion sparked into life again an hour later. They asked Meirich where they could find a brothel – as a policeman in this city he must surely know. He named several all the way to Strasbourg, and five guests set off. The rest fell asleep or had more drinks and ogled the stripper, who allowed them to touch her through the bars. Two masturbated by the cage as they caressed her body.

We'll get the lady later, Frank said, the three of us, just us three. Haberle dismissed the idea. He didn't want her because of the hygiene, the risk of disease; he wanted a clean young woman like the ones Frank had talked about.

"What about you?" Löbinger asked.

Silence.

"Out with it."

"I was in favour."

"The stripper?"

"Yes."

"But that wasn't possible, was it?"

"No. Looking and touching, but no more."

"So? Did you touch her?"

"Later. After the others had fallen asleep or left."

"Together?"

"Frank and I. She was too old for Haberle."

"Do you like women, then, Hans?"

Meirich didn't respond.

"Do you like women?" Löbinger said patiently.

"Yes, but . . . they don't like me."

"What about men? Boys? Do you like them too?"

"What do you mean?"

"People say you're a poof, Hans."

Meirich gave a weak snort. "Nonsense."

"Someone once saw you in the woods with a young rent boy."

"Oh, that was my nephew."

"Your nephew's a rent boy?"

"Was. He's dead now. I was trying to help him, but . . ."

There was a moment of silence before Löbinger said, "Back to your party. Let me just try to picture this. You're standing next to each other by the cage and touching her?" Meirich must have nodded because then Löbinger said, "Unbelievable."

"Yes," Meirich said.

"What then?"

"We left."

Nadine was the last of a string of young women they tried it on with, in discos, in bars, in the Bermuda Triangle near Martinstor where young people were drinking in the streets. Each time Frank approached a woman he was sent packing, despite the smiles and charm. Some just turned their back on him, one laughed in his face. He became increasingly angry.

Then they saw Nadine.

She was standing by Martinstor, saying goodbye to Serge, her ex-boyfriend. Serge headed towards the pedestrian zone and Nadine went over to the cab rank. But there were no taxis.

Then everything happened very fast. Haberle stopped the car beside Nadine, assuming that Frank would speak to her. Instead Frank got out and, under cover of the car, put his hand over her mouth and pulled her in. What's going on, Meirich said. Are you mad? One for all and all for one, Frank said, laughing, as he gagged Nadine with a handkerchief and tied her up on the back seat with his belt.

"I thought . . . I didn't want that, but she smelled so good, was so pretty, and Frank pushed her over to me and it was just so easy and . . . *logical*, and she didn't put up any resistance, and I thought if she's not resisting, then . . . And so Frank starts undressing her and Dietmar says he wants to be the first, that he'll only join in if he's the first, and Frank says, fine, you can have first dibs, you can deflower her, and Dietmar says, I know where we can go, and he starts singing, I know where we can go and I'm having first dibs, and Frank laughs and pushes her into my arms, she's totally naked now and I feel her . . . her body, and Frank laughs and Dietmar sings and . . ."

Meirich stopped. Löbinger said nothing.

Outside it was now dark; the streak of light above the Kaiserstuhl had disappeared. The rain stopped for a few minutes, then got heavier again. Louise didn't want Meirich to keep talking, she didn't want to keep listening. She didn't want to hear any details, know what they'd done to Nadine. She wanted to leave, but there were Surveillance officers in her apartment, and outside . . . Frank Nicolai might be waiting outside. She couldn't go to Ben's as she didn't have a key. And it was too early for the car park in St Georgen.

That left H.Q. She had stuff to do there anyway.

And at midnight, St Georgen and Ben – everything else forgotten.

She turned and looked at Löbinger. "Do you know where to get good ćevapčići?"

Seconds passed.

"No," Löbinger said.

Meirich looked at her. "Try Tennenbacher. It's just around the corner. Tennenbacherstrasse. Towards the station, first right."

"Tennenbacherstrasse," she repeated.

Meirich nodded.

"You can't leave before we've got him," Löbinger said.

"I know." She clambered over D.V.D.s, books, clothes, then stopped at the door. "How did Nadine get out? From the basement?"

On Sunday afternoon at around two o'clock she was hungry. Haberle set off and he, Meirich, took a shower in the apartment. Frank was supposed to keep watch downstairs, but he fell asleep. When Haberle returned with rolls and coffee, Nadine had gone.

They spent hours searching for her and then they came across the barn in Grezhausen. He, Meirich, discovered the blood. They kept searching, in the woods, along the Rhine. At some point Haberle and Meirich returned to the barn, where they bumped into Eddie. They chatted to him, he ran off towards the river and so they called Nicolai, who caught him.

Louise nodded. "What if Nadine hadn't escaped? What would you have done with her then? Had breakfast and taken her home?"

Meirich said nothing. He didn't have to answer; it was obvious.

Meirich, the policeman, who knew what would happen if they left Nadine alive. Haberle, who panicked easily. Unpredictable Frank. Two who would have turned away; one who would have taken it to its conclusion.

"I think he wanted it from the beginning," Meirich whispered. "He didn't just want to . . . rape her. He wanted to kill her."

"And now he wants to kill me," Louise said.

30

"**N**ow's not the time," Marianne Andrele said.

They were sitting in Andrele's office. She'd redone her hair and changed her clothes: dark skirt, dark blouse, golden brooch. A press conference had been fixed for 9.30 p.m. with Andrele, Bermann and the police spokeswoman. Kripo boss Reinhard Graeve and Hubert Vormweg, the chief of Freiburg police, would also be present. Press enquiries were coming in all the time, and reporters and camera teams were waiting downstairs by the entrance. There was a lot of explaining to do. Three men had abducted and raped a girl, beating her to within an inch of her life, and one of them was a Kripo officer.

"Do you understand what I'm saying?" Andrele asked coolly.

Louise did understand. Now wasn't the time and within two minutes it would be forgotten for ever. It would remain a secret.

"I'd like to be different," she said.

Andrele gave her a searching look.

"I thought I was different. But I'm not."

"Different from whom?"

"Different from . . . the others. Different from how I am."

"*How* do you want to be?"

"I want to not make mistakes."

"That's a hopeless enterprise."

"Yes," Louise said.

"Think who we're talking about," Andrele said. "A policeman who's committed two of the most serious crimes possible: abduction and rape. The fact that he's a policeman makes it even worse."

"This isn't about Meirich, it's about me."

"Only because that's how you want to see it. Because you want to make life that much more difficult for yourself."

"Perhaps. But I don't want to have to live with secrets. I don't want to be comfortable. I want to be consistent."

Andrele got up and shuffled her documents together. "You look terrible and you sound terrible. Get into your car, drive to see your family in France and come back in a week. By then we'll have Nicolai and the world will look like a better place."

"Sit down," Louise said.

Afterwards she went into her office.

Ilic wasn't there. Louise sat at her desk and stared at his chair. She wondered whether he'd gone home. When she would see him again.

Decisions, goodbyes, conclusions.

She got up and watered plants, to give herself something to do and in case Ilic neglected them over the coming days. Her hand shook as it held the watering can. Even here, in the safest place in the city, she was afraid of Nicolai.

Or maybe it was just her bad conscience.

You can't do this to me. After all these years.

She sat down again.

The formalities were quickly dealt with once Andrele had understood that Louise wouldn't be tempted by her offer, but was determined to confess. A deal like the one she'd made with Rolf Bermann one winter's Sunday two and a half years ago: today, still on duty; tomorrow, not on sick leave, but suspended after the relevant conversations with the heads of section and Kripo.

Until which time she would retain possession of her badge and gun.

Bonì now heard a gentle, rhythmic dripping; water was running from one of the plant saucers. A small puddle was forming on the floor beneath the windowsill. She allowed it to spread.

Louise seemed to have come full circle: she'd returned to where she was two and a half years earlier. What had been the point of withdrawal, the months of rehabilitation in the Kanzan-an, the conversations with the psychologist Kathrin Rein and her seven months with Ben if she was now at the edge of the abyss again? If she let herself get carried away, hit a colleague while on duty, risking everything just because she lost control.

At least she was still in control of the booze.

And that, she thought, was the difference from before. This was something to build on, for the future.

The press conference in the police canteen was a first indication of what to expect in the next few days. Freiburg had its huge scandal: a Kripo officer as kidnapper and rapist.

Around sixty people from the media had turned up, more than they'd had for years. The air was sticky, the neon light too bright and because in haste too few chairs had been set out, some had to stand. One question after another, provocative, confrontational, sometimes aggressive or scornful. New questions even as answers were still being conveyed, particularly those which could only be answered fully in a few days' time.

The room was full of accusations of a cover-up, shoddy police work, a protracted investigation. Some things, Louise thought, they had to put their hand up and admit to, whereas others were ridiculous. But the reporters didn't know the chronology of the investigation.

Andrele, Graeve and Vormweg stayed calm, didn't lose composure; the press officer struggled with the rapid cut and thrust. Bermann, who arrived at H.Q. only at 9.40 p.m., found it very hard to restrain himself. His face was red with fury, and on a couple of occasions he snapped at the individual asking the question. But perhaps this wasn't a bad thing, thought Louise who was standing close to the glass entrance. You couldn't tell how hard it was for Andrele, Graeve and Vormweg to stomach that this case involved one of their own, but with Bermann you could.

There was more behind his mood, however. Bermann kept looking at her and she suspected his mind was on Frank Nicolai. Nicolai, who'd asked for her name and address.

"How about the third man? What can—"

"Didn't I already tell you that we can't say anything about him because he's still a fugitive?" Bermann growled.

"I just want—"

"Did I or didn't I?"

"Yes, but—"

"Haven't you understood yet?"

"All I want is—"

"Next question," Andrele said.

"The woman in the green blouse," the press officer said.

A deep, pleasant woman's voice, a sympathetic question: How is Nadine Rohmueller?

While Graeve answered, Bermann's gaze roamed the room then alighted on her again.

He arrived about half past ten.

"We've no idea where the bastard is."

She nodded.

He sat on Ilic's chair, swivelled a few centimetres to the left and then to the right. "The French have found his car in Colmar. His wife is refusing to assist us. Engele says he has no idea where he might be, as he hadn't seen him for years before the party."

"He called Meirich from Germany. He's not far away."

"Yes," Bermann said, swivelling left, then right. He stared at the poster with the Asian children, then finally said, "Come to our place tonight."

"Thanks, but I'm staying with Ben."

Bermann looked at her. "Who is that now? The man in your life?"

Yes, she thought: who was Ben Liebermann? A man who'd been in her life for the past few months. The only man in that time. This meant little but also a lot, and it was cowardly to call him this, but everything else sounded ludicrous when you were forty-four. My boyfriend. My partner.

"One of us," she said. "He used to be with Kripo, then he worked for the border police in Israel and in the Balkans. I met him last year in Croatia."

Bermann grinned fleetingly. "You weren't in Croatia last year, so you can't have met anyone there. So he doesn't exist. You're going to stay at our place."

She smiled. Good old Rolf Bermann.

How strange, she thought. The men came and went in her life; only Rolf Bermann remained.

He of all people.

31

It was raining cats and dogs when Bonì arrived in St Georgen just before midnight. As ever she parked on the other side of the road, as ever she got comfy in the driver's seat, and as ever she looked at the guard hut. This was by now a familiar sight: the bright rectangle in the darkness beyond the rivulets of water on the windscreen. Ben's blurred outline; this time he was wearing his official cap. She smiled. From one moment to the next a feeling of calm spread through her body. She'd arrived. Somewhere.

When her mobile beeped Louise reached for her handbag and the ćevapčići wrapped in tinfoil. When she got out the rain pounded her umbrella and in the distance she heard the midnight bells. She crossed the road carefully to avoid stepping in any puddles. She loved this strange ritual, however imperfect, provisional and tenuous. Not even the heavy rain could dampen her enthusiasm. Midnight in St Georgen: two people, unsure where their lives were heading, meeting in an empty car park and enjoying the experience.

From behind her a vehicle turned into the car park, where there were already two other cars. Rush hour in St Georgen ... Ben seemed to move and pull down his cap, although through the veil of rain it was hard to tell precisely. For the first time she would see him in action – a novel element in the familiar ritual. She stopped a few metres to the side of the cabin so as not to get in the way. The ćevapčići felt warm in her hand, well, just about lukewarm, but woe betide you, Ben, if you complain.

The car's engine switched off, and a man got out and approached the front of the cabin. Bonì didn't see the pistol until the man raised his hand, three or four metres from Ben. Barely a second later a shot thundered through the rain and the pealing of the bells, and Ben was knocked backwards. Then came another shot, and another. He must be on the floor; he'd vanished from sight.

Having dropped her umbrella and the ćevapčići, Louise was scrabbling in her handbag when the man turned and aimed the pistol at her. He was still on the move, now heading towards her, and she thought it was too late, too late for everything, too late to grab her gun, too late to scream, too late for her and Ben.

"Hello, Louise," the man said. Her legs had already given way.

As he pulled her up and took her handbag she momentarily caught the scent in her nostrils. It had almost faded, but it was still recognisable: "Pasha" by Cartier.

Mick, she thought. It's only Mick.

She swallowed the urge to vomit.

"I thought it was high time we met, seeing as it's all over. Don't you think so, Louise?"

Bonì didn't reply. She'd begun to tremble and could feel the cool rain on her face and head. All of a sudden she was freezing. It's only Mick, she thought again. Her eyes darted to the guard cabin. A bright rectangle in the dark, just like before, only now there was a crack in the glass at the back.

"Don't you think so too?" Frank Nicolai repeated.

She fell to her knees again and threw up.

Nicolai laughed.

When she'd finished he handed her a tissue. This too seemed to emit the scent of "Pasha", even sweeter and more intense, but that couldn't be possible, she thought.

She pressed the wet tissue against her mouth and nose.

"Well, what have we here?" Nicolai said.

From the corner of her eye, Louise saw him bend down and open the aluminium foil. "Is that his dinner? Ah, how romantic!"

He pulled her up again.

"Come on, let's go and see how he's doing, shall we?"

He pushed her towards the guard cabin. The front of it had shattered and now she saw the blood, blood everywhere, on the narrow counter, the shelves, the lower half of the back wall, the floor. In the corner of this small space lay his cap, the peak facing upwards as if it had been placed there. She saw a light-coloured shoe, a dark, damp leg, an arm and a hand full of blood.

"He doesn't look very well, what do you think?" Nicolai bent forwards slightly. "No, he's really not very well, Louise. Is that a problem?"

At that moment fear shot through her body. To begin with everything had happened too quickly to feel fear; there were more important things than the fear of what Frank Nicolai might do to her.

But now it had taken hold.

She sensed him looking at her. The fear threatened to paralyse Louise, make her inferior, and she didn't want to be inferior to him, at least let her avoid that. With sufficient determination, she thought, she would never be his inferior, she might in fact secure a minor victory, even if she lost in the end. There was a crumb of comfort in this thought.

But the fear remained.

She lifted her head and looked him in the eye for the first time. An attractive, friendly-looking man: broad chin, fresh complexion and regular features that dripped with rain. His eyes were bright and intense, his blond hair was soaked and, yes, he did have a charming smile.

"Hello, Louise," Nicolai whispered. His rapacious voice sent a shiver down her spine.

The car, an old Renault, had a French number plate. On the passenger side the window was broken and shards of glass lay on the seat.

Nicolai opened the driver's door, threw her handbag into the car and pulled a lever. Louise heard the lock of the boot click open.

A few years ago it had been Annetta, now her.

"Not in the boot," she said.

"Oh yes," Nicolai said.

Louise turned and began to run towards the road. A few metres on she felt a powerful blow to her right shin and lost her balance. She fell onto her left shoulder and stayed on the ground. Her shoulder blade throbbed with pain, as did the spot beneath her left collarbone where a bullet had lodged a few years before. And with the pain came the memory. The bitch is alive, the man who'd shot her said.

The bitch, she thought, was going to go on living.

"So," Nicolai said. "Think you can run away, do you?"

He kicked her in the side with the tip of his shoe and she realised she would have to obey if she wished to avoid ending up like Eddie and Dietmar Haberle.

Nicolai dragged her to her feet yet again. He pushed her towards the car and opened the boot which contained a tatty blanket, a warning triangle and jack. Annetta had been taken in the boot of a car to a snowy wilderness near Munzingen. She was already half dead. Raped, beaten, half dead.

But Louise wasn't Annetta.

"In you get," Nicolai said.

She lifted one foot over the edge of the boot, tumbled inside and curled into a ball. Her side was aching and when the door of the boot slammed shut she briefly found herself gasping for air. Total darkness and the feeling that she was unable to breathe for fear and pain.

Louise thought of Gérardmer, and of Ben in Gérardmer.

Although the fear remained, her breathing returned. Ben would never wear an official cap. He didn't have a pair of light-coloured shoes. He hadn't come to work in St Georgen this evening.

Louise could guess why.

Ben Liebermann and Uncle Pierre, the absinthe expert.

*

Twenty minutes of darkness, a long, straight road at speed – she knew where Nicolai was taking her. Above the muffled drone of the engine Louise could hear him singing, whistling and laughing, then at some point he started talking. She couldn't make out what he was saying. He didn't appear to worry about getting himself to safety. All that interested him was her and what he planned to do to her.

Louise had started feeling around the boot. The warning triangle and the jack were too heavy and unwieldy. She had rummaged around in the damp, musty blanket and checked every nook and cranny, but so far had unearthed nothing except C.D. sleeves, scrunched-up paper, two empty drinks cans and a box of matches. Nothing she could use as a weapon.

And that was that.

At the very end of the drive the road became bumpy and the car stopped. Louise heard Nicolai get out and open the barn doors. He came back and drove in. Seconds passed without anything happening, then there was a click as the lock of the boot was opened.

Louise didn't move.

Nicolai lifted the door to the boot from the side. She couldn't see him; all she could see was that he wasn't standing behind the car.

Then she heard his voice.

"The magic moment, Louise." He laughed. "Come on, then, get out. But please don't throw up again."

She sat up. Her left shoulder and side were hurting, as was her head, perhaps from the lack of oxygen, or from her pulsating fear. The urge to vomit returned briefly, but then ebbed.

Louise took a deep breath. The air smelled of straw, soil and wood. Of rain and dampness.

The double door to the barn was closed and inside it was dark. The overcast sky meant that no stars were visible through the gaps and holes in the walls. Maybe the darkness was a help. She couldn't see Nicolai, but he couldn't see her either.

Then he switched on a torch and pointed it at her face. She narrowed her eyes to a squint.

Now Nicolai was standing by the car on the left, between the light on her face and the road as well as the houses of Grezhausen. Even though he had no intention of escaping he wasn't reckless.

Bonì couldn't make out his face. All she saw was the source of the light, a sharp, blinding circle.

"Do you know this feeling, Louise?" he said. "As if everything boiled down to one moment, your entire life, everything you've done or not done, everything that's succeeded and everything that's failed. Everything culminates in a single, long moment, and what's to come after is of no interest because *nothing* will come after, nothing of any significance. That is the magic moment, Louise. Don't you believe that something like this exists too?"

She sat up fully and lifted one leg over the rim of the boot. She'd thought that the torch was a hindrance, but now she realised she could work it to her advantage. In the darkness Nicolai would have spotted a lit match, but perhaps not in the beam of the torch.

"Do you believe that too, Louise? Everything you've done and haven't done? Twenty tedious years with the same woman, stuck in a boring job. Then the evening at Michael's . . . You must have heard about it? Did Hans tell you? You went to visit him, I saw you, I was barely fifty metres away, Louise, when you went to his apartment. You were quicker than me, but in retrospect that's all part of it too, you understand? Of that one moment, Louise, which is going to reach its climax here, which will give everything a meaning, which will explain why over all these years one thing happened rather than another. The fact that you were quicker than me is the reason why the two of us are here at this moment – now do you get what I mean?"

She slid closer to the edge. It hadn't crossed their minds that he'd already gone to Herdern. That he was there the whole time they spoke to Meirich.

"The moment began with that evening at Michael's, Louise. The girl at Martinstor, her escape, the fact that I had to kill the boy and Dietmar, that you almost caught me in Colmar – all that was part of this moment. That's what it was about the whole time, as if there were some book of fate where two lines converged – yours and mine. Do you get what I'm saying?"

"Yes," she said as, shielded by the rim of the boot, she struck a match with a discreet movement of her finger.

"You think you can lull me into a false sense of security, don't you? That's what you think, isn't it, Louise?"

She laid the match on the scrunched-up paper. "Yes."

Nicolai laughed.

Banishing her fear and her pain, Boni climbed out of the boot. She wasn't going to lie in there like Annetta any longer. She took a couple of steps towards Nicolai.

"When something like that happens you suddenly realise what's inside you, Louise. What was there all these years without you ever feeling it. Yes, come to me ..."

She took another step in his direction. She needed only to get between him and the boot. As soon as the car was on fire ...

"First I thought that those hours with the girl were the culmination. The climax of the magic moment. When I could do with her as I pleased, you know—"

"Torturing a defenceless girl."

Seconds passed without Nicolai saying anything. She thought she heard a crackling, like burning paper.

"That was the problem."

He'd wanted her to fight back. He'd hit her, kicked her, harder and harder to *make* her fight back. He'd wanted her to resist so he could lose control. To enter a frenzied state of violence and counter-violence, where anything was possible, even his own defeat. To identify his calling in a spiral of ecstasy, loss of control, sheer rage. Let out what was inside him.

But she hadn't fought back. And he hadn't lost control.

"Ultimately boring, Louise. Like life in general."

She thought about this word. Boring. A long nightmare for Nadine, but ultimately boring for Nicolai. Louise had thought the man responsible must have enjoyed torturing Nadine, but clearly she'd been wrong. For Nicolai, the torture only had a purpose if it provoked resistance. If not, he found it boring.

What a terrible word.

She put a hand up to her eyes. "The light's bothering me."

The blinding circle sank until it was pointing at her chest. Now she could see Nicolai, a dark shape above the light. He'd cocked his head slightly as if he were gazing at her thoughtfully.

"The girl was good for one thing, though," he said. "All of a sudden I realised what I'd been living for, Louise. At a stroke I knew what was inside me. And it has to be let out, don't you think so? Whatever it is that's inside you?"

"Violence?"

"Violence, lust, love."

"What? Love?"

"Yes, Louise. You love the person you kiss, don't you? When you touch another person you love them, at least for a few seconds or minutes . . . With her I wanted to lose myself in lust, violence and love."

"But by offering no fight, Nadine didn't play along with your game."

She saw him shrug. "She was paralysed by fear."

"But you continued all the same."

"How could I have known beforehand? And I have to admit that I did have some fun. Especially when I saw the way Dietmar and Hans went about it." He laughed. "Is there anything more ridiculous than a man fumbling with a woman? What primitive creatures. All that mattered for them was just for once in their life to stick their cock into a forbidden hole, Louise. Nothing more."

Now she could smell burning paper. Flames were crackling. Nicolai seemed to have noticed it too. The source of light wiggled around to the side of her, then pointed at the car, before returning to her.

He giggled. "Oh, made a fire, did you, Louise? So you think everything's going to be fine? Do you imagine you're going to get out of here and life will go back to normal?"

"Yes," she said.

A small fire that barely extended beyond the rim of the boot. The musty old blanket wouldn't burn. In the light of the flames she saw Nicolai's hip, his hand. He grabbed the blanket, threw it on the fire, then slammed the boot shut.

"Brave girl."

The light of the torch glided across her body.

"Brave old girl. How old are you. Pushing forty? You've kept in good shape, Louise, I have to give you that. But you'd have been too old for Dietmar. Hans would have you if he could, but an eternity would have passed . . . when I think of what you'd have to do for him to be able to get it up." He laughed.

Nicolai was standing up straight. The torch was pointing towards the road and the village. Anybody out walking would be able to see it through the gaps and chinks in the barn walls.

But who would be out walking in Grezhausen after midnight?

Nobody would see the light. Nobody would hear if she cried for help.

Her only hope was if someone found the dead security guard. Ben perhaps, if he came on duty after all. He would see the ćevapčići and guess where Nicolai had taken her. Where else apart from the barn? Nicolai was on the run, there was nowhere else.

"Why did you go to Colmar? Why did you want to kill Nadine, given how boring you found her?"

As if he'd read her mind Nicolai switched off the torch. She heard his footsteps, but they weren't coming closer.

"I asked myself the same question, Louise."

Now he was standing to the side of her, in front of the barn doors, which she could no longer make out in the darkness. She thought about which way they opened. Outwards, and you bolted them shut on the outside. Dennis had said that Eddie had slotted a piece of wood through the handles. Had Nicolai managed somehow to secure it from the inside? Or just closed the doors?

Again she heard his footsteps, still roughly the same distance away. He was walking in a circle around her.

"Perhaps because in the end she did put up a fight. She resisted, Louise, she fled and then there were the old women, a wall of resistance, a very brittle one, I grant you, but it excited me. I admit, it's a bit like a child who gets bored with their toy but is then desperate to play with it if you take it away from them." Nicolai had stopped close to the wall where Nadine had lain. "I wanted to play and I wanted to win. It was exhilarating, Louise, a mixture of lust, fear, anger, speed, an adrenaline rush. A race."

"To get Nadine?"

"Yes."

Nicolai continued pacing. She wondered how he was able to see her. *If* he could see her.

Maybe he'd started playing again.

"There was also the fact, of course, that she was the only one able to identify us. You understand that I'd have liked to have prevented that, mainly because it was all part of the fun. But more important was the feeling that she was finally offering some resistance, and that seriously got me going. Breaking resistance, Louise ... Perhaps I could have tried it with her again in Colmar. Killed the old biddies and then tried it again with the girl."

"Violence, lust and love instead of boredom."

"Exactly," Nicolai said.

He resumed his pacing, circling her slowly. The distance remained at an even four or five metres, as if he were moving in the darkness with great assurance. Once she fancied she saw something move, but she could have been mistaken. She didn't stir. In front of her the Renault, to the left the doors, to the right the rear wall. Whatever you do, don't lose your orientation, Bonì.

"Then the resistance got stronger, you were there, the French police – a dream. I'd started living, Louise, after Saturday night everything became more intense. You can't choose what's inside you, you know? It's simply there. You can block it out or suppress it, but then you're like Dietmar, Hans or all the other bores who wander around town like zombies. Or you acknowledge it and let it out. Then you start *living* . . . What's inside you, Louise?"

She shrugged. "You tell me."

"Maybe the same thing that's inside Hans?" He laughed. "Do you change sides occasionally? Sometimes do what's forbidden, what only others are usually allowed to do? Wicked things?"

"Such as?"

"Killing me, Louise."

She snorted. "But very slowly."

Nicolai laughed. "You're not going to be paralysed by fear, are you, Louise?"

"No."

"You're going to fight back."

"Yes."

She sensed something beginning to change inside her. The fear was subsiding. Perhaps because now she knew that something *was* actually inside her: the will to fight. She couldn't do it any other way, she *had* to fight, even though she knew that the other way would be more sensible. Enduring what Nicolai would do to her in the hope that he would get bored and eventually leave her alone. Become distracted as he had in the basement in Oberrimsingen.

Louise was calmed by the thought that all she could do was resist with every fibre of her body and wait for her chance. It gave her a feeling of strength. She wasn't paralysed by fear. She had a choice and she'd made her decision.

"Are you afraid of the dark, Louise?"

"No."

"Do you think you can escape from me in the dark? Is that what you think? Yes?"

He'd stopped somewhere behind her. She resisted the impulse to turn around. Although she didn't want him at her back, it was more important not to lose her orientation.

To her right the wall, in front of her the car, to the left the doors.

"Switch the torch on again, then."

"No, no, not yet. The darkness helps. It reduces inhibitions. Your feelings are more intense in the darkness. And it's fairer on you, don't you think?"

She said nothing.

At that moment the torch went back on. Nicolai laughed. "A little joke, Louise. So you don't feel too secure."

"You don't frighten me."

"That's good. Very good."

Silence filled the barn for several seconds.

Then she could hear him breathing right behind her. In a flash his arms closed around her, one arm at her neck pulled her head back, cutting off her air, while the other ran over her body, felt for her breasts, tugged at her blouse. She reached back with both her hands and pulled his hair as hard as she could. Nicolai yelled, an excited sound somewhere between laughter and fury.

He let go of Louise as quickly as he'd grabbed her and wriggled from her grasp. She heard him panting a couple of metres away.

"A promising start, Louise."

She sank to her knees without making a sound.

"Louise?"

"Yes?"

"Would you like me to undress you, or will you do it yourself? Perhaps you'd like to start."

"Dream on."

"Fine. Shall I tell you about them? My dreams?" She could hear his footsteps again, moving slowly to the right towards the wall opposite the doors.

"I'm not interested."

"That's how I like you, Louise. Rebellious to the last."

Bonì listened to his footsteps for a few more seconds then leaped up and ran towards the doors. She heard Nicolai's laughter, his rapid, hard footsteps, his voice: Do you really think you can escape me, Louise, do you really believe that, you bitch? The torch went on, a circle of light frantically darting across the wooden wall, up and down to the rhythm of his footsteps, then the circle of light disappeared again, but those few seconds had been enough to point the way. As the dark surface raced towards her, she put her arms in front of her head, tensed her shoulders forward and launched herself into the doors, which squealed as they flew open. Grabbing one of the doors with both hands, she swung it back, heard it crash into Nicolai, heard a cry that expressed anger, pain and surprise but no more laughter. She felt the impulse to keep on running, further and further, to run in the cool rain that would wash everything away, through the woods to the Rhine, which was so quiet and peaceful here, and wait by the water for the morning, for the sunlight . . .

But she knew that Nicolai would catch up with her after a few metres.

She found the plank in the mud when Nicolai pushed open the door. The torch lit up again and as she took a backswing all she saw was blazing light, which for a moment looked like the sun.

Then the light fell.

32

He came to as she was tying her scarf around his bleeding head. In the dim glow of the Renault's interior lights she saw his pupils brighten and dilate. From blackout to consciousness. From darkness to the light. Feebly he moved his hands, which she'd handcuffed to the steering wheel, and whispered, "I'll be back, Louise."

"In fifteen years."

"Fifteen years pass quickly."

She'd switched on the ignition and sidelights, which lit up the wall of the barn roughly where Nadine had lain. Where Eddie had sat.

Nicolai closed his eyes and took a deep breath. "So close, Louise. You're so close to me. I can smell you. I can taste you. Have you made the call?"

"Yes."

He opened his eyes. "For a moment I really believed you'd understand me. You'd join in. Do wicked things for a change."

"It's easy to be mistaken."

He laughed faintly. "You weren't afraid."

"Not at the end."

"I sensed it. I thought you'd join in. Power, lust, love, Louise . . . I really was mistaken."

She shrugged.

"Don't go away."

"Watch out for your foot."

Nicolai moved his left leg in and she shut the door. Again her eyes were drawn to the place where Nadine had lain. A naked, abused girl, wrapped only in a red blanket. How distressed she must have been.

How distressed when two boys came who didn't help her. Who wanted to hurt her too.

She turned to Nicolai who was looking at her through the window. He said something, but too softly. She waited for him to say it again more loudly, but he didn't.

Then she turned and went to the barn doors.

It had stopped raining. The air smelled of damp earth and had cooled. Freezing, Louise pulled her ripped blouse tighter and fastened her denim jacket. But still she froze.

At least it numbed the pain in her shoulder and side.

No lights on in Grezhausen – actually there was one, a very faint light at the Holzners' on the edge of the village. And a couple of kilometres away in the opposite direction were plenty of blue lights on the motorway.

She waited to the side and in the beam of headlights watched Frank Nicolai being taken from the Renault and put into a patrol car. He seemed to be looking for Louise, but dazzled by the light he couldn't see her. Fifteen years – she would do her utmost to ensure his sentence was not a day less. A man without compassion, a murderer and rapist of sound mind. Someone who'd taken the conscious decision to hurt other people, to kill. As a witness at his trial she would make sure this wasn't forgotten. And see to it that Hans Meirich's responsibility for the crimes wasn't downplayed. Years of loneliness, anxiety, over-burdened by work, alcohol, depression, the influence of Frank Nicolai, an evil manipulator who had led two sick people astray – the lawyers would try it. And she would try to stop it succeeding.

She would also ensure that Eddie's and Dennis's guilt wasn't swept under the carpet. After all that's how it usually began, with children. The Nicolais, Meirichs and Haberles of this world didn't just fall from the sky. They became who they were over the course of many years. Surely the only way of breaking this development was by refusing to excuse what people did as children.

"Bonì?"

An older police sergeant had come up to her. Bags under tired eyes, a wrinkled and worn-out face. It took her a moment to recognise him. Paul Oertel from Breisach station. Paul "Pensioner" Oertel.

"Kripo will be here soon." He didn't sound as sceptical as he had earlier.

She nodded.

"Do you know what happened to the security guard? Is he dead?"

"Yes," Oertel said.

Louise nodded again.

She was still freezing. A young constable from Breisach had given her his coat, which she was wearing over her denim jacket, but she still felt cold.

"It's over now," Oertel said.

"Yes."

"Come into the car where it's nice and warm."

Louise shook her head. After all that had happened it wasn't that simple. Get into the warm car, drive home, go to bed, get up, continue one's life.

"Bonì, it's all over now," Oertel reiterated, sounding embarrassed.

Only now did she realise that tears were running down her cheeks. She didn't know why. Perhaps the tension was gradually dissipating. She found a tissue in her trousers, wiped away the tears and blew her nose. "I need to be alone just now," she said.

"It's not good to be on your own after something like that."

Louise tried and failed to smile. She turned away.

"Don't go, Bonì, please."

"Bermann will know where to find me."

Walking did her good, the woods and the darkness did her good. The dampness of the path, the branches and the leaves. The warmth slowly returned to her body.

Only now, while walking, could she permit herself to think that it was over. Kidnapping, rape, three murders – two perpetrators in custody, one no longer alive. Yes, it was over, somehow.

For Nadine, on the other hand, it would never be over. For her parents. For Haberle's daughter Emily. For Eddie Holzner's mother. Catastrophes had burst into their lives, changing them for ever. Three men had decided to give free rein to their urges, thereby destroying the world of a handful of other people. They would go on living, but very differently. The recollection of what had happened, the horror, the loss would dominate their lives from now on. Her colleagues, especially Bermann, could put it all to one side. She was not so adept at this.

Yes, it was over.

No, it would never be over.

The Old Rhine was still and sedate with the occasional gurgle, as if swallowing itself, and the odd splash, as if fish were jumping. Louise had heard that more than sixty species of fish lived in the Rhine, although she didn't know if jumping fish were among them. But she liked the idea of it. Outside, on dry land, the most terrible crimes were committed. In the water fish jumped.

She had called Ben, but he hadn't answered his phone.

She sat on the riverbank, near to the spot where they'd found Eddie's body a couple of days earlier. Opposite, barely visible in the darkness, lay the island that Holzner used to swim to with Eddie. At least Holzner had sometimes tried to be a good father . . . Apart from the sounds of the Rhine it was totally silent. There was probably no-one else around in a radius of two miles. Perhaps Bermann, if he was already on his way.

And Nicolai.

She felt his hands, heard his voice, saw his eyes. Nicolai, who she had allowed to come close, to give herself a chance against him. Now he was back with her and would stay a while longer.

Louise tried calling again. In her head she heard the languid ringing of a telephone in a room with grey stone walls. It rang seven or eight times before somebody picked up and she heard Uncle Pierre's gruff French.

Ben was asleep.

"I thought as much. He's not used to the absinthe."

"Absinthe? Rubbish! Give them the sun, the air, the altitude and the Boche fall into a deep sleep. They lay their heads on the table and don't wake up until the birds are crapping on them."

She smiled.

"He didn't want to leave," Uncle Pierre said.

"The air makes your legs heavy."

"Yes. Are you coming to visit?"

"In a couple of hours. Have you got a room for us?"

"We ran out yesterday. I'll put a lounger in the garden, beside the table. Then you can tip the chair and he'll have a soft landing."

"You don't like him."

"Your aunt says I don't like anyone."

"Only the birds."

Uncle Pierre chuckled. "Only the birds."

Then she was alone again, with Nicolai, the fish and the Rhine.

Maybe it was a help, the Rhine, with the pain at least. Louise stood up and stripped to her underwear. The water was cool from the rain. Although the current made her slightly anxious, she waded in. She swam upstream along the bank. Fighting again already, she thought. But fighting against the water felt good. And she *had* to fight. Drifting wasn't right somehow. Surrendering to the current. If you drifted you ended up somewhere you didn't want to be.

No, she had to fight, graft against the current. That's just how it was.

"I don't believe it," Bermann said from the riverbank.

She laughed.

Acknowledgements

I should like to thank all those who have helped me in writing this novel, especially Chief Inspector Karl-Heinz Schmid of Freiburg police.

The quotation at the beginning of the book comes from Nathaniel Hawthorne's *The Custom House, and Main Street* (Library of Congress, 1899).

OLIVER BOTTINI was born in 1965. Four of his novels, including *Zen and the Art of Murder* and *A Summer of Murder* of the Black Forest Investigations have been awarded the Deutscher Krimipreis, Germany's most prestigious award for crime writing. *Zen and the Art of Murder* was shortlisted for the 2018 CWA International Dagger. He lives in Frankfurt. www.bottini.de

JAMIE BULLOCH is the translator of Timur Vermes' *Look Who's Back*, Birgit Vanderbeke's *The Mussel Feast*, which won him the Schlegel-Tieck Prize, *Kingdom of Twilight* by Steven Uhly, Robert Menasse's *The Capital* and most recently *Love in Five Acts* by Daniela Krien.